This book should be returned to any branch of the Lancashire County Library on or before the date shown

CPP

- 2 MAY 2014

22 SEP 2015

27 OCT 2016

- 6 SEP 2018

2 4 SEP 2018

2 7 NOV 2018

1 7 DEC 2018

2 1 MAY 2019

24 SEP 2019

24 SEP 2019

Lancashire County Library
Bowran Street
Preston PR1 2UX

Lancashire
County Council

www.lancashire.gov.uk/libraries

D0996822

LL1(A)

IF FRIED CHICKEN COULD FLY

IF FRIED CHICKEN COULD FLY

COULD FLY

Paige Shelton

CHIVERS

British Library Cataloguing in Publication Data available

This Large Print edition published by AudioGO Ltd, Bath, 2013.
Published by arrangement with the Author

U.K.   Hardcover   ISBN   978 1 4713 4803 7
U.K.   Softcover   ISBN   978 1 4713 4804 4

Copyright © 2012 by Paige Shelton-Ferrell

This is a work of fiction. Names, characters, places and incidents are either the product of the author's imagination or are used fictitiously, and any resemblance to actual persons, living or dead, business establishments, events or locales is entirely coincidental. The publisher does not have any control over and does not assume any responsibility for author or third-party websites or their content. The recipes contained in this book are to be followed exactly as written. The publisher is not responsible for your specific health or allergy needs that may require medical supervision. The publisher is not responsible for any adverse reactions to the recipes contained in this book.

All rights reserved

11823576

Printed and bound in Great Britain by
MPG Books Group Limited

*For my wonderful editor, Michelle Vega.
I'm so glad you aren't afraid of ghosts.*

ACKNOWLEDGMENTS

A special thanks to:

My agent, Jessica Faust. I still pinch myself sometimes just to be sure.

Michael Kennedy-Yoon and Katherine Kennedy, who baked my son the most delicious red velvet cake and then were willing to share the recipe.

Charlie and Tyler, my favorite guys. Our trip to Tombstone was a blast!

Fellow authors Riley Adams, E. J. Copperman, and Jenn McKinlay. I tip my hat to you.

When I was a little girl my parents made sure we frequently visited our relatives in Rolla, Missouri. There's something about a place with family that sticks with you forever. The cooking school building in this series is based on a church building on the outskirts of Rolla. A few years ago my son and I were trudging through the cemetery next to it looking for my great-grandmother who died a tragic and gruesome death. Sometimes you don't even know you're getting ideas for books.

So, thank you Mom and Dad, the Grzybs, the Rothwells, the Lights, the Roaches, and the Sheltons. I love you all!

And an extraspecial thanks to Mrs. Lois Bowen, who many years ago made sure I had my great-great-grandmother's funeral program and a picture of her on her eighty-second birthday. She was known as Missouri Anna and I hear she was pretty amazing.

Chapter 1

If the items in the cast-iron skillet hadn't burst into flames just as Gram was dunking the coated chicken breast into the hot bubbling grease, we might not have found the dead body so soon.

As it was, we were in the middle of our evening class — Chicken: Sometimes You Gotta Keep That Skin on, Baby! — when the fire, with flames that licked the ceiling, lit fast and hot. Gram yanked her arm out of harm's way and exclaimed, "Hells bells a-ringin'!" as the singed breast flew through the air and landed at the feet of one of our students, Mabel Randall, who stamped on it with her bright pink sneaker–clad foot.

Gram and I were coolheaded enough to reach for a couple handy extinguishers and take care of the fire in a quick and professional manner. We'd practiced, after all. No matter how careful you were, you just couldn't open a cooking school and not be prepared for such maneuvers.

The chicken class was one of our part-time evening courses and had only five students, who ranged in age from fourteen to seventy. We offered the evening classes because, though everyone wanted to learn how to cook like Gram, not everyone wanted to take it as seriously as our daytime students. The fifteen "daytimers" were all working toward a much-coveted certificate that would assist them in gaining positions as chefs in some of the best restaurants in the country. Other than Mabel, the other four "nighters" in attendance froze in place and watched as Gram and I pulled the keys and then the triggers on the bright red extinguishers, and shot down the flames.

Once the fire was out, replaced by white foamy powder and distinct stinky smells, we received a hearty and relieved round of applause.

"You okay, Mabel, Gram?" I said.

"I'm fine, Betts," Mabel said as she wiped her brow with the back of her hand. "Make sure your gram's not toasted."

I stepped toward Gram and grabbed the arm I'd seen in the middle of the flames.

"Oh, phoo, I'm fine. Didn't even take the hair," she said as I inspected her for harm. She seemed no worse for the wear.

"That was amazing," Stuart Benson said, his eyes big behind thick lenses. Stuart was short, bald, and practically blind, but none of that kept him from being the most adorable old guy I knew, and a pretty darn good cook, too. I didn't know his exact age, but I thought he must be close to seventy.

"Thank you, Stuart, but it should have never happened in the first place. I suppose that's why you always have an extinguisher close by." Gram inspected the mess. "I'm afraid we'll have to cancel the rest of class. I'm sorry about the chicken disaster."

Grumbles of understanding spread through the long kitchen. Mabel and her fourteen-year-old granddaughter, Amy, offered to stay and help clean up, but we sent them on their way and promised Mabel we'd buy her some new pink shoes. The other students, Jenna Hopper, a local bartender, and Miles Street, owner of the town pool hall, had been flirting anyway; they could probably figure out something to do with the time.

"Well, hang a hide, Betts. I don't think there's much permanent damage, but we'll have to have the fire marshal come out and look at things tomorrow," Gram said as the last of the students exited the kitchen through swinging doors that led to the reception area. "Come on, help me grab stuff to get started on cleaning it up."

Two ceiling tiles would have to be replaced, and grease seemed to be all over the range and the floor around it, but since everything else in the immediate area, including Gram's favorite skillet, was covered in white powdery foam, we couldn't be certain of the full extent of the damage. There were still plenty of cooking space and clean stovetops, but the sooner we got rid of the mess, the better.

Gram's Country Cooking School was located in an old bingo parlor that Gram had frequented back in the eighties with one of her boyfriends. I'd heard that before it was a bingo parlor it was a church, which I could easily picture. The building sat on a short hill; it was long and thin and had a peaked roof. It was also right next to an old cemetery. The cemetery was a big Broken Rope summer tourist attraction. Among others, Jerome Cowbender, famous southern Missouri outlaw, was buried there. So was Sally Swarthmore, famous Missourian who, in the late 1800s, took an ax to her parents.

A small reception area was located in the front of the building. Full swinging double doors led from there into the long kitchen where eight large butcher block tables filled the center of the well-furnished space. At each end were an extralarge refrigerator, an extralarge freezer, and pantries. Against the walls were a total of six six-burner gas stoves; worktables; and shelves full of pots and pans and other utensils, such as spatulas, spoons, and Ginsu-like sharp knives. There was a seldom-used classroom with about a dozen desks and chairs at the other end of the kitchen. Farther along were Gram's and my offices, followed by the non–food supply room, which held everything from aprons to every kind of kitchen cleaning supply known to man- and womankind.

Though we had the supplies and always cleaned up after classes, we also had a full cleaning crew come in every night. It was this cleaning crew that Gram cussed as we opened the door of the supply room.

"Aw, Betts, what do you suppose happened in here? When did the cleaning people start doing this?" Gram put her fists on her skinny hips and stood in the familiar stance that was all Gram — left toes forward, right toes pointed to the right.

It looked as though someone had just thrown, willy-nilly, mops, towels, sponges, and buckets to the floor. Where once there had been an organized room full of supplies, there was now a disaster.

"I don't understand. I've never seen it like this. Do you suppose they were in a hurry last night?"

"This is worse than a hurry; it's destructive," Gram said.

I gently toed an overturned white bucket.

Gram gasped. "Betts! Is that a hand?"

I looked at the spot where the bucket had just been.

"Oh, Gram!" Yes, it was a hand.

Gram and I dove in and cleared the mess. Now we were throwing towels, brushes, and bottles full of cleaners every which direction. Seconds later we uncovered the body of one Everett Morningside. We knew who he was because he had been Gram's newest suitor and they'd planned on a late-night dinner that evening. A dinner that clearly wasn't going to happen, because there was no doubt that Everett Morningside was no longer in any condition to eat. He was dead, presumably killed by the plastic bag over his face and tied around his neck.

"Oh, oh no!" Gram said as she reached for the bag.

My mind was jumbled with fear and concern, but I still managed to grab her arm. "Don't touch it, Gram. We've messed up the scene enough."

She looked at me with tears in her eyes and nodded. But then she pulled her arm from my grasp and hurried out of the room. I thought she might be calling the police, but she returned only a few seconds later.

"Aw damn, Everett. What happened?" she said as we both stood over the body.

The entire scene was surreal and bizarre, but I was suddenly more worried about Gram than poor Everett. I'd heard her described as "one tough cookie," "a tough old broad," and "tougher than nails," but finding her date dead in the supply closet was bound to cause her some distress.

"You okay?" I asked as I reached for her hand.

She nodded.

We looked at Everett for another long few seconds. It was difficult to process, difficult to stay in the room, and yet almost impossible to leave. We should have been screaming or freaking out or hyperventilating, but for those long seconds, I stared at Everett's body and tried to understand how something so unreal could possibly fit with reality.

He was a hefty man and his belly made a round even mound. He was also one of Gram's youngest "friends," and probably hadn't been more than sixty years old. He wore a black suit with a buttoned-up vest, which was what he always wore. He was the newest owner of the Jasper Theater — Broken Rope's one-auditorium theater that had been around for over a hundred years. It had seen burlesque and live-action shows, and now it played the current films, well, current to Broken Rope at least. The big cities were a few months ahead of us when it came to new releases. Fitting with the theme of the town, Everett dressed like a gentleman from times past.

"When did you talk to him last?" I said.

"We talked on the phone last night around nine to confirm the dinner date tonight. Who in the name of all things wicked and horrible do you think did this to him?"

"I have no idea, but I think we'd better call the police." I swallowed some fear. I'd inherited some of Gram's unshakable demeanor, but Everett's seemingly violent and intentional death was finally beginning to rattle my nerves. Suddenly, my knees were shaking and I couldn't quite catch a full breath.

"Of course," Gram said with a sigh. "Poor Everett." Then, almost in a whisper, she added, "This won't be good for business."

I was taken aback at her reaction, but I

chalked it up to the stress. Plus that was the least of Gram's worries. We had a waiting list of students for our numerous courses. Anyone who tasted her cooking, or talked to someone who tasted her cooking, or heard about her cooking, wanted to learn how she did what she did.

She'd taught me, law school dropout and her only granddaughter, free of charge. Since law school hadn't been all I'd wanted it to be, and she and my parents had decided I would wander aimlessly through life if I didn't find something to do, she asked me to help her at the school. I have been trying to keep up ever since. As horrible as it was to even consider, the dead body was going to put a big kink in our routine but probably not our business.

Broken Rope, Missouri, was full of gruesome stories and odd tales of death, after all. It was our history of knife battles, gunfights, hangings (it was when this method of death didn't go quite as planned that the town got its name, but that's another story), and homicidal scorned women that formed the base of our busy summer tourist economy. Even though at that moment I was more concerned about poor Everett than anything else, later I'd realize this would prove to be just another

17

strange happening to add to the morbid charm that was Broken Rope.

We bypassed the office phones and hurried back through the long building to use the phone in the reception area. The school was located in the country, right on the edge of Broken Rope, but Main Street and the jail where our local police had their small office were only a curve in the two-lane highway and about three minutes away. We could probably watch them drive up before we hung up the phone.

"Yeah, we had a fire and we got a body here," Gram said into the phone. "No, the body isn't a result of the fire. They're two different incidents. Yes, we're pretty sure he's dead. Uh-huh. Uh-huh. He's in our supply room. No, the fire wasn't in the supply room. Oh for goodness' sake, just send some cops and firemen." Gram slammed down the phone and looked at me as she put her hands on her hips again. "Sometimes I wonder if the fake cops have infiltrated the ranks of the real ones. What was with all the questions?"

"Procedure, I guess," I said.

"Procedure my foot," she said, and then disappeared back through the swinging doors.

The fake cops she mentioned were the

ones who dressed like sheriffs and law enforcement officers from the late 1800s and early 1900s. During the summer and with all the other actors/characters, they would walk up and down the boardwalks of Broken Rope, their spurs jingling, and good-naturedly tip their hats, gently pretend to harass the tourists, and stage fake gun-fights. My brother had been a pretend sheriff six years earlier, the summer he was twenty-one, but they took his badge and fake gun after he got drunk one night and scared a family from Boston out of their wits. He interrupted their dinner, pulled his plastic gun, and told them they were being arrested for having such a sexy daughter. Yes, his methods for attempting to get a date had proved to be a bad moment for all of us.

The good news was that the family from Boston didn't push the real police to press charges. The young lovely thing in question also slapped him, which was entertaining to a number of women. Even with his poorly thought-out behavior Teddy was too attractive for his own good, and he left an angry trail of broken hearts in his wake.

They're here, I said to myself as I saw a real police car pull up in front of the school, well illuminated by the building's outside floodlight above the front door. It was just one of the many changes Gram had made to the building.

When she bought it, she had the inside completely gutted and rebuilt to accommodate the cooking school, so if there'd ever been a pew or a bingo card in sight, they were long gone now. When Gram's second husband (my grandfather was her first husband) died from injuries sustained from falling down a well, she was left with lots of money. For a long time she hadn't done a thing with it, saying that she'd know how to spend it when the time was right.

The time had been "right" shortly after my brother's fake sheriff incident and my escape from law school (our parents had been particularly challenged by their children that summer); as she drove by the abandoned building one day, she decided immediately that she would build a cooking school. "Hell," she'd said, "everybody, dead or alive in this town, wants me to cook for them anyway. Might as well get paid to show them how to do it. Plus," she added to my parents, "it'll give Betts something to do."

I hadn't protested. In fact, I was thrilled with the idea. For a brief time I was humiliated at my poor life choices and my return to Broken Rope with my tail between my legs, but Gram was my favorite person in the universe and I loved to cook, and someday I might almost be as good as she was. It seemed mostly perfect.

Until today at least. With a body in our cleaning supply room, I experienced a fleeting thought that we might need an attorney, and if I'd stayed in law school I'd be pretty experienced by now. Also, if I'd stayed, there might not be a cooking school, so therefore no supply room and finally, no dead body.

I devoted a few minutes every day to beating myself up and second-guessing my decisions. It was a hard habit to break.

But the assessment of my present situation was rudely interrupted by a ghost from one of my past situations. The two police officers who got out of the car were familiar, which wasn't too unusual. Broken Rope was small enough that I knew pretty much everyone or recognized some feature about them that hinted at which family they came from.

One of the officers was Jim Morrison, like the singer, but not really. This Jim Morrison had looked the same for the last ten years: bald, big-shouldered, and somewhat soft around the middle. He was approaching fifty and wore Clark Kent glasses, but his wife once told me he never did manage the transformation into someone Superman-like, though he was a good guy.

It was the other officer who was the ghost — if not literally, certainly figuratively. Cliff Sebastian was my first love. We'd known each other all our lives, dated when we were at Broken Rope High School, and then ended the relationship when we both went to different colleges. I'd dated since then, but I'd never cared for anyone as much as I had Cliff. In fact, there were times, when I felt like being extradramatic, that I was certain he'd ruined me for anyone else. Though we lost contact over the years, my family continually snuck in updates about him: "Pass the beans, Betts. Oh, did you hear that Cliff Sebastian finished architecture school and is moving to San Francisco?" Or "Would you run to the store and get me some milk, Betts? Oh, and did you hear that Cliff Sebastian still isn't married?" Or "Betts, brace yourself, Cliff Sebastian is getting married to a medical school student." That last one was sprung on me about ten minutes after I made it home with the new title of Law School Dropout.

No one had ever snuck in, "Oh, and did you hear that Cliff Sebastian is now a Broken Rope police officer?" That seemed like a pretty big update, so either my family was slipping or they didn't want me to know that Cliff was back in town. With a wife. And probably some kids. It wasn't that I minded him having a family so much — I just didn't want to have to be around it, and I really didn't want to have to be nice to it . . . *them*.

But hang on. Something didn't fit. Something was wrong. I stepped closer to the window and rested my forehead against it as I stared hard. Cliff Sebastian was a successful architect in San Francisco. He was married to a woman who must be a physician by now who surely wouldn't have the sort of career in Broken Rope that she'd have in San Francisco.

Maybe it really wasn't him. Even with the bright building light, it was dark outside. But why did the person, dressed like a real and modern police officer, who was walking toward the cooking school front doors, look so much like him?

If it was Cliff, he hadn't changed over the years as much as he'd just slightly expanded. He still had stick-straight brownish hair, though it was shorter than it had been in high school. He was still tall, but instead of thin, he was trim, his shoulders wide, his stomach flat, his legs long and muscled, and Lord help me, his face still dotted with a dimple on his right cheek. He used to be adorable, and now he was just plain old handsome. I lifted my forehead from the glass and then dropped it again, not hard but hard enough.

As Jim and the Cliff-lookalike came through the double front doors, I straightened up. By this time I'd become completely self-involved and had forgotten the reason we'd called the police in the first place.

"Isabelle," Jim said as he led the way. "We got a call, we think from your gram. Was there a fire, and is there a dead body in the school?"

Cliff-lookalike stayed to Jim's side and back a step or two.

"Uh-huh. Hi, Jim," I said as I found my feet and boldly stepped forward. "Who's your new officer?"

"Oh, this is Cliff Sebastian. Cliff, this is . . ."

"Isabelle Winston. Hi, Betts," he said with a half smile. "We went to high school together, Jim."

"Oh, that seems about right. Cliff's come back to town. Funny how so many people come back to Broken Rope."

"Yeah, funny," I said. "Hi, Cliff."

"You haven't changed a bit, B."

He kept shortening my name, finally

reaching the derivation that I'd only allowed him to use. No one else had called me B. And after we broke up, no one dared.

The swinging doors flew open. "Well, there you are. Who is that yahoo you have answering the phone at your office? Oh, never mind," Gram said.

"Sorry about that, Miz. We're here now. You say there's a body? Where is it?" Jim scratched the side of his bald head.

Gram's given name was Missouri Anna Winston. Most people called her either Gram or Miz. My dad, her son, called her Miz Winnie and my mother called her Mom. But everyone knew who she was, no matter what name was used. My full name is Isabelle Anna Winston. Someone, though there's a continuing family argument as to who, called me Betts when I was little, and it stuck.

"Yes, there's a body. It's horrible, Jim. That's why I . . . oh, hang on. Who's this?" Gram, though skinny, was strong as the proverbial ox. She pushed Jim aside and looked up at Cliff. "Cliff Sebastian, is that you?"

"Yes, Miz, it is. Good to see you."

Gram chewed at her bottom lip as she studied Cliff. Then she looked at Jim and then at me and then back at Cliff.

"Well, I'll be," she said.

CHAPTER 2

"Miz, there's a body, right?" Jim said as he scratched his head again.

"Yes, there is." She gave Cliff one more look and then turned to Jim. "The fire was in the kitchen, but it's out now. The body is in the back, in the supply room."

"Let's go," Jim said. He led the way out of the reception area and through the swinging doors. Cliff gave me a strained nod and followed Jim.

"Well, what do you think of that, Betts?" Gram said.

"I think we have a dead body in the school and we need to know what happened."

"No, I meant . . ."

"I know what you meant. Gram, Cliff and I dated in high school. That might as well have been a hundred years ago. We're both almost thirty years old and have lived our lives separately. I'm surprised to see him, but this is his home; in an odd and sometimes cruel twist, people do come back here because for some reason, it seems, some of us just can't live outside the boundary of strangeness that is Broken Rope. I think . . ." If I'd continued to vocalize my thoughts, I would have said that I thought I was going to have to figure out how to live in my hometown and avoid someone besides Ophelia Buford who had been my own personal version of Nellie Olsen since I was five years old. Because even though it had been over a decade since Cliff and I had dated, just seeing him made my stomach flutter and my breathing speed up. I would have to find a way to avoid him — a married man, probably a parent — at all costs. I would have said: *Damn.*

Gram patted my arm. "Actually, dear, I just wondered what you thought about Cliff working for Jim, that was all. But I see now that we're going to have some other issues." Finally, she also disappeared through the swinging doors.

"Damn," I said. Trailing the rest of the crowd, I pushed through the doors, too.

Gram stopped outside the supply room. She put her hands on her hips and peered down as I stayed back a little. At seventy-eight she was still as skinny and as strong as my parents claimed she'd always been. She said she hadn't lost any height, but my father says he thinks she used to be a couple inches taller than her current five foot five. She always wore jeans, even in the middle of the southern Missouri hot and humid summers. Her T-shirt and sweatshirt collection had happened by accident. Decades earlier she was given a University of Missouri T-shirt and a Kansas State T-shirt on the same day. She'd promised the gift givers that she'd alternate them even though she was a Missouri fan through and through. The trend stuck, and she had closets full of tops from colleges and universities throughout the world. Today she wore a blue T-shirt from Drake University. She wore her gray hair short and boyish because "messing with my hair is a pain in the back end and I just don't want to do it anymore."

I still remembered when her hair was long, thick, and auburn, just like mine. Apparently we had more in common than our love for cooking and our hair. I didn't see the resemblance, but my dad says I'm the spitting image of the young Missouri Anna Winston, which is sometimes like being able to time travel into the future. I hoped I lived as long and had as much energy.

"You found him like this, Miz?" Jim asked from the room. I swallowed hard, stepped forward, and peered over her shoulder.

"No, he was covered in stuff. We cleared him off when we saw his hand," she said.

"Do you know him?"

"Yes, he and I were going to have a late dinner tonight. He's Everett Morningside, the newest owner of the Jasper."

"I know who he is. I just wondered if you did. Does he always dress like that?"

"Yes." I heard sadness in her voice.

"I can't be sure, but it looked like he was asphyxiated with the plastic bag," Jim said to Cliff.

"We oughta call Morris and then get to work gathering evidence," Cliff said.

"I can call Morris," Gram said.

Morris Dunsany was the county coroner and medical examiner. Broken Rope wasn't the largest town in the county, but with its history of strange deaths and the summer tourist bump in population someone decided that Morris's office would be best placed here.

Jim said, "We'll need to get your and Betts's fingerprints and anyone else who might have been in here." He cleared his throat. "Actually, we'll probably need prints from all your students — well, let's find the time of death and then we'll see who was in the school at the time. We'll start there."

"That's a pretty big list of people," Gram said.

"You had classes today and tonight?"

"Yes."

Jim looked closely at the body. "Okay, well, can you call the night students and get them back here? Give me their contact information, too. I'll also need your daytime students' numbers and addresses as quickly as possible."

"I'll call the nighters right after I call Morris. I'll make you a copy of my phone list," Gram said. I admired her ability to function clearheadedly.

A buzz sounded from a speaker in the office. Someone had just come in the front doors.

"Who would that be?" Jim asked.

"The firemen?" Gram said.

"I'll come with you." Jim stood, wincing slightly as he held a hand to his lower back. "Cliff, stay here and make sure the scene isn't further compromised. I'll go with Miz to make the calls and see who's here."

I was going to go with Jim and Gram, but I stayed put instead and leaned on the doorframe, forcing myself to ignore the dead body. I cleared my throat a couple times, but Cliff barely looked my direction, his professional focus on Everett. Finally, I said,

31

"Okay, Cliff, I have to know. What are you doing back in Broken Rope? Why are you a police officer? I thought you were an architect."

He stood but with less effort than Jim. He motioned me out of the doorway and backward into the small hall. He snapped a latex glove over his hand — his left hand that most definitely had a wedding band on the third finger — and then pulled the door closed behind him. Once we were both in the hall, I stepped back farther. The space was small and he seemed to take up too much of it.

"I didn't like being an architect, Betts. When I was tired of where I was — San Francisco — I just wanted to come home. And I always wanted to be a police officer. Perhaps it was a dream left over from childhood, but it never went away. I decided it was time to live my life the way I wanted to."

"As opposed to the way someone else wanted?" I asked, prompting him to tell me more.

"I suppose," was all he said as he looked away.

"How long have you been back in town?"

"Not long. I did my training in Springfield and Jim hired me a week ago. I, uh, hear —

well, I see — that you came back home, too."

"Yeah, the magnetic pull of Broken Rope is too strong to ignore. Actually, it is working out well — other than today, I guess." I looked at the closed door.

"Good. I always thought you'd make a great attorney, but working with Miz is better, don't you think?"

"Much better."

Cliff rubbed an ungloved finger under his nose and looked like he had something else he wanted to say but was struggling with how to say it. We spent a strained moment staring at each other. It was difficult for me to look away, and I assumed it was just as difficult for him, though it couldn't have been for the same reasons. Surely, his heart wasn't pounding as he thought back to our high school days and the time we spent together. Considering the serious and horrible situation, it was ridiculous enough that I was having such an awful reaction; it would be downright disgraceful if he was, too.

Get a grip.

"Betts, come on up front," Jim said as he appeared in the hall behind me. "Cliff, stay there."

I broke the stare-down and hurried back

33

through the long building. A dead body and the return of Cliff Sebastian all in one day.

I didn't know if I could handle all the excitement.

CHAPTER 3

The buzz had announced the fire marshal, a man who'd only recently moved to Broken Rope. Evan Mason had come to town via St. Louis. Apparently a statewide plea for a new Broken Rope fire marshal had gone out after Fred Hutchinson retired six months ago. Evan, having lost the rest of his family in a terrible car accident, took the job to "get a fresh start." He was quiet but friendly enough when he'd come into the school once before to check one of our natural gas hookups.

After Gram showed him the scene of the fire, she and Jim called the coroner and the five students who'd been recently dismissed.

Before long, the students were back, and the small parking lot out front was full enough to resemble the late-night crowd from the bingo parlor days.

Cliff stayed with Everett's body and Morris and two EMTs joined them in the back.

The five students sat on stools in the kitchen and observed as Evan stood on a ladder and peered into the ceiling. He stopped me as I walked by.

"Ms. Winston," he said as he looked down. He had a head full of curly blond hair but in the dark of the ceiling space it almost looked like he was wearing a halo.

"Yes?" I said as I looked up.

"You will have to replace these ceiling tiles, but next time something like this happens, you need to call me immediately, even if you think the fire is out. There's evidence that something sparked up here but then must have died out on its own. If that spark had taken off, the fire could have spread before you knew about it down there. In fact, I'm surprised it didn't."

"Oh. Sorry. Of course, we'll do better next time." My already nervous stomach turned at our mistake. If we hadn't found Everett's body, we probably wouldn't have called the fire marshal until the next day. Even at that, we might have just tried to clean things up ourselves. We would definitely have to do better next time.

"The damage isn't bad enough that you need to close down. Just ventilate well and get rid of all the gunk as quickly as possible, okay? If Officer Morrison gathers everything he needs to gather, you should be good to go." He smiled.

"Thank you," I said.

"Betts, you need to get fingerprinted," Gram said, sticking her head through the opening in the swinging doors.

"Excuse me," I said to Evan. "I've got to . . ."

"No problem."

"How much longer do you think they'll need us here?" Stuart asked as I walked by the brooding and clearly agitated group of nighters. We'd tested their patience this evening.

Stuart, despite his vision problems, owned a small shoe repair shop on Main Street. He'd also started making and selling leather hand-tooled belts decorated with Broken Rope themes, things like hanging platforms and nooses. We'd considered it a huge victory when he signed up for cooking classes because it got him out of his shop. Mostly, he was there, hovered over something he was working on, a magnifying jeweler's visor over his head. I'd pass by his place sometimes at night and see him working and want to tell him he could use more light.

"Hopefully not much longer. Has Jim talked to you yet?" I said.

They all shook their heads and mumbled, "No" or "Not yet."

"After he fingerprints me, I'm sure he'll want to talk to you. I'll try to rush it along."

"Will we have to get fingerprinted?" Amy, the fourteen-year-old asked, her eyes wide with excitement. Amy had only recently come to live with Mabel. She was Mabel's daughter's daughter and had been through something horrible, but none of us knew the details. No one was allowed to mention Mabel's daughter who'd left Broken Rope for New York City and a questionable lifestyle some years earlier. Mabel was doing her best, but Amy's recovery was slow and difficult.

Mabel owned the town's cookie shop called Broken Crumbs. Her successful business had been the thing that helped Amy the most. Suddenly, the young girl had a job, things were required of her. Mabel said that things sometimes didn't get done correctly but that Amy was getting better. The night cooking classes were another distraction so Amy didn't spend too much time thinking about her past. I liked the girl but could see she was troubled.

"I don't know, Amy, but hopefully you'll get home soon," I said.

Amy's eyes widened more. She suddenly

looked concerned instead of excited. She looked at Mabel who seemed to ignore whatever she was trying to communicate.

"What do they think happened?" Miles asked.

"I don't know," I said.

When Gram had called the students back to the school, Jim told her to give as little information as possible. She hadn't mentioned the murder or the victim, but once they'd come back, they'd been quick to figure out there was a big problem that involved a dead body. It only took a few more moments for them to learn that the body belonged to Everett.

"This is truly horrible," Jenna said. "Everett was a good man." She wrung her hands and her eyes were glossy with unshed tears.

"Yes, he was," I said.

Amy looked at Mabel again. This time, Mabel didn't ignore her granddaughter but shook her head and gave Amy a stern look. I wondered what was going on.

"Betts, now," Jim said from the doors.

I took a deep breath and excused myself from the students. Too much had happened in the span of about one hour. I wanted the evening to be over, and Everett not to be dead in our supply room, and Cliff not to be a police officer in Broken Rope, and the fire not to have ever started. So many things were out of control and I didn't like the feeling one bit.

Neither did Gram. She sat on the corner of the desk, next to what must have been Jim's fingerprinting supplies. She seldom looked her age, but at the moment she looked old, tired, and ornery. I thought she had been doing okay, but now I wondered if she'd just put herself on autopilot to make sure what needed to be done got done.

"How're you doing, Gram?" I asked.

"I've been better."

"I know. Sorry about all this." I put my hand on her shoulder.

"I feel terrible for Everett, of course, but I'm concerned about everyone else, too. Who came into my school and killed someone? Why Everett? And could it just as easily have been someone else? What happened, Betts?"

"Don't know, but Jim and . . . Jim and his crew will figure it out."

"I think we should shut down the school until this is solved. For safety's sake."

I thought about that a long minute. I supposed we could close and everyone would either understand or put up with it. But that was a decision that would affect the whole town, not just the cooking school.

We were three short days from Broken Rope's summer season, which would be kick-started by our annual cook-off. We had fifteen daytimers who'd spent their money and time to receive one of Gram's Country Cooking School certificates. Four of those students were participating in the cook-off. If we closed the school, there would be no viable way for the students to prepare their meals under our supervision. The cook-off would probably have to be canceled, which would upset not only students but tourists, too, many of whom were already on their way to the Southern Missouri Showdown, as the day was traditionally called.

Additionally, we always saved Gram's champagne cookie recipe for right before the cook-off. It was a fun, delicious recipe that gave the students something to focus on that wasn't as serious as the cook-off but was a form of celebration instead. We could just give the students the recipe outside of school, but that defeated the purpose.

Though Gram's Country Cooking School wasn't accredited by the American Culinary Federation, a certificate noting that a student had completed his or her full nine-month daytime course work was becoming a valuable tool for obtaining some of the best cooking jobs. In the world of food

41

preparation, there was always a revolution occurring. Restaurateurs wanted as many options as they could get. We would still give the students their certificates, but they'd be cheated out of two of the big highlights — the cook-off and the cookies — that we'd promised them when they came to the school nine months earlier. Gram and I didn't like breaking promises.

Gram knew how to cook food that she and her parents and her parents' parents fixed and ate. Gram made food with butter and cheese and flour coatings. Her food wasn't light on calories or light on flavor. It was full and hearty and made taste buds stand up and pay attention and then swoon with delight. And when her students presented a certificate from her program, restaurant owners knew that they were hiring someone who'd learned the ins and outs of amazing fried chicken, creamy sauces and soups, potato dishes of all kinds, breads, and desserts that kept customers coming back for more.

In the real world, Gram's skills and methods were almost becoming things of the past, of a time when people didn't write down recipes but just added some of this and some of that, a time when cooking secrets were passed down through generations — passed down verbally and in the kitchens of country homes, kitchens that didn't have electricity or natural gas. So in the restaurant world, Gram's skills were fast becoming a lost art.

She was the first one to say that eating food cooked in lard wasn't smart to do every day, but every once in a while eating should be all about flavor and comfort. That's what we did: flavor and comfort, with a little lard added for good measure. Even for only a few days, it didn't seem fair to close the door to our students.

As for the nighters, we could postpone or cancel further classes and refund their tuition, but there was more to it than that. The current nighttime class was made up of the five judges for the cook-off. They were just as excited to judge as the other students were to cook. They could still judge even if we canceled their class, but that didn't seem fair either.

The cooking school also had a catering order to fill. Gram called the catering business a nice accident, because she'd never made catering a goal. But when she saw that students could get more experience by filling the orders, she thought it was a good addition. The library's read-a-thon was tomorrow and Gram had committed the students to red velvet cupcakes. I could handle making the cupcakes by myself, but some of the upcoming orders might be more of a challenge.

After playing all these things through my mind, and realizing that, even with the horrible murder of Everett Morningside, I needed to step it up and be more to Gram and the school than I'd ever had to be, I said, "Gram, the fire marshal said that if Jim clears us and we can get the worst of the mess cleaned up, it will be all right to continue operating. If Jim says it's okay, let's just cancel tomorrow and take it from there. I can make the library cupcakes. The day-timers won't mind missing one day. It might be good for them to relax anyway. I'll call Mom and let her know what's going on and have her call the students. We'll decide what to do after that. We have a lot coming up. No disrespect to Mr. Morningside, but we can't let our visitors or the rest of the town down."

She looked at me, her eyes thoughtful and wide. The old woman I'd seen a moment before was disappearing, and Gram would be back soon.

"You're right, of course, Betts. Thanks." She stood and patted my arm. "Now get your fingerprints taken and we'll get everyone out of here as quickly as possible."

"Right here, Betts," Jim said as he joined us at the desk and reached for what looked like an ink pad. "Sorry about getting your fingers messy. We have the high-tech computer fingerprinting stuff at the jail, but our portable kit is still old-fashioned."

"No problem." I let Jim take my hand. Finger by finger he rolled them each over the black ink and then a piece of cardboard that had squares designating which finger went where.

"Tell me about today, Betts," he said as he rolled.

"What do you mean?"

"Start with the morning and tell me what you did all day. When did you get here?"

"Am I a suspect?" I said. "Should I get an attorney?"

"Spoken just like someone who went to law school," Jim said as he peered at me through his thick glasses.

"I dropped out."

"Smart girl. No, Betts, you're no more a suspect than anyone else. I've got nothing except for a dead body. I'd like to get a snapshot of what happened at the school today. Who was here — in and out? Did you see or hear anything strange? Was the school empty for a period of time?"

In my head I rewound the day, back to when I woke up and had my normal first cup of coffee.

"I got here about nine A.M. I usually get here a little earlier — the daytime students get here at ten o'clock and I like a couple hours to do paperwork or prepare for the day. This morning I was a little late but not for any particular reason. Gram always gets here at nine thirty and she was on time."

"Did you go to the supply room in the morning?"

I shook my head. "Not that I remember. I wouldn't unless I thought the night cleaning staff had missed something. They seldom do."

"What time do they get here?"

"About midnight." I looked at my watch. "A couple hours from now."

"I'll talk to them when they get here, but I'm not going to let them clean up tonight. Maybe tomorrow. Okay, so you were a little late. Did you notice anything odd or out of place?" Jim started rolling the fingers on my other hand.

I thought backward again. "No, Jim, I don't think I did." But I thought harder. I had a faint inkling that something unusual had happened that morning, but I wasn't sure. I suddenly remembered that I thought

I'd heard Gram talking to herself in her office — adamantly. I'd peeked in, but she acted like I'd been hearing things. It was odd, but I doubted it had anything to do with Everett's death. "No, nothing."

"How about classes? How did they go?"

"The daytime classes went off without a hitch. We worked on some pie crusts in the morning and then red velvet cupcakes this afternoon. We have a catering order tomorrow for the cupcakes. We wanted the class to practice today. I don't remember any issues."

"Sounds good." Jim smiled. "Did you or Miz leave the school at any point during the day?"

"Yes, I went out for lunch and then a couple hours later to the store for red food coloring for the cupcakes. I thought we had plenty, but we didn't. I had to make the emergency run to the store."

"What about Miz?"

"I don't really know. She might have left at noon, but I'm not sure. You'll have to ask her."

"All right."

"Jim, you know Gram didn't kill anyone," I said.

He handed me a wet wipe for my inky fingers and said, "Betts, I don't know who killed Mr. Morningside, but someone did. Your gram didn't give me any reason to believe that she was the killer. In fact, I'd put money on the fact that we're going to be looking for someone none of us knows, a stranger. At least I hope so."

"We'll have another Broken Rope mysterious and bizarre death. It will be good for the tourist season." My stomach dropped. I'd told myself I had to be strong, but had I really said that? "That sounded awful. I think I'm just tired."

"I understand," Jim said cautiously.

I'd known Jim Morrison forever and never once had there been a moment of question in his eyes or his voice about me or whatever I had done. Even when I was a teenager and accidently forgot to pay for my gas at the Rusty Chicken corner convenience store Jim hadn't suspected I'd done it on purpose. He called my parents who greeted me as I arrived home.

"You forget something, Isabelle?" Dad had asked, reading glasses on the tip of his nose and the newspaper in his hands.

"No."

"Did you gas up the car?"

"Yes."

"Did you pay for it?"

"Of course."

"Think about it. Did you go into the store and pay for it?"

"Oh. Oops, I don't think I did."

"Yeah, Jim called. You're not a very good thief. Oren's working the store and he saw you. Plus, Jim was in the store. You might not want to steal gas when your cousin's working and the local police chief is grabbing a Snickers bar. Run on back there now."

I hurried back to the Rusty Chicken, paid for the gas, and decided then and there that crime in a small town just didn't pay.

But it seemed it might have today. Someone put that plastic bag over Everett Morningside's head. Someone killed him, right where lots of people came and went. I'd gone through my day with Jim, but I wasn't sure I'd remembered everything.

"It's all right, Betts. These kinds of things take everyone off their game in one way or another." With his left-hand slant, Jim wrote my name on the top of the cards he'd used for my fingerprints. He filed them in the back of the big black case that held the rest of his low-tech stuff. "I think we'll be able to get all the evidence gathered tonight. I've called in a couple crime scene techs. They're on their way. I should have everything I need by morning, but I'll let you know if I don't."

The swinging doors boomed open, startling both me and Jim. Gram came through the opening first. She was followed by Cliff and Everett's body on a stretcher. I didn't know the two EMTs pushing the stretcher, but I suspected one was from the Bennigan family — his big blue eyes gave him away. The other one was probably a Stover, or at least he reminded me of Bud Stover, the overseer of the other cemetery in town — the bigger one, which had its own share of famous dead people.

The group was rolling toward the front door and to the ambulance, I assumed to transport Everett to Morris's office, when the sheet they'd used to cover the body somehow slid off and onto the floor. Those Bennigan blue eyes got bigger and he and the other EMT tried to hurry and cover poor Everett again. An instant later, the crowded reception area became even more crowded as the front glass door also flew open.

A woman I'd never seen before looked at everyone, her eyes finally landing on Everett's still-uncovered body.

She was short and comfortably round. Her face was older but not very wrinkled, and her short gray hair was fine and almost fluffy as it danced on her head.

"Everett!" she exclaimed as she hurried to the stretcher and hugged his neck, plastic bag and all.

"Ma'am, can I help you?" Jim said as he took her arm and gently pulled her away from potential evidence.

"My Everett! He's dead! Someone killed him! Who?" She stood up straight suddenly and looked directly at Gram. "Are you Missouri Anna Winston?"

Gram nodded, confusion wrinkling her forehead.

"You did it. I know you killed him."

Gram suddenly looked more concerned than confused. "Ma'am, like Officer Morrison said, can we help you with something?"

"Who are you?" Jim asked.

"I'm his wife! And she . . . she's the one! She must have killed him!" The woman pointed at Gram.

Gram looked like she was going to say something else, but I hurried to her side and whispered something in her ear. She stopped talking and blinked at Jim.

I said, "Gram won't be saying anything else without an attorney present." I might have been a law school dropout, but I knew when it was time for someone to quit talking. "I'm sure you understand." I looked at Jim and Cliff as they looked at Gram.

They nodded as if they understood far too well.

CHAPTER 4

I'd ridden a stomach-roiling wave all evening. The horrible discovery of Everett's body, the shocking reappearance of Cliff, and now the frightening accusation from Everett's wife that Gram was a killer — all unexpected, all shocking, all quite horrible. By the time the cuckoo clock on the wall cuckoo'd that it was two in the morning, I wanted to punch Jim, smack Cliff, scold Gram for dating a married man, and rip the small wooden bird out of the clock.

"Why does a jail have a cuckoo clock?" I asked Jim, who was sitting behind his desk, across from me.

Jim looked at the fowl and shrugged. "Dunno, never noticed it really."

"You never noticed it?" I said. But I remembered that though Jim was a friend, he was also the top lawman in town. Since Gram was sleeping in one of the two small holding cells, it would be best not to antagonize him by questioning his powers of observation.

The jail was a mix of the old and the new. It was the official law enforcement office of Broken Rope and not meant to be a tour stop, but inevitably a few visitors would open the door and at least peer in. They'd see a couple small but clean holding cells in the back of the deep space, a few old desks topped off with modern computers — large flat-screen monitors and all — in front of the cells, polished wood railings, the obligatory stacks of paperwork, and a front wall decorated with old handcuffs. Somewhere along the way, someone started hanging the cuffs on the wall and the tradition continued. The wall gave the impression of both a law office and a kinky brothel. Truthfully, while I was well aware of the wall of handcuffs, I'd never noticed the cuckoo clock either, but then I hadn't spent a lot of time in the jail.

When he wasn't too busy, Jim was good-natured enough to wave in some of the tourists and give them a quick history of handcuffs and how important the ratchet mechanism had been for bigger-wristed lawbreakers.

To avoid confusion, we called the fake law office the Sheriff's Office. It was across the street and was manned by Jake Swanson, a law officer wannabe who'd not been able to pass the physical examination because of something with his feet. Jake was also my best friend. He was available to be the town's fake sheriff because he'd made a fortune in the stock market. He was officially richer than any higher power one could think of. He was short and thin, and as a poet he had become a tourist attraction in his own rights.

"Not many places could boast they have a poetry-recitin' sheriff," he often said. He had a way with words that defied his short stature and after spending any time around him, people mostly recalled his deep baritone voice and his handsome face. They usually forgot he was height-challenged the moment he opened his mouth.

Tonight Jim's good and patient nature was wearing on me. Gram and I had come with him directly from the school. We'd been trying to contact Verna Oldenmeyer, so Gram could be questioned with her attorney present. Verna and her husband were somewhere in the Ozarks, camping and fishing, and their cell phone coverage was spotty. My last conversation with her had been wrought with missing words and a funny buzzing in the background, but I thought

I'd managed to convey a plea to come back to town as quickly as possible. I thought she said she'd be there in about an hour, but two had passed and still no Verna.

Jim seemed unconcerned and went about paperwork as we waited. He'd left Cliff at the school to attend to Mrs. Morningside, further question the students, and secure the scene until the techs arrived and he was certain that all evidence was being collected properly.

I still hadn't called my parents or my brother because I didn't want to wake and concern them yet. The daytimers still needed to be notified, but I kept hoping that Verna would show up, Gram would be questioned, all this would be cleared up in a quick manner, and we could leave. If I could get Gram home soon, maybe I could just grab a few hours' sleep and get up and handle all the calls myself.

But every fifteen minutes the cuckoo clock kept reminding me that we were still there: *Coo-coo, coo-coo.*

"Jim, you know Gram isn't going anywhere. Let me take her home so she can get some decent rest. When Verna gets back, we'll come in again."

Jim leaned back in his chair, turned his neck so he could more easily peer at Gram.

"She's sleeping just fine, Betts. I think waking her might be the worst idea."

I looked over Jim's shoulder. Gram was fast asleep on her back with her mouth open. Her lips moved with a gentle snore. He was probably right; she seemed to be resting comfortably.

"I'm tired, Jim," I said. "I'd love to get some rest."

"Go on home, Betts. We just need Verna. I haven't locked Miz up, and I'm sure I'll let her go after I question her. If you'd just let me question her now, we could get this over with."

"I'm not an attorney," I said.

"Shoot, you spent two years learning all that stuff. You'll do just fine."

"Well, I certainly remember enough to know that it would be illegal to act as her legal representation. Wouldn't want any of your questioning thrown out because of that," I said sweetly.

Jim smiled slowly. "No, probably not."

"Come on, Jim, you know Gram didn't kill Everett Morningside. She's strong but not that strong."

"I don't know who killed Mr. Morningside, but he is, most definitely, dead. He was killed in your gram's cooking school. He was a married man who seems to have been dating Miz. These sorts of things make me itchy to ask important questions and such."

"Allegedly — to everything you just said, except the dead part. He's definitely dead."

"*Allegedly* — everyone's favorite word nowadays. They were planning on going out for dinner, weren't they?"

"As far as I know, yes, but they might have just been friends," I said.

"Miz could answer that if we asked her," Jim said.

I sighed. "She's not answering anything without her attorney present."

"You sound like a broken record. Or an attorney."

I sighed again.

"We can go around all night long, Betts. I'm content with letting Miz rest. She looks like she needs it." He glanced back at Gram again, who was deeply and peacefully asleep.

"If she'd killed him, I don't think she could sleep so soundly," I said.

"Some might say that they wouldn't sleep so soundly after finding a dead body in their business. She's — pardon the expression — dead to the world, seemingly without a care." Jim's eyebrows rose.

He was right, but she'd always been a quick and deep sleeper.

"Yeah, but she's old, Jim. She needs to rest in her own bed."

Jim smiled. "Your gram is the youngest old person I know."

"Jim, come on."

His face sobered. "Look, Betts, I don't think she killed Mr. Morningside either, but there are proper procedures to follow. I need to question Miz and I'd like to ask you some more questions, too, but I'm going to wait until Verna shows up because I respect the right to counsel. I got nothin', kiddo. Broken Rope might have a lot of mysterious deaths, but it is rare that we have a murder without any sort of indication who might have been the killer. The cell door's not locked, Miz is resting, and you're the only who seems to be having a problem. There's a top bunk in there. It's clean. Hop in and get some rest. I'm going to run down to Bunny's for some coffee and pastries for everyone. Verna will be here soon and she'll be bellowing about being hungry. Do not take Miz out of here or I'll arrest you for interfering with an investigation — bet you got far enough in law school to know what that means."

I blinked. Despite the fact that he was leaving the cell door open, Jim was doing almost everything exactly like a police officer should. I was impressed. Other than the teenage accidental gas theft, I'd only known him as a friend. Being a police officer in Broken Rope, Missouri, had its share of challenges, but I was suddenly pleased to think that we were, as a community, probably in good hands even if it meant Gram and I had to suffer his propriety.

"Yes, I know what that means."

"Good. If Cliff gets back before I do, tell him I need a report before he goes home for the night, or day at this point, I guess. Got it?"

"Yes," I said, dreading the thought of being in the same room with Cliff without any supervision other than my sleeping gram.

Jim stood, unconsciously touched the gun at his waist, and then put on a brimmed official police hat that I rarely saw him wear. He made his way out around the desk and then out of the jail building. For a moment, I sat and wondered if he'd been trying to tell me that it was okay to take Gram and go home — like I'd seen in movies when someone left out a crucial piece of evidence that they couldn't legally hand over but knew would be looked at if they left the room.

That thought fizzled quickly. Jim's instructions were clear: I wasn't to take Gram anywhere. He trusted that I'd listen to his orders and do as he said. He'd only left the cell door unlocked to be polite to Gram.

I sighed.

I stood and stretched as I walked back to the cell for a closer look at her. She was definitely sleeping deeply, seemingly not a care in the world, as Jim had already observed. The top bunk, though maybe clean, didn't look inviting at all, mostly because the only way to get to it was to hoist oneself up; there was no ladder or a bottom bunk head- or footboard to climb. I couldn't see pulling off such a maneuver without tipping the entire bed or smushing Gram.

I often wondered how Gram did everything she did. I'd never really seen her run out of energy. She never complained about being tired or of body aches from working too hard. She never needed a day off.

She would probably attribute her energy to her uncanny ability to fall asleep on command, but I thought it was just the way she was put together, the way she was hardwired, something genetic that I wasn't sure had been passed down to me. Though I hid it from her, there were days that I was tired and felt that my energy had been depleted. I loved working with her and never didn't want to be at the school, but I'd had moments when I thought about asking for an extra day off here and there. I never had, though, and never would. Gram knew my obvious faults; she didn't need to know about the ones I tried to hide.

"What happened, Gram?" I asked quietly as I leaned against the cell door.

Something made a loud rattled bang somewhere behind me.

I gasped and turned quickly. "Who's there?"

There was no one else in the jail. I knew there was a bathroom around the opposite wall. Even though it didn't sound like the noise had come from that direction, I hurried to see if someone was there.

The bathroom was empty. And clean, I noted.

But the sound had been real.

I glanced around the space with my best critical eye. The only thing I'd really paid attention to was the cuckoo clock. But from what I could tell, the bird was still in place, perched at the ready to extend from its hole and squawk again in about six minutes. And the clamor had had a metallic and heavy tone to it.

The two desks seemed no more disturbed than they already had looked: messy paper-work but organized, shiny, and new computer equipment. The chair I'd sat in was still in the same spot. Jim's chair hadn't moved from where he'd left it. The other desk's chairs seemed to be in their right spots, too.

I walked to the front of the room and found what I thought could have made the noise.

A pair of handcuffs, an old antique pair was on the floor. I was almost, but not one hundred percent, certain they hadn't been on the floor before.

"Huh," I said as I crouched to gather the cuffs. They were old and very heavy. I didn't know what sort of metals had been used over the years to create handcuffs, but these were solid and would be a burden to someone's wrists and shoulders if they had to wear them for too long.

They must have fallen off the wall because of a vibration caused when Jim closed the door, I reasoned. But they hadn't fallen off the wall until a few minutes after he left, I thought to myself.

"Delayed reaction?" I said quietly as I stood to place them back where they had come from.

They were rusted and had thick and wicked bars that closed around the wrists of captured criminals. The curved parts where wrists were placed seemed small and tight. I couldn't help but slip one of my own into the curve. There was nothing unusual about the size of my wrists, but the cuffs were tight and painful against the wrist bone. Time had certainly made handcuffs more comfortable and a better fit for different sizes.

As I studied the cuffs and contemplated whether or not more comfortable versions were deserved, Cliff came through the door, holding folders and a big black bag that resembled the one that Jim had used for the fingerprint equipment.

He paused when he saw me, glanced at my hands and said, "Jim told me I wasn't supposed to ever touch the cuffs."

"These fell. I was just putting them back," I said as I pulled my wrist from the loop. Even that maneuver squeezed the bone and sent a twinge of pain up to my elbow. I wouldn't show it, though. In fact, I was going to concentrate on not showing anything except a cool detachment. Who cared if Cliff Sebastian was back in town? Besides, I had bigger concerns than the ghost of my previous love life coming back to haunt me.

Cliff raised an eyebrow but then turned and took the bag and folders to his desk. He looked at Gram before turning back toward me.

"How's she doing, B . . . etts," he said, as though he'd remembered that he was the only one who called me B and it might now be an inappropriate familiarity.

"She's been asleep since we got here." I looked for an empty hook or nail, but there were so many cuffs it wasn't an easy task.

"That's probably good. She needs her rest. We need her alert so she can help us find who killed Everett Morningside."

I found a nail, but I had to maneuver the cuffs in between a bunch of others. I was sure I'd cause more to fall. "You don't think Gram was the killer, then?"

He hesitated. "I hope not."

He wasn't totally schooled in police-talk; he wanted to be careful with what he said and not commit to a particular conclusion.

I made sure the cuffs were stable before I turned again and looked at Cliff. His concentration was focused on a manila folder that he held like an open prayer book. I hoped he wouldn't look up for a second so I could get a good, critical, well-lit look at him.

There was no question that he wasn't a ghost. He was real, as real as Cliff had ever been. I wished that when he'd left Broken Rope all those years ago, he hadn't stayed so firmly in my heart. As I inspected him, it was as if something woke up in my chest, something opened and breathed for the first time in years.

Oh crap, I was in trouble. I put my hand on my chest and told my thawing heart to freeze right back up, because falling for a married man was not only a mistake, it was a *huge* mistake and could mess up lots of lives.

I didn't know this Cliff any more than he knew this Betts. We were over ten years older and had both traveled through our twenties, the time when you're supposed to figure out what you're going to do with the rest of your life. It was interesting to see that he'd changed paths just like I had. Being a police officer in Broken Rope was far from the world of architecture. My position as a cooking school teacher was pretty far from law school, too. Had we found our callings, or were we two of those people who can't ever find what they really want out of life so they keep trying different jobs and careers? I hoped for the former.

Cliff looked up suddenly and was surprised at my intense stare.

"What?" he said.

"Nothing."

He put the folder down and cleared his throat. "I suppose I owe you some sort of explanation for returning to Broken Rope."

"No, not at all. It's none of my business." I regretted the words immediately. Darn straight he owed me an explanation. I should have stomped my foot and said as much.

"Well, nonetheless, I do want to talk to you at some point. I have some things . . . things I should tell you, but now's not a good time."

"Sure, we'll talk."

Cliff nodded and looked as though he was about to say something else when the door flew open with a gust of personality and the distinct smell of fish.

"Verna, thanks for coming," I said as I hugged her, fish smell and all.

"I didn't have any choice, young'un. I was summoned, even if it wasn't by a summons." Verna laughed at her own jokes all the time. Usually it was because she was the only one who thought they were funny, but sometimes it was because everyone else listening was still adjusting to the volume and tone of her deep loud voice.

Verna Oldenmeyer was the woman who'd originally been the inspiration for my wanting to become an attorney. She was smart, big, brash, never bothered with her short red hair and never wore a stitch of makeup.

The smart part was what inspired me. When I was a young girl, I'd listen to her banter with anyone who was in her space. She'd win every time. I liked the idea of winning and had decided that it was because she was so smart that she won. When I learned she was an attorney, I wanted to be one, too. It was the dream, the career ideal, that I held on to for years.

When I dropped out, I thought Verna would be more disappointed than my parents, but she hadn't been disappointed in the least. Instead, she hugged me tightly the day after I got home and told me that her biggest secret was that she sometimes wished she'd dropped out of law school, too.

I didn't believe her, but I appreciated the lie.

When she wasn't practicing law, Verna was all about fishing or genealogy. If she didn't have a worm in the water, she was in front of the computer looking for direct links between someone from Broken Rope's past to someone who was currently alive. She came upon dead ends more often than not though. Since so many infamous Broken Rope characters lived on the wrong side of the law, they frequently died young or without family that would claim them. More than direct lineages, she'd find cousins-by-marriage or similar non-blood relations, but finding those connections had become one of her passions.

"We took you away from camping," I said.

"Yep. Left Ben snoring on the air mattress. Good grief, is that Cliff Sebastian?" she said to me as though he couldn't hear.

"Hi, Verna," Cliff said as he walked forward. He extended a hand, but I saw him prepare for the inevitable embrace. Verna might battle tough to win arguments, but she was still big on hugging.

She pulled him to her and his cheek was forced into the snap on the top pocket of her fishing vest. He was probably grateful she hadn't left a hook on it.

"What in blazin' are you doing in Broken Rope?"

"I moved back recently to become an officer with Jim."

"None of that makes any sense. Is he speaking Martian? Have I lost my mind, or has he, Betts?"

I shrugged.

"You'll take me and Ben out to Bunny's for pancakes and sausages and explain yourself, young man. Y'hear?"

"Yes, ma'am. Any time you're available."

"Well, I'll let you know. For now, we need

69

to attend to Miz. I do need something to eat, though. Vending machine anywhere?"

"Jim ran down to Bunny's. He's bringing back food and coffee," I said.

"God bless that Bunny for having no life but that all-the-time café. If it weren't for her, we'd all spend way too much time being hungry," Verna said.

On cue, Jim opened the door while balancing multiple cups of coffee and a couple white bags with grease stains on the outside.

"Verna, glad you could make it."

"I wasn't given much choice, Jim," Verna said as she took a bag and peered inside. Her eyebrows lifted in approval and she reached into it and pulled out a chocolate-glazed donut.

"Blame it on Betts. She wouldn't let us talk to her gram without you present."

"That's because she's a very smart girl. But you know you could have waited until tomorrow afternoon."

"Verna, there's a killer on the loose. I've got nothing at this moment except that the victim's wife claims that Miz was having an affair with her husband and that she killed him. I have to ask some questions, and I have to ask those questions right away. Sorry if your fishing trip was cut short."

Verna inspected Jim as she chewed. After

a moment she said, "Well, I suppose that makes sense. Damn shame about Everett. Nice man. Betts, go and fetch your gram. We'll set up some chairs in a happy circle and put something in the middle to hold the food and coffee."

This was Verna's way of giving orders. She'd defined my job, but it would be expected that Jim and Cliff would accomplish the other tasks.

They did as they'd been passive-aggressively told while I went back to the cell. Despite Verna's loud arrival, Gram was still sleeping so peacefully that it was a shame to wake her. I ducked under the top bunk and shook her arm gently. "Gram, wake up. Verna's here."

Gram's eyes fluttered open. "Isn't she supposed to be on a fishing trip?" She blinked. "Aw, shoot-fire, Betts, now I remember. Poor Everett. I'm a convict."

"Not quite yet," I said. "Jim and Cliff are going to ask you some questions, but don't answer anything Verna doesn't want you to answer. Got it? Let her lead the way."

"Yeah, I got it," Gram said as she sat up and unfolded herself from the bunk. "Not bad, comfort-wise."

"Yes, but your bed at home would be better, I bet."

"Betts," she said as she lowered her voice and whispered in my ear. "Did you clean anything up in the hallway outside the supply room today?"

"No. What do you mean?"

"Good. Okay. Let's get this over with." Gram led the way out of the small holding cell. I had more questions but didn't want to raise any further suspicion, so I kept them to myself.

There was no interview room in the jail. The only private space available was the bathroom. Neither Gram nor Verna wanted to have a conversation in there, so they went outside and conferred for about ten minutes.

When they came in, Gram took a chair next to Verna. I sat on Gram's other side and the three of us faced Jim and Cliff over a box we used to hold the bag with the late-night snacks. I didn't have an appetite and neither did Gram. Cliff pretended to be interested in a pastry and Jim just held tight to his coffee. He placed a cassette recorder on the box and pushed *record.*

"Broken Rope police chief Jim Morrison present with Cliff Sebastian, Missouri Anna Winston, Isabelle Winston, and attorney Verna Oldenmeyer." He recited the date, the precise time and then said, "Miz, which is how Missouri Anna is known, can you please tell me what you did today, from the time you woke up to the present moment."

Gram sighed. "I went through this, Jim."

"Yes, but we didn't have a tape recorder running at the time."

Gram looked at Verna who nodded and added, "If I stop you at any point, Miz, don't continue until I give you the okey-dokey."

I hadn't heard Gram's version of her day, so I listened closely. She'd gotten to the school at about nine thirty, taught the first cooking class, stayed at the school through lunch and then taught the afternoon class. She knew I ran to the store for some red food coloring, but she said she stayed at the school while I was gone.

"Miz, is there anyone who could corroborate that you didn't leave the school?"

"No. As far as I know, none of the students stuck around."

"Did you see Everett Morningside today — well, I guess that would be yesterday — before you found his body in the supply room?"

"No."

"Did you talk to him on the phone?"

"No. The last time I spoke with him was the night before, at nine P.M."

"What did you talk about?" Jim asked.

"Our dinner plans for tonight, I mean last night. You know what I mean, Jim?"

"Yes. Did you know Mr. Morningside was married?"

"Whoa, Nellie," Verna said. "Miz, don't answer that."

"Why not?" Jim asked.

"Because I said so."

Jim's face pinched. "Miz, were you and Everett in a romantic relationship?"

"Nope, not that one either," Verna said.

Jim sighed. "Okay, had you ever met Mrs. Morningside?"

Gram looked at Verna who shrugged and said, "Just yes or no, Miz."

"No," Gram said.

"How long had you known Everett?" Jim took a sip of coffee.

"Since he took over the old Jasper Theater about six months ago. He had that open house, you all remember?" We nodded. "He'd heard about my champagne cookies and hired me to make some."

"I remember that," Jim said. "They were good." He smiled.

I didn't remember Gram baking the cookies, but I remembered them at the open house.

Verna raised her hand and said, "I'd like

to ask everyone a question and I'd like it on the record. Before tonight, had anyone in this room met Mrs. Morningside? I've never seen or heard of her before, and I meet everyone. Everyone hates us attorneys until they need one, and I'm the only good one close by, so the world sucks up to me, even if they don't like my company. I would have met her if Mr. Morningside had wanted us to meet her. So, anyone else?"

"No, Verna, I hadn't met her," Jim said.

"Me neither," Cliff said.

"Nope," I said.

"Well, I do believe, Jim, that you might have reason to pick up another suspect. Too bad for Mrs. Morningside that Miz got me first. I'm sure she'll be searching for an attorney, too."

"Perhaps," Jim said.

"For now, though, I'm positive there's no reason to hold Miz or any of the rest of us for that matter. Thanks for the pastries, though." Verna stood.

"Wait," Gram said as she raised a finger in the air.

"What is it?" I asked.

"I did leave the school for a brief time."

Verna put her hand on Gram's shoulder. "Hang on, Miz. Tell me first." She sat back down and leaned toward Gram.

Gram whispered something, Verna whispered something, then did it again, Gram nodded, Verna nodded. "Go on, Miz."

"I stepped out briefly, but I didn't go far."

"Where did you go?" Jim asked.

"Just to the cemetery. Since I started the school, I've taken to visiting the gravestones. I enjoy grooming them a little, taking care of them a little. There are so many legends in that cemetery. I feel like I've gotten to know them — some of them were alive when I was a baby." Gram laughed.

I'd seen her visit the cemetery a few times, but it never occurred to me that she'd taken a liking to its inhabitants.

"Gram, aren't some of them criminals — bank robbers, killers?" I asked.

"Or maybe they were just misunderstood." Gram sniffed.

I didn't say anything else but hoped Verna knew it was time to stop Gram from heading further down that path. She did. She put her hand on Gram's shoulder again and shook her head gently.

"I do believe Miz has one other thing to add, though," Verna said as she rolled her hand through the air. She was probably trying to signal Gram to ixnay on the emetery-cay talk.

"Go on," Jim said.

"Well, I'm not sure, but I think I have something that might help."

"Good," Jim said.

Gram looked at me, pursed her lips, and then said, "There was a mess in the hallway outside the supply room. It was about half an hour after lunch. I spilled what was left of the red food coloring. It's why I asked you to run to the store, Betts. I spilled it and then got distracted by one of the student's questions about the cook-off. I forgot all about it. It wasn't there when we found Everett's body. I thought that either Betts must have cleaned it up or . . . or the killer did."

"Betts?" Jim said.

"I don't know anything about the spill," I said. "But why in the world would a killer clean up a food coloring spill?"

"Maybe he stepped in it. Maybe he made footprints, maybe he got his shoes stained," Gram said. "Maybe it was easier to clean it up than risk leaving a clue in a track or something."

"If that's the case, the killer probably threw the shoes away." I was thinking out loud.

"Betts, Miz, are you both one hundred percent sure you didn't clean up the food coloring?" Jim asked.

"Positive," I said.

"One hundred percent," Gram said. "I don't think any of the daytimers did and I'm positive none of the nighters did. I don't think anyone went back there after the spill. Anyone but Everett and the killer, I suppose."

"We'll ask them." Jim looked at Cliff who nodded. "I suppose this is something, Miz. Thank you."

"I hope it helps."

"Well, that's it for tonight, fellas, thanks for coming and I'll be here all week." Verna hefted herself out of the chair and smiled. "We were going to come home tomorrow anyway. The big day is almost here. If any of you need me, you'll find me easily. Cliff, I'll be calling you for the pancake outing."

"Yes, ma'am," Cliff said.

I stood and said, "Yep, come on, let me get you home, Gram." I grabbed her arm gently. I wanted to get her away from Jim and Cliff before she started waxing nostalgic again about misunderstood criminals.

It might not have been overly important to have Verna here for the questioning, but I was still glad I'd called her. If nothing else, going to law school had made me wary of talking to anyone in law enforcement without an attorney present. We all trusted Verna and knew she would do her best for Gram.

Jim rubbed his chin as he eyed me impatiently. He had more questions, but even he probably thought enough was enough for the night.

"All right. Well, I suppose I don't have to tell the three of you that Miz, and Betts for that matter, shouldn't leave town for a while." Jim stood. Cliff followed suit.

"Where in tarnation are we going to go, Jim? I've got a school to run and a cook-off to conduct. I won't be leaving Broken Rope. You know where to find me." Gram huffed and turned to leave. She was behaving more like the gram I knew and a sense of relief washed over me. She'd be okay.

"Miz, hang on, I'd like to chat with you in private. Betts's car will do. Betts, give us a few minutes, okay?" Verna grabbed one more cup of coffee and another pastry and followed Gram out the door.

"Betts, have you ever seen Miz out in the cemetery?" Jim asked the second Verna closed the door. He and Cliff were putting the chairs and the box back where they belonged.

"I'm not sure," I lied. I wasn't under oath, after all. "I don't recall anything like that, but I'll think about it. Why? Do you think that has something to do with Mr. Morningside's murder?"

Jim shook his head slightly. "I'm not sure, but it seems odd."

"Gram's old, Jim. She looks at the obituaries gleefully. She's glad to be alive another day. Old people do those sorts of things."

"Sure."

I must have rehung the handcuffs too precariously because they fell to the floor again with another loud thud. The sound duplicated what I'd heard earlier.

"What the —" Jim said.

"Oh, these fell earlier. I tried to put them back, but I guess I didn't quite get them on the nail well enough." I picked them up again and found a spot that seemed more secure.

"In all the years I've been in Broken Rope, not one of those cuffs has fallen off the wall. Were you looking at them?" Jim asked me.

"No. I was looking in on Gram when it happened. Scared me."

I turned to see Jim give me a curious look. He seemed unusually perplexed at some handcuffs falling from a nail in the wall. The wall was jam-packed with cuffs. His glance was almost accusatory, as though I'd done something horribly wrong.

"What?" I asked. I looked at Cliff, who gave me a small shrug.

"Nothing," Jim said. "Nothing."

I was almost certain I saw him shudder. I'd never seen Jim shudder. Seeing him do it sent a zip of chill up my spine and made me want to do it, too. Fortunately, Verna saved the day.

She opened the door and peered in. "You're good to go, Betts. Get your gram home and into bed. She's too old for this nonsense." Verna looked directly at Jim, who didn't bat an eye.

"Thanks for coming in, Verna," he said.

In truth, they adored each other. They'd worked together for so many years that they'd become almost like an old married couple — a couple with two opposite points of view about almost everything, but still their animosity was tinged with fondness.

I said my good-byes and tried not to allow my eyes to linger on Cliff too long. He didn't seem to struggle with ignoring me.

I stepped out into the night air. It was cooler than I expected it to be and smelled lightly of distant wood smoke.

"Who would be burning wood this time of year?" I mumbled aloud. Or was that the smell from the fire still in my nose? I didn't think so; I hadn't smelled it until I stepped outside.

I could see Gram sitting comfortably, her

eyes closed, in my old blue Nova as the crickets scolded those of us crazy enough to still be awake.

I sniffed deeply. Broken Rope was surrounded by the woods of southern Missouri. Some people still lived in those woods and a small group of those people had somehow remained off the grid. They still cooked over open fires and used candles to see at night. The smoke I smelled was probably from someone who'd either fixed a really late dinner or a really early breakfast.

I looked down the boardwalk, toward the Jasper Theater. The small marquee above the front ticket booth was lit with the title of the current film being shown, but the rest of the theater was dark and suddenly seemed very sad. The theater was located on an inner corner and was flanked by Stuart's shoe shop on the near side and the pool hall on the far side. Continuing farther, past the barber shop and at the end of the street was Mabel's Broken Crumbs cookie shop. Across the street from Mabel's was the saloon where Jenna worked. The saloon sold ice-cream treats during the day and beer at night. Jenna worked both shifts.

An alley ran behind the row of businesses. More Missouri woods and a few open spaces snuggled up to the alley. In only a few days, there'd be a hanging platform in the space at the end of the street and in between Mabel's and the saloon. The cook-off judges would eat atop the platform and hand down their judgments from above to the large crowd below. It seemed like a hundred years away, but it always did at this time. It was amazing to observe how Broken Rope went from quiet to booming in the matter of a couple days.

Tonight, other than the crickets, it was quiet. There was no traffic; Verna had already left and it would be rare to see someone out at this hour even when the tourist season hit full stride.

As I looked away from the theater, something flashed outside its big double doors. I turned my head to look again. The milky light from the old-fashioned streetlights didn't illuminate anything clearly, but instead gave a borderless-like glow to just about everything.

But the flash I'd seen suddenly transformed into a complete figure. I blinked to clear my eyes.

Who was dressed in the cowboy getup outside the theater? Seeing people dressed as he was dressed wasn't a rare occurrence in Broken Rope, but in the middle of the night before the tourist season officially started? Maybe someone was just trying to get into character — rehearse.

"Hey!" I said. "Who's there?"

The cowboy started to turn to look my direction, but his head never made it all the way around before he disappeared. The area where I thought I was seeing him went dark, as though someone had flipped a button on a television or a projector.

I blinked again and looked hard. The theater doors were painted a bright red, but in the darkness they just looked . . . dark. Perhaps the light from the streetlights had briefly played off the red doors? I was tired and the evening had been full of unwelcome and unexpected surprises. Perhaps my body and my mind needed to go to bed.

I hurried into the car.

"Thanks for taking care of me this evening, Betts," Gram said as I pulled on my seat belt.

"You okay?" I asked.

"I'm fine," she said. "Sad about Everett, but I'm okay."

I hesitated as I looked back toward the theater. There was nothing there, I was sure of it. The car windows were rolled down and I noticed that the wood smoke smell had dissipated, but I didn't think that had anything to do with what I'd seen, or thought I'd seen.

"Did you know he was married, Gram?" I asked as I pulled my attention back to her and started the car.

She sighed. "I don't want to talk about that right now, Betts."

I tried to hide my irritation. Technically, she didn't owe me any explanation, but she was my gram and we'd been close from the second I was born.

"I can't testify against you," I said.

She laughed and patted my arm. "You sound so professional, Betts. I know you can't testify against me, but you might be able to testify against whoever did this to Everett. I don't want to be secretive, but Verna made it very clear that the only person I was supposed to talk to about any of this mess was her. I listen to my lawyer."

"That's smart," I said.

"I know." Gram turned to look out her window as we drove home.

I glanced in the rearview mirror and saw nothing by the theater, but for a brief instant, I thought I saw an old cowboy hat blow across the street like stray tumbleweed.

I was looking forward to at least a few hours of good sleep.

CHAPTER 5

I did sleep, but not for as many hours as I would have liked. I got Gram to her house and into her bed before I went to my parents' house and roused them out of their sleep. With heavy eyelids and wild hair, my mom listened to me tell her about the evening's events. She sat at the kitchen table and took notes as I asked her to call all the daytime students in a few hours to let them know that classes had been canceled for the day but we'd resume the normal schedule the following day. I hoped Jim would give us the go-ahead. If he didn't, I'd come up with another plan.

Mom wasn't a morning person, particularly at that hour of the morning, but the panic of a murder and of Gram's predicament kept her alert and at the ready.

No one knew where my brother was, but that wasn't unusual. I left him a message.

Dad jumped out of bed, threw on some

jeans, and hurried over to Gram's. He'd make sure she got some rest and would be there when she woke up. He was the principal for Broken Rope's elementary, middle, and high schools, but he could take the day to be with his mom. My mom was the auto shop teacher at the high school, but the school year was coming to an end so most of her students' projects were completed. Her classes had rebuilt a motor from a 1969 Mustang and refurbished the rest of the car this year. The Mustang would be put up for auction after the cook-off, with the proceeds going to the high school athletic programs. I'd been seriously considering bidding on the car, but I hadn't approached the bank to see if I'd qualify for a loan yet. Plus my old Nova still ran pretty well.

We were a small community and the tourist dollars took care of most of our town's needs, but the schools didn't always see the benefits, so Mom came up with the rebuild-a-clunker idea, and it stuck. Over the last ten years, the rebuilt cars had paid for bus trips, uniforms, and equipment for the high school athletes.

The fact that my mom was the local expert grease monkey hadn't ever seemed odd to me. Even before her rebuild-a-clunker idea, she'd taught at the high school and tinkered with car stuff. "Some people, like your gram, like to spend time in the kitchen, Betts. I prefer to be under a hood."

It was Mom's other skill that made everything else she did or knew how to do pale in comparison. She knew everyone's birthday. Not only did she know the dates, it was how she remembered people, and it was sometimes how she greeted them. "Hello, Heather Binton, October 18, 1987."

It was embarrassing, but over the years she'd learned to control it a little and not always include the birthday with the greeting.

If you mentioned a date, she could list the people she knew who were born on that day. I knew it was weird and savantlike even though I'd grown up with it. It was roughest when an October date was recited. For some reason, Mom knew lots of people who were born in October.

So, after waking them and discussing who would do what, I finally made it back to my own home and into my own bed, where I slept for approximately four hours. When the alarm sounded I wondered if it would have been better just to stay awake.

I lived one block over from Gram and across town from my parents. It took about five minutes to get across town. Gram and I both lived in small 1950s houses. Our floor plans were similar except the stairs to her attic were in her front room and mine were off the kitchen that was behind the front room and at the back of the house. Each had one bathroom and two small bedrooms. I had a basement because the previous owners had wanted one so much that they'd dynamited under the house to create one. I'd heard the stories of the big explosion for years. My basement contained a washer and dryer, and it led to the outside with an old heavy single-panel garage door that I kept closed. My car wouldn't have fit in the space anyway.

My southern Missouri basement always smelled wet with humidity and I never went downstairs without shoes for fear I step on one of the big fat slugs that came out during the warm summer months. Gram could sweep one of those things twenty feet with just the right push of a broom. I hadn't mastered that skill yet, and one of my greatest fears was squishing one of them with my bare feet.

After a refreshing shower and a full pot of coffee I thought I might be able to function okay. While I was in the shower I missed a call from Jim. His message gave us the all clear to go back into the school but I needed to get the mess from the fire cleaned up as quickly as possible. I was glad to hear the news. We still had the catering order for the library, and I knew Gram would skin me alive if I didn't make sure it got taken care of. It would be much easier to prepare the cupcakes at the school than in my own small kitchen.

I hoped Gram was still sleeping but I doubted it. If she was awake, Dad was supposed to try to keep her home. I doubted that would work either, but it was worth a try. The students were originally supposed to make the cupcakes for the library read-a-thon. Since they'd been forced into taking a day off and unless Gram had wrestled her way through my dad, which was a possibility, I'd be making the cupcakes by myself. Gram's recipe for red velvet cake and cupcakes wasn't difficult, but after the practice session the day before, I couldn't remember if we still had enough of her "secret" ingredient. Gram would skin me alive twice and then pinch me hard if I didn't include it in the cupcakes. After a quick detour to the grocery store, I was still close to being on schedule.

I didn't know if it was the coffee or the sunshine of a new day, but a zip of optimism ran through me as I pulled out of the grocery store parking lot. I was deeply sad and sorry about Everett, but I knew Gram wouldn't be under suspicion for long. Everything would get worked out quickly and we could get back to mostly normal.

And then, as I was looking both ways before exiting onto Massacre Lane, I caught sight of Cliff. His return to Broken Rope had been something I'd driven out of my mind; I'd literally forced myself not to think about him since last night.

Seeing him surveying a parked car in front of the local herb supplement specialist's establishment caused another wave of dread to rock my stomach.

"Why did you have to come back?" I slapped the steering wheel.

Cliff glanced at the front license plate of the car and then walked around to the driver's side and peered into the window. He pulled out a pen and a notebook and started to write something. He looked great in a uniform.

This was not good.

Why hadn't I made a better effort to find someone else? Why wasn't I married with two children and Saturday afternoon soccer games? Why hadn't I let go all those years ago? Why hadn't I recovered from Cliff Sebastian, and even more important, why had

I allowed him to be something I needed to recover from?

Even when we dated, I wasn't all about Cliff. I had my own life, my own dreams. My brother tells me the problem was that I never considered that Cliff might have plans of his own and wouldn't want to be a part of *my* future dreams.

"You set yourself up, sis," he'd say. "You expected too much from him and when he couldn't give you exactly what you wanted you wouldn't compromise. You two would still be together if you hadn't told him you should cool it while you were getting your 'educations.' "

I wasn't sure if my brother was right about whether Cliff and I would still be together, but I *had* been the one to tell Cliff that we should put our focus on school.

I just thought he'd do what I did — dive in and ignore the social world around him until we could get back together.

I should have known better. Cliff was a much better multitasker than I was.

Thankfully, a horn beeped and pushed me on my way and out of my unpleasant stroll down memory lane.

I pulled into the school's parking lot at about 10:00 A.M. I had plenty of time to bake the cupcakes and get them delivered.

And, the bicycle leaning against the front door told me I would have help after all.

Jake Swanson's bike was a modern version of old-fashioned. It was bright green with a thick and curvy middle bar. The seat was cushioned and comfortable, and the handlebars were set high — sissy bars, my brother called them. When he was the fake sheriff, Jake kept a child's stick horse in plain sight, but when not in character Jake rode his bike all over town. It was what he attributed his trim build to. I thought he was just blessed with a metabolism that the rest of us would pay to have. He ate whatever he wanted whenever he wanted it and didn't gain a pound.

Though he was one year older than me, we met in high school when he moved to town at the beginning of his sophomore year. He was the new kid, neither big nor athletic, and had been a prime target for the bullies at the school. It was Cliff who'd come to his rescue, but it was me he'd really hit it off with. We shared a love of cooking and the law. We'd been in home economics and the Debate Club together. When I'd gone off to college, Jake had stayed in town, made money in the stock market, and devoted himself to the town's Historical Society and his character. He'd been making noises like he was going to open a restaurant someday, but his plans never seemed well developed.

I was glad to see the bike. Both the company and the help would be welcomed.

I knew the doors were locked, and Jake wasn't anywhere to be seen on this side of the school. I parked the car, grabbed the grocery bag, and peered into the cemetery. Jake was there, sitting on the ground, staring at a tombstone. He had his arms wrapped around his knees and his eyes were so focused forward that I wondered if he was meditating.

"Jake!" I shaded my eyes from the sun.

He blinked, looked my direction, and waved. "Isabelle. Come here."

I stepped over the low rope that separated the parking lot from the cemetery and walked carefully on the uneven ground, passing old tombstones, some simple, some ornate and beautiful. The cemetery groomers would be here soon to even out the grass and get rid of the weeds. I'd never taken a lot of time to study the criminals and victims of Broken Rope's shady past, but some of the tombstones were interesting and even humorous.

"What are you doing?" I asked as I reached him.

He stood, brushed off his behind, and pointed at the tombstone he'd been next to.

"Look," he said.

"It's Jerome Cowbender. Well, his final resting place, that is. He died young." The tombstone read: HERE LIES JEROME COW-BENDER. 1872–1918. HE COULD CHARM THE LADIES AND THE BANK TELLERS, BUT HE COULDN'T SHOOT DIDDLY.

"I know. I mean, look what's on top of the tombstone."

The tombstone was just an upright curved block of concrete that was worn and tilted slightly with time. I peered at the top slope.

"There's a coin there," I said as I reached for it. Jake slapped my hand away.

"Don't touch it. It could be important."

"Important to what?"

"I don't know, but it doesn't look like a normal coin. It's an" — he counted — "octagon. Who would put such a thing here?"

"It looks like a piece of gold," I said. "You sure I can't touch it and see if it's real? It might just be a piece of plastic."

Jake debated silently for a moment, his bright blue eyes squinting in thought.

"Let's grab it by its outsides. Let's not get fingerprints on the face or back of it."

"Why not?"

He looked up at me, his eyebrows coming together. "There was a murder here last night, right?" I nodded. "Thanks for calling to share the scoop, by the way."

"Sorry, I've been distracted."

"Yeah, I heard about Cliff."

"No, I haven't been distracted by Cliff!"

"Anyway, there was a murder here. A gold coin on the tombstone could be evidence."

I didn't make the same connection, but I honored his request and picked up the coin carefully and by its edges.

"It feels heavy, substantial," I said. "It's not plastic, but I don't know how to tell if it's gold or not. Do you suppose it's a doubloon or something fun like that?"

"I don't know what a doubloon is, but isn't it more associated with pirates than bank robbers?"

"You think this has something to do with Jerome?" I asked as we carefully transferred the coin from my fingers to his.

"Maybe. It seems odd doesn't it?"

Suddenly I wondered if I was the subject of a prank, something Jake concocted to get back at me for not calling him last night.

"Did you put this here?" I asked.

"What? No, I saw Miz and Everett, the man who was killed — thanks again for letting me know about the murder — looking at this tombstone yesterday. I came out to see if I could see what they were looking at."

"You did? When? Tell me the details."

"Oh, now you want *me* to share?"

"Jake, I'm sorry I didn't call you. I didn't get home before four A.M. or so and I'm running on a little sleep and a lot of caffeine, so that's the best I can do for now, but I will find a way to make it up to you."

He smiled as he held the coin in the air. "Thank you. I forgive you. And yes, I stopped by yesterday at lunch to talk to you. Miz and Everett were out here looking at Jerome's tombstone. Their tête-à-tête seemed serious and I had to yell at Miz twice before she turned and saw me. She said you'd gone out for lunch, but she wasn't sure where."

"So, Everett was here yesterday at noon? Gram was with him?" I said. "Are you sure that was yesterday?"

"Positive."

"That's . . ."

"What? What is it?" Jake asked.

"I don't know. I'll have to talk to Gram," I said. Did she forget that Everett had been here earlier yesterday? Did she lie? If so, why?

"What should I do with this?" Jake inspected the coin in between his fingers.

It took me a second to notice that he was still talking. "Put it back where you found it, I suppose," I finally said.

Jake placed the coin back on top of the tombstone. "Yeah, someone might have put it here to honor good ol' Jerome."

"Good ol' Jerome? He was a bank robber."

"My dear, for someone whose best friend is the town historian, you don't know nearly enough about Broken Rope."

"He wasn't a bank robber?" I said. "Are you going to tell me he was misunderstood?"

"Maybe. He was a bank robber, but he was much more." Jake brushed his fingers next to the coin, flicking some dirt off the tombstone. "You need a history lesson."

"How about you tell me all about it while you help me with some cupcakes for the library read-a-thon?"

"Cupcakes? Let me see." He pointed to the grocery bag that I was still holding.

I opened it and he peered inside. "Very good. You didn't forget Miz's secret ingredient."

"She could be handcuffed behind bars and she'd still hurt me if I forgot the secret ingredient," I said. I'd meant to make light of the moment, perhaps a forced levity because I was now even more worried about Gram's possible connection to Everett's death. But the comment wasn't met with a smile or a laugh from Jake. Instead, we were interrupted by a sudden gust of wind that seemed to come at us from all directions. Jake's short brown hair was pushed both forward and backward at the same time and my long ponytail got in my eyes from both sides. We looked around for something that might explain the disruptive anomaly. But after the wind gusted once, it was over. The day returned to sunny, calm, and was warming up quickly.

Jake looked at me and said, "What was that?"

"I have no idea."

We both looked around again.

"All righty then. How about we get to making those cupcakes?" Jake said.

"I think that's a good idea." I was more than ready to be out of the cemetery.

"Did you really say 'doubloon'?" Jake asked as we stepped around graves and over the rope.

"Yes. My mind is tired and that's the first thing that surfaced."

"Ha! The more I say the word, the more I like it."

I hadn't been prepared for the mess inside. It seemed worse in the daylight and smelled so sour and charred, I wondered if Jim should have shut us down. Would the students be able to prepare the cook-off meals in a couple days? As I opened windows for ventilation, I thought about taking the cupcake ingredients home and preparing them there. But there wasn't enough time to divert off course, so I hoped for another strong wind or two.

"Boy, Betts, this looks like it could have gotten bad quickly."

"I know. The fire marshal said we got lucky."

"I'm glad no one got hurt. I guess, except for Everett, that is."

"Yeah, except for Everett. I've got to get someone in here to clean this up, but for now we'll just work on the other side."

Fortunately, the bad odor seemed to clear away and was quickly replaced by good baking smells, and the kitchen area was so large that as we worked at the opposite end we could almost forget there was a mess in the near vicinity.

Cooking or baking with Jake was an unforgettable experience. He loved scents associated with foods and spices. He'd sniff the air around him as he stirred or blended or mixed and make comments like "Divine" or "Sublime" or "Weak" or "So not right." We pulled out many spoons when he was helping because he believed religiously in taste testing. Gram wouldn't let him double dip, and when she once caught him putting his finger into some cookie batter, I thought her head might pop off her neck. She scolded him and then told him that he was required to use spoons, one per dip, and then he'd have to clean them up. Since that moment, he had done as he was instructed.

He was quieter than normal today as I replayed the events of the previous evening. He listened intently, and we both forgot the history lesson about Jerome Cowbender he'd promised to share.

As I spoke, I became increasingly worried. Everett was dead, and if Gram had lied about seeing him earlier in the day, she might have known he was married. I thought back to Everett's wife and her certain accusation. The zip of optimism I'd felt earlier was unzipping and diminishing quickly.

Jake saw my concern, and as we put a batch of cupcakes into the oven he changed the subject with the same hope I'd had in the cemetery — to add some relief or levity to the situation.

"You want to hear about my date last

night?" he said as he leaned against a butcher block table and wiped his hands on a towel.

"You had a date? Of course I want the details."

"My date was the new kindergarten teacher, Sarah O'Neill."

"I think I know who she is and she's very pretty."

"Very. She's also very quiet and perhaps a bit reserved for my boisterousness."

"Perhaps you could use some 'reserved.' "

Jake waved away the thinly veiled insult. "We'll see. We did have fun, but it most definitely wasn't lurve at first sight."

"Love at first sight is a bunch of hooey, Gram would say."

"This from the person who hasn't given another man a fair chance since the second she laid eyes on Cliff Sebastian." Jake put his fingers over his mouth. "I'm sorry. That was not fair and probably mean considering he's back in town." His apology was sincere.

"That's okay. You're probably right." I adjusted my ponytail.

"No. No, I'm not. I have no idea what made me say that. Forgive?" He fake-punched me in the arm.

"Yeah," I said. "I suppose."

"Good. I really am sorry. I don't know

anything, by the way, if you wanted to ask. I haven't met his family. I just heard he was back yesterday. That's the real reason I stopped by — today and yesterday, to make sure you're okay. Miz didn't tell you?"

"I'm fine. Thanks. No, she didn't say a word."

Something made some sort of musical bell sound. "Oop, that's me." He pulled his cell phone out of his pocket. "Hello. Uh-huh. Sure. Okay, on my way." He disconnected. "Gotta go, love. The tourist office is being slammed with large-group tour calls. They need some help answering the phones. You okay without me?"

"Got it covered," I said.

Jake stood on his tiptoes and kissed my cheek. "Sorry for all the drama. Call me — I'll check in with you later today."

I nodded and watched him hurry out of the kitchen. He loved Broken Rope, and he thrived in the summer when he could don his uniform and pretend to be someone else. His association with the Historical Society had been one of the best things to happen to the town. And he had turned his volunteer role into something much larger. Not only was he the poetry-reciting fake sheriff, but he'd also tackled the enormous task of organizing the town's messy piles of historical archives. His hard work and loyalty didn't stop there, though. If the commission needed help with the phones, or anything for that matter, Jake was there to lend a hand.

Despite my distracted mind and the messy kitchen, the cupcakes turned out to be perfect: the right color red, light, chocolaty, and topped with a cream cheese frosting that Jake would have loved to sample. Gram's recipes were almost fail-proof, and I'd made them all so many times that even distractions didn't throw me off my game.

Gram had never minded sharing her recipes, but writing them down had been one of her biggest challenges when she opened the school. She'd learned to cook by watching her mother and her grandmother. They cooked using their intuition, adding just the right ingredients at just the right time, and all without the use of measuring equipment. "People pay better attention when they have to use their noggins, Betts," she'd say. "If you don't have to think about the proportions of ingredients to each other, you get a lazy brain. I don't abide lazy brains."

So before her students baked one cookie or fried one piece of chicken or mashed one potato, Gram spent some time talking to them about the chemistry of food, of ingredients. She wanted her students to be able to think, to know what to do if something didn't work as it should. When should you add flour, an egg, more sugar? When should you add less? Why is the secret red velvet cupcake ingredient vinegar?

And she was right. When you had to think about what you were doing, you paid better attention to how things blended together, and when your experience mixed with your intuition, somehow food transformed and became better.

When the cupcakes were done I went back out to my car for a silver serving platter I thought I'd left in the trunk. It was there, but it was also dirty, hidden under the jumper cables and probably shouldn't be used for the library event. Nonetheless, I took it inside to see if I could clean it up enough.

As I walked back into the school, a scuffing sound caught my attention. All at once I turned, saw a person sitting in the chair in the corner, threw the platter into the air, and screamed. The platter dropped to the floor, its crash punctuating the scream.

"Who are you?" I demanded.

I'd scared him as much as he'd scared me. His dark eyes widened, and before he stood he'd jumped in his seat. Once he was fully upright, he held his hands in a halt position.

"Apologies, ma'am. I didn't mean to scare you." His southern drawl was thicker than Gram's bread pudding.

It wasn't totally unusual that someone I didn't know was in the school. But my car had been parked pretty close to the front door. I would have seen someone go through the doors, unless whoever it was snuck in while I was digging out the platter and the trunk door was up, hiding the school from my view. It had only taken a second or two for me to wrangle the platter, but that might have been enough. The fact that there'd been a murder the day before also probably contributed to the surprise-induced adrenaline running through my system and goosing my heart rate.

"Who are you and what do you want?" I said.

"I'm looking for Missouri Anna," the cowboy said. He put his weight on one hip and casually stuck his thumbs in his belt, but I could tell he was still shaken up, too.

There was something about him that made me think of the glimpse of the vision I'd seen outside the Jasper the night before. He was made up of all the same colors, and my initial thought last night had been that I was seeing a human figure.

He wore a beige shirt and brown leather chaps over tan pants. His black boots were worn and dusty and his hat had seen better days. His face was striking because his features were so sharp and he'd grown and groomed a mustache like the cowboys of old; it rode the top of his lips and then made a wide curve on each side of his mouth down to his jawline. Still, though, there was something about him that left a wonky sense of unreal in my gut. He stood in front of me and he was most definitely real, but it was as though he were somewhat faded. He must have been a new summer character/actor.

"She's not here. Can I help you?" I reached down for the platter.

"No. I need to talk to Missouri." He crouched down, too, but didn't reach to help me with the platter.

I sniffed. Wood smoke.

"Do I smell smoke?" I said aloud, as we both stood again.

"It's possible," he said. "Apologies for that, too."

"No, no, it's okay. Sorry, if that was rude. Anyway, my grandmother isn't here at the moment. I'd be happy to give her a message."

He looked at me a long time, his dark eyes disturbingly intense. "You're Missouri's granddaughter?"

"Yes." Very few people called her by her full first name. "How do you know my gram?"

He looked at me again. It was as though he had to think hard about what to say before he said it. "Long story."

"I'd be happy to give her a message."

His getup was so authentic. I'd often thought many of the actors made their old-fashioned clothes look too crisp and clean. This guy wore wrinkles in all the right places and it looked as though the clothes were worn a little thin. The other cowboys could take a lesson or two from him.

"No. I'll come back by later," he answered more quickly this time.

"Can I give her your name?"

He inspected my face again but then smiled and then tipped his hat like he'd practiced the maneuver and said, "No, thank you. Sorry to have startled you. Ma'am." Then he turned heel and walked out the door, the smell of wood smoke going with him.

I was stunned still for a moment, not sure

what to make of the visitor. He hadn't told me who he was, and the more seconds that ticked by the more I felt like it was my right to know. I followed his path out the door. At least I wanted to see which direction he'd gone. But I didn't see him anywhere. There were no other vehicles in sight. The parking lot was empty except for my car. The road didn't have any traffic.

I concluded that he must have gone into the woods on the other side of the cemetery. That would explain the smoky smell and why I hadn't seen another car, maybe.

But it didn't explain what I'd seen outside the theater last night.

None of it sat right with me, but there was nothing I could do about it. I had cupcakes to deliver. I went back inside, closed and locked the door, searched the entire school for any other surprise visitors, and hurried back to the kitchen.

As I finished organizing the cupcakes onto clean serving platters, something rattled the walls and made the pots and pans clank together violently, but it wasn't the return of the intriguing cowboy. At first I wondered if we were having an earthquake, but it turned out to be a much angrier force of nature.

Gram had walked to the cemetery side of

the school and was pounding on and peering in one of the open windows.

"For crying out loud, Betts, open the blasted door and let me in!"

CHAPTER 6

"Your father took my keys. I had a spare set to the car but not to the school. Do you have any idea how angry I am at him?" Gram's mood was foul at best. She'd tried to reach me on my cell phone to make sure I was taking care of the cupcakes, but for some reason my phone hadn't rung.

"You were up late, Gram. You needed a day off. Dad was just doing what he thought was best."

"I wish everyone would quit treating me like I'm fragile. When in all of your days, Betts, have I been fragile?" Gram flung her hands to her hips. Today she supported the Nebraska Cornhuskers, her red T-shirt a bright topping to her jeans.

"Never," I said, "but these are unusual circumstances."

"I didn't kill Everett. I didn't kill anyone. I'm sad that someone was killed in the supply room of my school, but I've lived long

111

enough to see plenty of dead people. You'd be surprised."

"Speaking of Everett, Jake was here earlier. He said he saw you and Everett together yesterday at lunch. You were out in the cemetery looking at a tombstone."

"Was that yesterday?" Gram said quickly. "I don't think it was. Maybe Jake was mistaken about the day."

She'd responded so quickly and easily that I knew she'd rehearsed the lines. I didn't know if I was more upset about the fact that she was avoiding the truth or that she was avoiding me. I was concerned, of course, that she was making things up to cover for her possible involvement in a crime, but my feelings were also hurt. Gram and I had a pretty great relationship. If she thought so little of it that she didn't know she could be one hundred percent honest with me, then I couldn't help but feel like maybe we weren't as close as I thought. She sensed my concern and stepped around the butcher block and put her hand on my arm.

"Betts, we have a lot to do. Let's not talk about all this nastiness right now. Maybe later, okay? I'm fine, though. You, your dad, and your mom don't need to worry about me or protect me. I'm a big girl."

I nodded. She was making amends, but

she still wasn't telling me the truth. We had to get the cupcakes delivered or I would have pushed it more. We switched into work mode, finished arranging the cupcakes on platters, and then carried them out to her car.

As we were loading them I said, "Oh, we also had a visitor just a little bit ago."

"Who?"

"He was a cowboy — well, a new character/actor, I suppose."

"Here? What did he look like?"

I shrugged. "Like all the cowboys, I suppose. Except this one had a little more cowboy in him. He seemed naturally rugged, not phony like some of the others. Sort of." He'd been a contradiction because though he seemed more authentic, he also seemed less . . . something. I couldn't pinpoint it, but it was as though he'd been made of faded colors. I didn't want to describe him that way. "He smelled of wood smoke."

"What did he want?" she asked.

"He wanted to talk to Missouri. I don't know many people who use your full first name. Do you know who I'm talking about?"

"No," she said.

"Really? He sure seemed to know you."

"Come on, Betts, let's get these cupcakes to the library."

"Did the cowboy have something to do with Everett?"

"No. I mean, I don't know. I don't know who you're talking about."

Gram kept her eyes away from mine. The hurt I'd felt a few minutes ago was transforming into anger. What was she keeping from me, and how could it not have something to do with Everett's murder? If I hadn't been so committed to the read-a-thon, I would've refused to budge and demanded that Gram tell me what was going on. Instead, I told myself to save it until later. I'd get the truth — or the whole story — from her before the day was out. I just wasn't sure what method I'd use to wrestle it free.

We had an old white panel van we sometimes used for deliveries or groceries or whatever, but the cupcakes would fit fine in the back of Gram's old Volvo station wagon. She insisted on driving, probably so she could turn up the radio and continue to avoid me.

It was either that or her love of country music. Gram loved Tim McGraw and Toby Keith. The local country radio station, the only local radio station in fact, played these two artists frequently. When the radio didn't come through, Gram would hit the CD button. Currently, Toby Keith was singing something about a bar or a girl, or a girl in a bar; Gram seemed to know every word.

The library was on the other side of town from the cooking school. It was in a skinny three-story old brick building that was at one time a hospital for the mentally ill; "insane asylum" was the politically incorrect description and the one we all most used. The county hospital was active up until the 1950s when the population grew and shifted in southern Missouri. The need for a larger mental health facility forced ours closed and a new facility was built in Springfield. Along the road in front of the building, a large stone wall announced that you were fast approaching the entrance of the library, still named the Fallow Facility as it had been in its hospital days. Halfway along the perimeter of the wall, the entrance was marked by two tall black wrought-iron gates that were now secured in the open position. Through the entrance, there was a long drive that snaked up toward the main building. The property had been used for a few Hollywood movies because when the backdrop of thunder and lightning was added, there was no hint that the place was a peaceful library. It could just as easily still be a haunted and horrifying facility for long-gone and probably mistreated insane people.

But today was sunny and the parking lot and open field to the side of the building were jam-packed with children and their parents. As she entered through the gate, Gram brought the speed down to something respectable.

"Sarabeth told me to pull to the back door. Right around there." She maneuvered the Volvo and we unloaded the cupcakes, placing them on one of the long tables in the front area of the main floor that was full of beanbag furniture and small chairs. The outside of the building might still have been ominous, but the inside was bright and cheery and made one want to pull out a book and sink into a beanbag.

"Miz, I heard about poor Everett. Found in your supply room! Such a shame!" Sarabeth was as old as Gram and had been Broken Rope's librarian since the beginning of time. She was round and agile and always wore dresses with flowered prints. For years she'd also worn shoes with heels, but for the last five years her footwear of choice had been sneakers. Her size belied her quick agility and made her look kind of mean and rough. But she was one of the sweetest women in town, unless you harmed one of her books. Then the wrath of Sarabeth was frightening and ugly. She'd track down past-due books by showing up at offenders' homes and demanding the book be given to her before she left the premises. There was a story around town that her longest stay had been two days. No one had confirmed the legend, though. No one wanted it not to be true.

"Horrible," Gram said. "Just horrible."

"Does Jim have any leads?" Sarabeth asked.

"Not that I'm aware of," Gram said. Clearly, Sarabeth hadn't heard all the details yet. She wouldn't have been shy about asking how Gram's questioning had gone if she'd known about it.

As we finished arranging the cupcakes so they looked nice next to some pitchers of water and a jar of peppermints, I looked up to see Cliff, now out of his uniform, walk past the large front pane-glass window. He was dressed in jeans and a short-sleeved nice blue shirt. He also held on to the hand of a very small, very adorable little girl.

My heart did two things at once; it thought the child might be one of the cutest it had ever seen so it kind of soared. But mostly, it sank. There it was, that thing I was dreading: seeing Cliff with his family. I and my heart didn't like that part at all.

"What is it, Betts?" Gram asked.

"Huh?"

"You squeaked or something."

"Nothing. Sorry about that." I pulled my glance away from Cliff and the little girl with the head full of short unruly brown hair. But, as though a string was attached to my head and someone tugged on it relentlessly, I turned to watch them again. They were making their way to an area where someone was dressed in a costume from a Dr. Seuss book. Broken Rope was good at anything that required a costume.

"Oh, I see." Gram's eyes followed mine. "Go say hi to him, Betts. It might be better for the two of you to have a conversation that wasn't centered around your grandmother's guilt or innocence. You won't be able to avoid him forever," she said quietly enough so that Sarabeth wouldn't hear.

"I'm fine," I said.

Gram laughed. "Whatever you say, dear."

"Miz, someone dropped off some old cookbooks. I thought about putting them on the shelves to lend out, but I'd really like for you to take a look at them and let me know if you think they're any good. I need to get outside, but do you have a minute to look at them before you leave? They're just in the back in my office."

"Sure," Gram said after she surveyed Cliff's location again and lifted her eyebrows at me. "I don't have to be anywhere for a while."

I rolled my eyes, but that only made her smile bigger.

"You need to get used to him being back, Betts. The sooner, the better," she said, quietly again.

As she turned to follow Sarabeth, I debated escaping out the back door and hiding in Gram's car. It was the chicken way out, but that didn't bother me so much. I realized, though, that Gram was right. Broken Rope was too small to continue to hide whenever I saw Cliff with one of his family members. Besides, it would be easier to start with a daughter than a wife.

I ventured away from the food tables and outside into the throng. I wouldn't force the issue, but if I ran into them, I'd be polite.

The read-a-thon was more a celebration of the end of the school year than a place for kids to sit quietly and read. Mostly, parents and younger children attended to see what Sarabeth recommended for good summer reading — the time away from swimming pools and baseball games that produced the dreaded phrase "I'm bored." Besides the Dr. Seuss character whose name I still couldn't remember, there were tables with all sorts of puzzles, a rubber duck pond, a puppet show, and other various activities that appealed to children of all ages.

It only took a minute or two to run into Cliff and his daughter. His look of surprise seemed genuine.

"Betts, hi! What're you doing here?"

"Catering." I nodded toward the building.

"Great. We'll have to go in and check it out, won't we, Ashley?"

The little girl with unruly hair nodded. She was definitely adorable but didn't look a bit like Cliff. That meant his wife was adorable, too.

I can do this. I can do this. I can do this.

"Betts, this is my niece, Ashley; she's Cora's daughter. Ashley, this is my friend Isabelle Winston." Cora was Cliff's younger sister. I knew she'd gotten married, but I didn't realize she'd had a child — more proof that my family was slipping when it came to keeping me up-to-date regarding Cliff's or his family's life.

My insides imploded a little and relief washed over me. I giggled and said, "Oh, I thought she was your daughter."

"No, I don't have any kids," he said casually.

Now I felt ridiculous. I bit my cheeks to keep from more giddy laughter and just nodded.

"Nice to meet you," Ashley said, proving her manners were rungs above mine.

"Nice to meet you, too."

"Can we go to the duck pond, Uncle Cliff?"

"Sure, kiddo. Talk to you later, Betts?"

I nodded again.

As I watched them walk away, I had a sudden urge to kick my heels in the air and give a woot of glee. And how unbelievably immature would that have been? I imagined what Jake would say if he were here.

You are out of control, Betts.

He would have been right. But Cliff's telling me he didn't have kids was an unexpected bit of good news.

My momentary happiness was interrupted by the high-pitched wail of a siren. Everyone turned toward the open gates. Jim steered his police car, under control at a slow speed but with the lights and siren on full power.

"What the . . . ?" I muttered as I maneuvered my way through the crowd of small people. Was this some sort of event? Part of the party? Maybe so the kids could get a look at a police car? Was the fire truck close behind? Not that I could see.

Jim parked his car, turned off the siren but not the lights, and stepped out. His face was serious and told me he wasn't there for fun. Cliff and Ashley hurried toward him. Jim said something to Cliff as he searched the crowd and then pointed at me.

Suddenly there was a voice in my ear.

"Your gram would never have killed that man," the voice said.

I turned to see the cowboy, still in the same getup and still smelling of wood smoke.

"I know . . . Who are you and how do you know Gram?"

"Don't let them arrest her. She's the only one who can help me and can help them figure out who killed Everett."

"No one's going to arrest anyone," I said.

Jim walked directly to me. Cliff followed behind him as he held on to Ashley's hand.

"Isabelle, where's your gram?" Jim asked as he stopped and put his thumb in his belt buckle next to his gun.

"Why?"

"Where is Miz?" he demanded. He didn't pull his gun out of the holster, but even in the midst of the panic that was spreading

122

through my limbs, I had the sense to be offended at the mere hint that he could if he wanted to.

"She's in Sarabeth's office. Looking at some cookbooks."

Jim made a move to walk past me, but I grabbed his arm. He looked at my grip and then back at my eyes with something that didn't need words attached. I was to let go of him immediately. I did.

But I also followed closely at his heels, with Cliff, Ashley, and the cowboy close on mine.

"Jim, what's going on? Should I call Verna?"

He didn't answer, so I turned and said the same thing to Cliff. He gave me a stern look and shook his head with two quick moves. I was suddenly angry at both of them. What was going on that they couldn't be civil to me? This was not the way things were done in Broken Rope.

"She couldn't kill him, Isabelle. Somehow you need to convince them," the cowboy said.

"How do you propose I do that?" I asked as I tried to keep up with Jim. Cliff shot me another look that got further under my skin. How dare he reprimand, even though it was with just his eyes.

"I don't know, but we need her to help find the real killer," the cowboy said.

"What are you talking about?" I said.

"I'm not talking," Cliff said, his eyes now more questioning than punitive.

"Not you. Him."

Cliff's eyebrows came together before he blew by me and walked next to Jim. Ashley was hanging on to Cliff's hand and her short legs lifted high and quick with the two men's pace.

Jim pulled open one of the big swinging front doors and continued to march toward Gram. Children and parents moved out of our way; the cowboy was following me, bringing the smoky scent with him.

I needed to track down Verna as quickly as possible, but I couldn't manage a call until I knew what Jim would do with Gram.

Jim yanked open the office door. Gram was sitting behind Sarabeth's messy desk, a thick cookbook open in front of her. She looked up casually at each of us.

"Jim, Cliff, Betts," she said, and then her eyes landed on the cowboy. "Uh-oh."

"Missouri Anna Winston, could you please stand up," Jim said. I could hear both anger and pain in his voice.

"What's this about?" Gram said as she stood.

"Missouri, you're under arrest for the murder of Everett Morningside . . ." Jim recited the Miranda warnings as I watched, but I couldn't digest the words. Gram was really being formally arrested for Everett's murder? What had they found?

"Isabelle, do not let them arrest her," the cowboy said again.

"What exactly would you like me to do?" I said loudly.

I didn't know if it was the volume or the tone of my voice, but suddenly everyone stopped what they were doing and looked at me.

"I just want you to stay out of the way," Jim said.

Cliff looked at me with his eyebrows tight together.

Gram said, "Just call Verna, dear. She'll get this taken care of quickly."

"I'm not talking to any of you," I said. "This . . . this guy keeps telling me not to let you arrest Gram. I have no idea how to prevent that."

"What guy?" Jim said.

"What are you talking about?" Cliff said.

"Uh-oh," Gram added.

"This guy whose name I still don't know." I pointed at the cowboy who stood next to

125

me and rubbed his chin as he looked at Gram.

"Threw me for a loop, too, Missouri. I thought you were the only one," the cowboy said.

"The only one what?" I said.

"There's nobody there, Betts," Cliff said.

"Very funny, Betts," Jim said as he took Gram gently by the arm and began to lead her out of the office. "You pick this moment to act foolish?"

"Stop talking, dear," Gram said as she walked by. "And you" — she nodded at the cowboy — "better explain yourself to her. It looks like I'm not going to be able to."

I watched Jim escort Gram out of the library. Cliff, still holding Ashley's hand, followed behind them. Ashley, who had observed the entire scene from her short stance and seemed to be entertained by the adults, smiled and waved at me as they walked away.

I turned to the cowboy and said, "Who the hell are you and what was all that about?"

The cowboy took off his hat and said, "I'm Jerome Cowbender. Pleased to make your acquaintance."

I wasn't sure whether to laugh or scream.

CHAPTER 7

"You're playing the part of Jerome Cow-bender this tourist season?" I said as we sat across from each other in Sarabeth's office.

Before I could focus on the cowboy, I called Verna and my parents and asked them to get to the jail as soon as possible. I told them I'd join them eventually. I let Sarabeth know that I was pretty shaken up and needed some time to gather myself. I asked if I could sit in her office. She'd said that was fine, and because she didn't seem to see the cowboy sitting in the chair across from me, I didn't mention him to her.

I wasn't lying; I was shaken up. I was literally shaking with fear and nervousness. My throat was tight and my stomach was turning painfully. I was trying to keep myself together because I needed answers. If Gram wasn't going to give me any, maybe the man sitting across from me would.

"No, ma'am, I'm Jerome, or I guess I'm

his ghost. At least that's what Missouri tells me."

"She tells you?" Obviously, something strange was going on, but I wasn't ready to believe it was something as weird as the ghost of Jerome Cowbender.

"Yes. I don't feel dead, but I died some time ago. Tragically. Someone shot me in the back. I don't remember it, though. Not yet at least. Every time I visit, it takes me a little time for some bits and pieces of my memory to tie back together. Sometimes I'm not around long enough to get much back."

"I have no idea what to say to that except that you must be an actor playing Jerome Cowbender this summer. There's no other reasonable explanation."

"No, I'm the real one; what's left of him at least. Here touch me." He extended one of his heavily calloused hands over the desk. "It's going to be strange, mind you, but it'll probably convince you."

I hesitated but only because I knew that if he didn't feel like a normal human being I'd have to accept that his story might have some truth to it. I knew that since no one else, except maybe Gram, could see him it probably meant he wasn't human, but I was more willing to think I was losing my

128

marbles than believe he was a real ghost.

"Go on, I can't hurt you. I can't really hurt anyone. Not anymore."

I took a deep breath and then reached to his hand, and hesitantly put my finger to one of his. And my finger went right through him. I did it again, and again.

"Holy sh—" I could feel my heart pound in my chest. "I don't understand. How is this possible?"

"I don't know."

"You don't know? Could you start from the beginning?"

"The beginning of what?"

"How do you know Gram?"

"Oh, that. Missouri says that when she was a newborn I saved her from a fire. Well, my ghost did. It was the first time I came back. She says I've been 'haunting' her on and off since I died."

"You saved her from the fire when you first came back? You mean you were a ghost?"

"Yep . . . well, understand that right now I don't remember the fire; I just remember her telling me about it. The longer I'm here, the more I remember from when I was alive and from my visits as a ghost, but there're no guarantees."

No guarantees? Apparently not. Ghosts

weren't really supposed to exist, were they? Wasn't there some sort of rule that ghosts only belonged in scary stories and big imaginations? The fact that I just might be talking to one tilted everything I thought was real. Something suddenly becoming real that wasn't supposed to be irrevocably changed my perspective about everything. I just wasn't sure what my new perspective was. Confusion only scratched the surface of what I was feeling and thinking.

"She says that she was only a day old when the fire broke out in her family's home. They lived outside town in a two-room shack that got hit by lightning. I was . . . it's hard to explain, but I was 'pulled' back, a part of me was anyway, and I somehow got her and her momma out of the fire. That was the first time and the only time as a ghost, according to Missouri, that I've been able to physically move things."

"You don't remember that?" I asked.

"I remember Missouri telling me about it. At the moment I don't remember doing it."

I'd heard the story of the lightning and the fire, but no one had mentioned that the ghost of Jerome Cowbender, the infamous bank robber, had been the hero who saved two of my family members. "You've been a part of Gram's life since then?"

"Yes. I come and go. It's unpredictable but sometimes I come back when something bad has happened."

I thought. "The fire? Did the fire — pardon the pun — spark you to come back this time?"

"I don't rightly know, but Missouri and I will figure it out eventually. I know she was in the jail last night. When I realized why, I thought maybe I was supposed to help clear her name."

"Last night was less serious than today. Now Gram's been officially arrested for the murder of Everett Morningside," I said. "If you have any information that would clear her, you should probably tell me."

"I don't have much right now, but maybe I'll come upon something."

"How?"

"Again, I don't rightly know just yet, but give me a little time. Missouri couldn't kill anyone, at least not if they weren't threatening her or her family. I'm sure we'll figure it out."

We?

"Who, besides me and Gram, can see you?" I asked.

"I don't know of anyone. I didn't know you could until this morning at the school when you scared the spit out of me."

"I saw you last night. Were you outside the theater?"

"Yes, I was looking for Missouri. I knew where she was, but I couldn't get into the jail."

"Couldn't?"

"Yes, I tried pretty hard last night. I just can't. I remember trying other times before but never made it in. Must have something to do with having been an outlaw."

I laughed, but it was uncomfortable. I was having a conversation with a ghost, a ghost of an outlaw who seemed pretty harmless at the moment and pretty matter-of-fact about his days of criminal behavior.

It was the fact that I'd seen Gram look at him and talk to him that made me think I probably hadn't lost my mind. If I'd been the only one to see him, I would have been more concerned about my mental stability.

Even though I didn't feel that I was one hundred percent aboard the notion that a ghost existed, I was ready to almost-all-the-way believe that *this* one did. And, if I really thought about it, a ghost residing in Broken Rope, Missouri, a place with a strange and deadly history, might not be too much of a stretch anyway.

There was a good reason Jerome seemed so authentic; he was the real deal, sort of.

He was as real as the ghost of someone could be at least. However, there was always a chance that I was rationalizing my confusion and the ghost was just a figment of my imagination. If that was the case, I would need some mental health help. The irony of recognizing my potential craziness in an old insane asylum wasn't lost on me, which made me think I wasn't crazy. Crazy people probably didn't recognize irony.

"In my explorin', I came upon a little something, though. It might be important and it was about me."

"I guess you should tell me what it was, Jerome. Unless you can make yourself appear to Jim, I'm going to have to be your voice." I gulped. Believing that the ghost was real was one thing, but speaking for said ghost would be a whole different challenge.

Jerome looked at me a long time as he traced the lines of his mustache with his finger and thumb. His eyes were dark and intelligent, though I'd never associated intelligence with the people who'd made the history that Broken Rope built its tourist economy on. That was probably a mistake, I thought, and something I would need to reconsider.

He leaned forward and put his elbows on his knees. "Apparently, somewhere, when I was alive, I buried a treasure, a whopper of a treasure, to tell the truth. Gold. I stole it, I think. I don't know for certain that the treasure had something to do with Mr. Morningside's murder, but considerin' what I saw yesterday, I'm thinking that gold is somehow involved."

"The gold piece on your tombstone — did you see it? I saw it today. Did you put it there?"

"I didn't put it there, but I did see it. Everett also owned the Jasper Theater. Last night, well early this morning when I figured out what was going on, I spent some time roaming around in there. There was a piece of paper on Everett's desk that mentioned something about me and the treasure. I couldn't see the whole thing so I don't know what it was all about. We need to ask Missouri, but I'd be willing to bet that Everett might have been onto something."

"You really did steal gold?"

"I don't remember. I'm just going on what I happened to see on the paper."

"Jake."

"What?"

"Jake, my friend, can help us. He knows more than anyone about the history of Broken Rope. He'll know more than anyone about your criminal behavior."

"Good. You'll talk to Jake. But we've got to remember one other thing, Isabelle."

I nodded.

"If Everett was onto something, maybe Missouri was, too. We'll need to ask her questions, but she might need protecting, too."

I hadn't made the connection, but as I thought about what Jake said about seeing Gram and Everett together by Jerome's tombstone and all the time they seemed to have spent together, I thought he might have a point.

No one would hurt Gram. Everyone loved her. But if a treasure really was involved, fondness for Gram might not help much. Money drove people to do desperate things; a treasure full of gold could bring out the greed in almost anyone.

Of course, I hadn't wanted Gram arrested for Everett's murder, but maybe having her behind bars was one way to keep her safe. Who knew what might happen?

This was Broken Rope, Missouri, after all.

CHAPTER 8

I tried not to dwell on Jerome's appearance and his subsequent disappearance. The visit to the library had been full of more unexpected surprises: Cliff with his niece, Gram's arrest, and making the acquaintance of a ghost.

Shortly after he scared me about Gram's safety, Jerome left. He told me he was going to have to go and then he disappeared without a sound and all at once. He didn't fade from view, and he didn't go one part at a time. He was gone in a blink — quicker actually. As the smell of smoke went with him, I became acutely aware of the scent of spearmint from a pack of gum on Sarabeth's desk.

Once Jerome was gone, doubts about his existence bloomed. With him out of sight, it was probably only normal to question if he'd really been there at all. I couldn't be sure, but I knew I didn't have time to dwell on anything.

I made a hasty departure from the library, steering Gram's Volvo down the winding drive and out through the open gates. Sarabeth had managed to downplay Gram's arrest, and the read-a-thon event hadn't missed a beat. By the evening, word would spread that the arrest had been real, not an act for the event or the quickly approaching beginning of the tourist season. Missouri Anna was in real trouble and that would be something everyone would want to talk about.

The trip back to town was quick. I parked in front of Jake's office, noticing that my parents' car was parked across the street at the jail. I didn't see my brother's or Verna's cars, but I couldn't worry about that now. My parents would take care of whatever Gram needed for the time being.

I hurried over the wooden boardwalk and knocked on the old double door. Jake would be keeping the doors locked to ensure that everything was neat and tidy for our visitors. His bike was chained to a hitching post, so I knew he was either inside or close by. He'd be working on his poems or cleaning or working in the back of the building amid the town's historical archives. I spent plenty of time in the front part of his office, but the archive area was foreign to me — documents back there were yellowish and smelled old or of dust, though it was unwise to mention the word *dust* to Jake. He took it personally.

"Betts," someone said from my right. I turned to see the last person I ever wanted to see. Ophelia Buford was marching toward me, her high shoes clomping loudly on the wooden walkway.

"Opie," I said in greeting. It was her nickname, and much to my constant surprise, she didn't find it insulting. She was wearing something from the same era of Jerome Cowbender's living days, but hers was scant on material covering her chest. Her waist was cinched so tightly that I wondered how she could breathe.

Every year Ophelia played a different town character. She had the time. She was my age, and her family was rich — rich in ways like buying new cars every six months and traveling so much that it seemed they were away more than they were home. They lived in a big house on lots of land in the country, about ten minutes away from the cooking school. They called the property Tara. Every year we had to convince Ophelia that Scarlett O'Hara's story had nothing to do with Broken Rope, and we just didn't need her to dress up as her favorite character.

It looked like we weren't going to have that problem this year. Ophelia's wig was big and blond, not brunet, and her less-than-conservative dress was bright yellow, not the green of the ill-fated draperies she tried so frequently to duplicate.

"I heard about your gram, Betts," she said as most of her came to a stop. Some things still jiggled, and it was difficult not to look at them.

"I'm sure it'll all get figured out, Ophelia," I said with a sigh. Conversations with Ophelia were full of passive-aggressive undertones, probably on both our parts, and it was required that I be at the top of my game to banter effectively. At the moment, I didn't have it in me.

"Well, they found fingerprints I heard. Such a shame, such a shame. Your gram always has had something of a temper, you know."

I didn't know they'd found fingerprints. How did she know? But I bit the inside of my cheek. I wasn't going to let her bait me, not today, not right now.

The door swung open, and as Jake took in the sight of me and my rival, a big smile lit his face.

"Ophelia Buford, as I live and breathe,

you are something to behold," he said, thickening his southern drawl and winking. "Who are you?"

Ophelia had always liked Jake, and Jake had always tried to see the world from Opie's eyes — eyes that had been tainted by too much money, not enough parental attention, and lots of rejection, including a heavy dose of it from my old boyfriend, Cliff Sebastian. If Opie's and my relationship hadn't been doomed from the first day of kindergarten when she bit me and I slapped her, we were certainly going to go down the wrong path when we were sixteen and Cliff dumped her for me.

"This year I'm Sally Swarthmore," she said proudly, things still jiggling.

"Really?" Jake said. "The ax murderer?"

"Perhaps she was just misunderstood," I said quietly, and raised an eyebrow at Jake.

"No, as a matter of fact, she wasn't misunderstood in the least. She was a killer and she offed her family in a fit of rage that is legendary. If you'd pay attention to the history lessons, you'd know," Jake said, raising his own eyebrow.

"Yes, the ax murderer," Ophelia said proudly. "I just need to find the ax, which is where I'm headed now. I'm getting a real one at the hardware store. I got it approved

— if I keep a safe distance from tourists. Although I wonder now, with the recent murder and everything, if they'll take away my ax rights."

I ignored her.

"Well, you look fabulous," Jake said sincerely.

"Thank you," she said to Jake. She turned to me. "Betts, I'm also sorry about Cliff's return to Broken Rope. I know it has to be difficult for you. I had coffee with him yesterday and told him he should have let you know before he just showed up in that handsome uniform. He must not have thought it necessary." She didn't make the tsk-tsk noise, but I heard it in my head nonetheless.

I looked at her but still didn't say anything. Jake touched my arm lightly to remind me of something I'd asked him to do years earlier. Whenever Opie was in the vicinity, I had an almost undeniable urge to beat her senseless. I'd come too close a couple times; in unladylike thuggish moments, I'd even pulled my fist back once or twice. Fortunately, either I'd stopped myself, or Jake had stopped me from finishing the punch. I'd asked him to pinch me lightly whenever she was around, so I would remember to remain nonviolent. It had worked pretty well, but at that moment I felt my fingers begin to curl into a fist.

"Well, TTFN," Opie said with a wicked smile before she pushed past me and continued clumping and jiggling down the boardwalk.

"Ugh," I said.

"Relax," Jake said. "She does and says all that stuff just to get you fired up. You buy into it too easily. If you just didn't act as though it bothered you, I'm sure she'd stop."

"You really think that?"

Jake shrugged. "You took her boyfriend, Betts. That's a pretty good reason to hold a grudge."

"We were in high school."

Jake shrugged again.

"And what was Cliff doing having coffee with her yesterday?"

Jake sighed. "Well, I suppose you won't be able to act as though she doesn't bug you until she really doesn't."

I took a deep, cleansing breath. I had a plateful of things to worry about already. I didn't need to let Opie get under my skin.

"Jake, Gram's been arrested. I need some history lessons."

"Really? Oh, I'm so sorry. What did they

find, and how are history lessons going to help?"

"I think they found her fingerprints on the bag over Everett's head. It'll make a pretty good circumstantial argument, but now I need to know more. Remember that gold piece you found on Jerome Cowbender's grave?"

"The 'doubloon'? Sure."

"Jerome supposedly buried a gold treasure. I need to know as much as I possibly can about him and the treasure. I think it might have something to do with Everett's death."

Jake's head tilted to the side and his eyebrows came together. "I don't understand, Betts. What's going on? Does an old buried treasure really have something to do with all of this?"

I hadn't had time to think about it much, but I'd decided I was going to have to tell Jake about my close encounter with the dead kind. He was someone I could trust implicitly. If I didn't tell him, I would have to operate in half-truths and elusiveness. I didn't want to do that with my oldest, best, and most loyal friend. I needed for him to know. I needed his help. Even if he didn't believe my story, he'd give me the benefit of the doubt no matter what.

"Jake, I need you to bear with me no matter what I tell you next, okay?"

"Always."

"Jerome Cowbender is most definitely dead, but he and I have had some . . . contact recently. In fact, he, well, his ghost, and Gram have known each other for almost all her life." I paused for Jake's reaction. He was looking at me intensely, but I didn't see any doubt. "He told me that Everett Morningside — and maybe Gram — was probably looking into the treasure, which might be why Everett was killed and why Gram's life might be in danger. I need to try to find that treasure, or information about the treasure, or information about Jerome." I sighed. "I guess I just need to know what there is to know. Maybe we'll be able to find the right killer. Maybe we'll find a treasure, but I highly doubt it. It's all I've got — the gold piece on the tombstone and the ghost of Jerome Cowbender. It's all pretty flimsy. I need more and I think you can help."

Jake blinked, tilted his head again, and then blinked again. He opened his mouth and then shut it. He bit at his bottom lip and then stretched his neck.

"Come on in, Betts. Let's see what we can figure out," he finally said as he held the door wide open.

Once I was inside, Jake peered both directions down Main Street and then closed the door and locked it.

"I've always wondered about the ghosts of Broken Rope," he said. "Oh, I've never seen one, but I presumed they were around. Come on, let's see what we can find."

I smiled, but I was also so relieved that I wanted to cry a little. Telling him had been the right thing to do. We'd figure this out together, no matter what grave we had to rattle.

CHAPTER 9

Jake had organized Broken Rope's archives in a way that was both neat and precise as well as mysterious. He claimed that he knew where everything was and that there was an alphabetical and by-date reference system, sort of. All I could see was a tall-ceilinged room that was full of stuff — neatly organized stuff but stuff nonetheless.

The room was bathed in a yellowish light, which was soothing and, he once told me, kind and gentle to old things. The chandelier that gave off the light was in itself a part of Broken Rope's history. At one time it had hung in the saloon (back in the liquor-only days, no ice cream). Its big white glass dome had once covered a candle that didn't illuminate much but made a great fire hazard. Somehow a bullet ricocheted off a piece of the chandelier and killed the saloon owner who was, at the time, a woman named Retta O'Brien. She'd come to town, running from some bad choices, and hadn't wanted to join the ranks of prostitution so she'd disguised herself as a man. She bought the saloon with a bank loan she wouldn't have been given as a woman and ran the place as Rhett O'Brien. No one knew her secret until she was killed, and the coroner shared the surprise news. The chandelier was immediately looked upon as bad luck, so the next owner took it down and threw it away. Someone, with a vision for history, retrieved it and saved it in the back of a store. It had been discovered and given to the society about ten years ago. Jake wired it for electricity and now it hung with a sign attached: 1889 — A RICOCHET OFF THIS CHANDELIER KILLED RETTA (RHETT) O'BRIEN IN A GUNFIGHT OVER SOME NO-GOOD CHEATING FOOLS PLAYING A CARD GAME. CARD GAME UNKNOWN.

The room had other lighting, too; fluorescent lights hung from the high ceiling, but they weren't as noticeable as the large chandelier in the middle.

A large table took up most of the spacious room. Jake called it his worktable. He had it constructed by a local woodworker and it was the biggest, smoothest table I'd ever seen. Jake said it cost him a fortune, but he wouldn't tell exactly how much. It was surrounded by stools that fit comfortably underneath it when they weren't in use. As particular as he was, if you didn't push in your stool when you were done at the table, he'd scold you and make you turn around and take care of your mistake.

There were a couple of smallish windows high up on the back wall, but they were always closed. Jake said the windows caused him worry because of possible pollutants or whatever they might let into the room. They weren't big enough for an adult to fit through, but if a small child were brave or stupid enough to climb a ladder up the outside wall, they might be able to fit and make their way inside. But once inside, they would be greeted by packed shelves and file cabinets as the only methods of making it to the ground. The climb down would be precarious at best and result in a certain broken bone or two at worst. There was also a back door — a steel security door with three deadbolts. Fire code dictated that he had to have the door, but Jake wasn't going to make it easy for anyone to get through it.

Between Verna's genealogy work and Jake's innate curiosity, the two of them had become good friends, sharing things about dead people that had never tripped my trigger. Verna had spent many hours with Jake in the archive room as they pored over things that were hard to decipher or understand. But I'd never spent a lot of time in the room or listened closely when Jake spoke about what was on the shelves or in the file cabinets. I'd never had much interest in the history of Broken Rope. Our history was so much a part of our present day that once I listened to the stories we shared with the tourists, I didn't have much desire to pay attention to something new.

But today was different. Today I wanted to learn as much as I could about Jerome Cowbender.

As we sat on stools, I told Jake about my encounters with the ghost of Jerome and how real, though not completely human, he'd seemed and behaved. I told Jake about the distinct wood smoke smell and the sense of authenticity Jerome's ghost carried with him.

Jake listened closely.

"You believe me?" I finally said when he had remained silent as I finished my story.

"I don't disbelieve you. I'm certain Broken Rope is haunted, Betts, but I've never seen a ghost myself. I'm jealous that you might have. I'm still not one hundred percent sure you've seen a ghost so much as . . . as . . ."

"What, Jake?"

"As maybe just had a haunted experience."

"What's the difference?"

"You might be picking up on vibes but a full-fledged ghost? I just don't know. I want to believe everything you ever say. I know you've never lied to me, and I know you have your wits about you. I also know you want to help Miz. As much as I want to believe, it still might take me a little time to get there. Either way, I'm here to help." Jake hopped off the stool. "I do think that whatever you experienced, and whoever it was that was relaying this experience to you was most definitely onto something. I was checking out Jerome's tombstone because I'd seen Miz and Everett looking at it, sure, but there's more. Everett had recently visited me, too. Right here in the archives. He came in about a month ago and started asking to look at everything I had about Jerome. I had no idea why, but I was thrilled to find a willing pupil."

Jake fingered through a stack of items that was on a low shelf. "Because he'd been coming in, I had a chance to look through pretty much everything I have and make one big Jerome stack. Normally, I keep things filed by dates and names, but Jerome was all over the place, I'm embarrassed to say. Anyway, now he's right here — or what I have of him is. I might have more and I'll keep looking." Jake heaved a stack of items from the shelf to the table.

Every piece was wrapped in its own plastic cover and the stack was a good six inches high. Some items were about poster board size, other items small. A piece of plastic about the size of a business card rode the top of the pile.

"What's that?" I grabbed for it first.

"That's a button from one of Jerome's coats."

I looked through the plastic and rubbed my fingers over the button. "I didn't know they had metal buttons back then."

"They did. It was this single button that made me originally question Jerome's reputation. This is not a common criminal's button. It is from a nice suit of clothes, nicer than what most of the Broken Rope men wore at the time. My research shows me there's much that says he wasn't just a common criminal."

"Any chance you could tell me what's here so I don't have to look at every single thing? I feel the need to hurry."

"Sure. Sort of at least. I know the high points, but I'll research the other things, too, and let you know later. For now, Jerome wasn't from Broken Rope. He came here from Boston."

"Boston?"

"Yes, Boston. He was considered a gentleman there, but I need to brush up on those details. I will. Anyway, for reasons unknown when he first moved here, he left Boston and traveled west."

"Lots of people did that," I said.

"Yes, but it wasn't until he'd lived here awhile that other Broken Rope residents figured why he left Boston. He was on the run from the law. He'd been accused of killing a man and instead of facing what he thought would be a certain guilty verdict, he escaped jail and ran — or rode — away."

"So he was an outlaw, then?"

"Yes, at one point. But when the citizens found out about his shady past, they decided to forget about it because they all liked him so much. He was a loner, lived out in the woods, came into town for supplies, and at one point had some cattle. Everyone liked him so much that they forgave him of the crime he insisted he hadn't committed. It was Broken Rope, after all."

"You said 'at first' he was an outlaw."

"He was eventually cleared of the crime in Boston. Word didn't travel quickly back then, but I found an article that printed in

Boston after the time of his death that cleared him. Unfortunately, I don't know if he ever knew, and by the time he was shot down by the sheriff, he'd taken on the full title of local thief in Broken Rope."

"What happened?"

"That's the part Everett was trying to figure out. What happened to turn this nice, quiet man into a thief?"

"And?"

Jake shrugged. "Still not sure. Close to the time Jerome started stealing things, there were articles in *The Noose* about him coming to town more often and doing 'good deeds.' It was as if a switch was flipped and he one day turned bad."

"Strange."

"Maybe you could ask him? In fact, if you could get a full historical account of his life, I'd be forever in your debt."

"You do believe me."

"Well, let's put it this way, if you get me a full historical account, I'll definitely believe you."

"He doesn't remember his life. He says the longer he's around, the more he remembers, but he's never sure how long he gets to stay."

"Why is he here? I mean, why now?"

"He thinks it has something to do with

helping Gram. Since he saved her from the fire, he thinks he's supposed to show up when she needs help."

"Why does that make sense to me?" Jake laughed.

"I don't know, but it does, doesn't it? What about the treasure? Or the legend that he was a bank robber but that he couldn't shoot a gun well?"

"Again, a little sketchy, but I'll do my best." Jake thumbed through the stack of archived items and pulled out something that was contained in an 8 1/2 × 11 plastic folder. "Here are two more articles from *The Noose,* our newspaper. You can't take them out of the plastic, but I did what I could to translate what first looks like gibberish. Here're my translations. One article might explain his reputation and hints at the good deeds. The other one plays a whole different tune." He pulled out some papers from a pocket behind the main one. "Read."

The papers encased in the plastic did look like they were written in gibberish, faded gibberish, actually. Jake must have painstakingly used a magnifying glass and borrowed some patience from an old dead monk to translate what he had.

I cleared my throat and read the first article. "Broken Rope resident, Jerome

Cowbender, was mistaken for some local bandits yesterday. Mr. Cowbender happened to mosey into town right at (?) when the local Bank and Trust was being robbed. Some robber scoundrels [I think that's the word] left the bank with bags full of money and fast horses. Mr. Cowbender drew his weapon and commanded them to stop. When they didn't, he started shooting, causing bullets to fly willy-nilly around Main Street but not causing harm to any living beings, be they good guys or bad.

"A misunderstanding ensued when Sheriff Earp [not of the famous Earps. I might have the name wrong] shot at Mr. Cowbender. Fortunately, his shot was off a little that day, too.

"No one was hurt and the misunderstanding seems to have been cleared up."

I put the paper down and looked at Jake. "Jerome was killed by the sheriff in a *later* gun battle, right?"

"I do believe that is true."

"So he wasn't a bad guy *again* until he was? And this makes no mention of the treasure."

"I know. Here, now read this one." Jake pointed at the other article.

I read: "If anyone knows the whereabouts and wherefores of local resident Jerome

Cowbender, would you please come forward and tell Sheriff Earp. Mr. Cowbender is wanted so's he can answer some questions about some missing gold pieces."

"Where were the gold pieces from?"

Jake shrugged. "I don't know. Journalism wasn't as thorough as it is now, but I think Everett was onto something. He came in the day before he was killed and asked to go through the archives again. He'd been respectful of all the documents so I let him be. I worked up front. I have no idea what he looked at. Except . . . now something's missing."

"Huh?"

"Something's missing." Jake held an empty plastic folder.

"What do you mean?"

"I think Everett took whatever was in this one. I went through everything this morning and this folder was empty. My system isn't set up yet so that I know what was in this specific folder. It's my goal to number everything and have a short description of each item in a computer file, but I'm just not there. In light of everything, I feel kind of terrible."

"Jake, you're a one-person operation here. You've done an amazing job with all this junk — okay, it isn't junk, sorry. But no one else has your vision and if any town needs this sort of organization, it's Broken Rope. The fact that you even know that Everett took something is helpful," I said. "Besides, I bet I know what it was. Jerome said he had been looking around the Jasper last night and saw a piece of paper mentioning him and the treasure on Everett's desk. He only saw part of it — he can't move things — so he doesn't know what else was on it, but he's sure he and the treasure were mentioned."

Jake half smiled. "That's probably it. I don't remember what it could be, but maybe I can look for it elsewhere. Thanks, Betts. I suspect that it will tell us about more than just a piece of Broken Rope's history, it might — might — help us figure out who the killer is."

"Or maybe more about the treasure. I didn't think it was important at first, but we'd better tell Jim about the gold piece on the tombstone. Or . . ." I bit on my cheek as I looked at Jake.

"What?"

"Gram lied to the police about seeing Everett earlier that day."

"So you don't want me to mention that I saw them either?"

"It would be wrong of me to suggest such

a thing," I said.

"Oh, quit being such a law school drop-out. I know Miz didn't kill anyone. I'm not going to tell the police anything that might make her look guilty, don't worry about that. We'll keep the gold piece to ourselves for a while."

"Thank you, Jake."

He waved away my gratitude.

"We also need to get into the Jasper and see if we can retrieve that piece of paper," I said.

"It's locked up tight right now. I think Jim searched it for evidence and is now looking for someone to run it on tourist opening day."

"And I really, really need to talk to Gram again."

"Hang on. One step at a time, Betts," Jake said. "Maybe we could see if we can get into the Jasper. I might know a trick or two. Let's start there."

"Good idea," I said, glad to put my energy toward something on my growing to-do list.

Jake shooed me out of the archive room so he could refile without distraction. As I waited for him, I looked out the front window and confirmed that my parents were still at the jail. It looked like my brother had also joined them. I wondered

158

briefly where he'd been.

I craned my neck and looked down the street toward the Jasper. It was dark and seemed sad and lonely. Even the small marquee that announced the currently playing movie wasn't lit anymore. While it wouldn't do much harm to have it closed, it would be a disappointment for some of our visitors. The Jasper wasn't only a place to see movies; it was also a Broken Rope historical landmark. Visitors loved the old photographs inside as well as the mosaic designs on the auditorium walls.

The pool hall was directly next to the theater. I'm not usually into gossipy things, but it was difficult not to notice local bartender and one of Gram's current nighters, Jenna Hopper, exiting the pool hall. Normally, someone leaving the pool hall wasn't cause for much interest, but Jenna behaved curiously enough to get my attention. She looked around as if she was concerned about being seen, fluffed her hair, and then hurried away.

I smiled. I'd suspected the potential romance between she and Miles; this scene made me think I was on the right track.

"Mmm."

"What?" Jake said as he joined me at the window.

"Nothing. Just looking around."

Jake looked out the window, but Jenna walking toward the saloon wasn't all that interesting.

"Okay, let's go," Jake said as he unlocked the door and held it open.

CHAPTER 10

"The Jasper was built in 1872," Jake said as we tried one of the two sets of large front doors. All four doors were locked and didn't budge no matter how many times we pulled. "It was specifically built to house a burlesque troupe."

"Burlesque was like a variety show with lots of cleavage?" I said.

A ticket booth extended from the center of the building. I put my forehead to the glass but couldn't see how the ticket seller made it back and forth from the main building. There must be a door, but it wasn't distinguishable.

"Heavy on the cleavage," Jake said. "One part of Burlesque was all about sex, the striptease. Think about it, what women were wearing at the time. They were covered from head to toe. Imagine the draw of a woman in tights who could move some big feathers to give the illusion that she wasn't covered

161

up on the top. It was all about sex, but there was still good music and bawdy humor, too."

"Women in tights? I thought the women were really uncovered."

"Sure, but it happened in steps. I actually think it was burlesque that progressed women's fashion to the point of bearable. Burlesque lasted through the sixties, the nineteen sixties. Even though it objectified women in its own way, I think it helped free them from some horrible clothing."

"I never thought about it like that," I said.

"I know, but you seem such a willing student right now. I'm taking advantage of the moment." Jake smiled and put his hands on his hips. "We're not getting in this way. Let's check around back."

"They locked the doors." Stuart Benson had emerged from his shoe repair shop. He stood in the doorway and rearranged his jeweler's visor as he spoke. "Because of the murder, I assume."

"Thanks, Stuart." I waved.

"No problem. Be careful. Remember there's a killer on the loose," Stuart said before sinking back into his shop and closing the door.

"That was eerie," Jake said.

"To the back?" I said as I shrugged.

"To the back."

There was an alley behind all the buildings along Main Street, but the only way to access it was at the end of the blocks. We'd have to walk down the street and around the buildings. As we passed the pool hall, Miles tapped on the front window and signaled us inside. He held a bottle of window cleaner and an old rag. Maybe Jenna had been helping him clean?

"Should we? We don't really have time," I said without moving my lips.

"Sure," Jake said. "Miles is a good guy. Let's see what he wants."

The long walnut bar inside the pool hall was pocked with time; scratches, stains, and gouges hinted that it had seen its fair share of rowdy moments, spilled drinks, and an occasional fight or two. A long brass footrest also extended the length of the bar; it shone brightly. Miles was particular about the pool hall's cleanliness, and a number of times I'd seen him on his hands and knees polishing the footrest. He swept the eight pool/billiard tables continuously and mopped the entire checkered linoleum tile floor every night. A mirror covered the wall behind the bar — a bar that no longer held alcohol but did have floor refrigerator cases full of sodas, sandwich ingredients, and candy bars of all flavors. The customers loved the cold candy bars.

Smoking had been illegal in public places in Broken Rope for years, but sometimes when I was in the pool hall I could smell the remnants of the days when men and boys and a few women leaned over the tables and aimed their cues with one eye open because the other one was closed against the smoke drifting upward from the cigarette between their lips.

"Betts, how's your gram?" Miles said as he made his way around to the backside of the bar and set down the cleaning supplies.

"I'm sure she'll be fine, Miles," I said. I wasn't sure if he was asking about her welfare after finding Everett's body or if he'd heard she'd been arrested.

"Good. I'm just so sorry about Everett. He was one of the nicest men. I don't understand . . ."

"You got to know him pretty well, then?" Jake asked.

"Sure, he was right next door. He'd frequently come over for lunch. And sometimes Miz joined him for dinner."

Gram and Everett were having sandwiches at the pool hall? Those were their hot dates? Didn't sound very romantic.

"They have dinner together often?" I

164

asked, but I only sort of wanted to hear the answer. It didn't take the short time I spent in law school to know that when questioning someone regarding something potentially criminal, it wasn't wise to ask a question you didn't already know the answer to. But what difference would it make if I knew how often they'd seen each other? I was unsure enough to be wary but curious enough to ask.

"I don't know. A couple nights a week and at least once on the weekends for the past few weeks. They seemed to get along pretty well. I thought they made a cute couple."

Miles was probably close to forty, but his short and shaggy brown hair made him seem younger. Everything about him was thin: his face, his close-set brown eyes, his nose, and his body. He always wore loose-fitting pants, either black or khaki; T-shirts in the summer; sweaters in the winter. He reminded me of movie portrayals of a stereotypical absentminded professor, but he wasn't absentminded at all. He'd moved to Broken Rope and purchased the pool hall about five years earlier. I knew he'd never married, but I didn't know anything else about his private life. His care for the pool hall had turned it into a popular place. His sandwiches made him a strong competitor for Bunny's diner, but I didn't think she minded.

I thought back to when Mrs. Morningside made her entrance at the school. Miles and the other nighters had been in the kitchen area, and though they might have heard the commotion, they must not have caught on to the details. Miles might not even know that Everett was married.

"Did you ever chat with them?" I asked.

"Not really. They'd sit down at the end of the bar. They ordered food and then ate it while they looked at papers. I thought they might be writing a book or something, but I realized they were reading things, not writing them."

"Did you get a close look at the papers?" Jake asked.

"No, never. They weren't rude about it, but they certainly didn't want me to see what they were looking at. They'd always go back to the Jasper after eating. I'm so sorry he's gone. I was tired last night, and I feel like I was less than patient with the police calling us back to the school. I apologize. That's really why I wanted to talk to you, Betts. Sorry if I was rude."

"I appreciate that, but no problem. Really. Thanks, Miles."

"Sure, sure. Let me know what I can do,

okay?" Miles said.

"I hope you're still planning on judging the cook-off."

Miles blinked. "That still going on?"

"I've decided that it is. It has to. The cook-off is more than Gram, more than the cooking school. It's the kick-off to the tourist season. The students who've been working so hard would be cheated out of the competition, and the winner always puts it on his or her résumé. The townspeople would be disappointed, and the tourists who've already planned to be here for the event might be beyond disappointed all the way to angry. We have to have it."

Miles nodded slowly. "I get that, I just thought . . . Well, of course I'm still in."

"You'll be at the judge meeting tomorrow morning then?" I said.

"Yes, bright and early."

"Thanks, Miles. See you later."

Once clear of Miles's being able to either hear us or read our lips, Jake said, "Did you know that Miz was spending so much time with Everett?"

"I had no idea. She's never been one to talk about her boyfriends. I knew they were friends and possibly romantic friends, but Gram's not one to act moony unless Toby Keith or Tim McGraw is involved. But lunch and dinner at the pool hall? While they looked at papers? How romantic could it have been?"

"You need to talk to her, Betts. Maybe you, she, and Jerome can have a tête-à-tête. À tête."

"Maybe."

We passed the empty barber shop and finally the last business on this side of the street, Mabel's Broken Crumbs. Mabel knew her way around a cookie. Gram was the first to admit that Mabel knew cookies better than anyone, Gram included. I often thought that Gram liked Mabel enough to keep her own cookie recipe selection small and low-key. If push ever came to shove, Missouri Anna could probably round up enough cookie recipes to put anyone to shame.

Just before we turned the corner, something flashed at the side of my vision. I wondered enough about what I saw to take a step backward and look into the cookie shop. It was normal that it wasn't too busy this time of day, but usually I could see Mabel or Amy behind the display or cleaning the small dining area.

At first I didn't see anyone, but suddenly it seemed that both Mabel and Amy appeared from behind the display and were moving past the cash register and toward the back of the store. It was difficult to interpret exactly what I was seeing, but Mabel had Amy by her arm and seemed to be moving her forcefully, roughly along. They disappeared behind the door to the kitchen without knowing I'd seen them.

"That was strange," Jake said.

I didn't realize he'd been watching, too.

"It made me uncomfortable," I said. "Should we . . ."

"I'm not sure what we could do. Maybe Amy was hurt and Mabel was hurrying her to the back to help her. We all know how much work Amy has been for Mabel, but the girl seems to be getting better. She's more pleasant to talk to, and she seems happier. I think what we just saw might have been something that was none of our business. However, I do think we need to watch for signs of something else." Jake's words were reasonable, but his tone was doubtful.

I'd go along with it for now, but the red flag had been raised, and from now on I would watch both Amy and Mabel more closely.

"Come on," Jake said as he nudged at my elbow.

The alleys of Broken Rope weren't like alleys of big cities or any-sized cities, really.

The spaces were wide and bordered by Dumpsters that were emptied on a regular basis. The entire space was kept clean and there were no typical alley dwellers in sight. There was also a number of storage sheds next to the Dumpsters. We were a theatrical town, and some of our props weren't required for the full year. Some businesses were able to store their things in basements or attics, but others needed the sheds that held items such as old-fashioned signs or costumes or whatever.

Jake led us along the alley, past Mabel's, past the barbershop, past the pool hall, and to the back of the Jasper, which even if we hadn't known where we were, an old sign that hung from a second-story window grate told us we'd reached our destination. The sign looked like it had been constructed and painted in the late nineteenth century, but I knew it was just a reproduction, something the owner before Everett had put on the front of the building. It said simply, THE JASPER THEATER and had never fit well with the theater's ornate decor. When Everett bought the business, he removed the sign and replaced it with a small plaque. He'd mentioned that the building had enough things to look at; it didn't need a tacky sign, too.

There was a similar two-door system at the back of the Jasper as there'd been at the front but with only one set of doors. They were locked, too, but we weren't surprised.

"I'm going to boost you up and you can try the window."

"That's your trick? The window?"

Jake blushed, which was a rare occurrence. "Yes, I used to sneak into the theater when I was a kid, when I first moved here. The window leads, or used to lead, to a film storage room. If you timed it just right, you could exit that room and make it into the auditorium before the projectionist even knew you were there."

"You scoundrel, you. You think you know someone . . ."

Jake rolled his eyes and threaded his hands together. "Climb."

I grabbed hold of a brick protruding from the building and stepped into Jake's hands. I barely faltered as I shot up to the window. I pushed up on the bottom sash, but it wasn't going anywhere.

"Okay, let me down. It's either locked or painted shut."

"Shoot," he said as I reached the ground again. "Well, short of breaking the window then, I don't see a way in," Jake said as he put his hands on his hips.

"Me neither." The thought occurred to me to do as much, but there didn't seem to be a good-enough reason to break, enter, or trespass. Searching the Jasper was a hunch. Granted, the hunch was stronger because Jerome mentioned seeing the paper on Everett's desk and Miles said that Gram and Everett had been looking at papers of some sort, but breaking laws unless absolutely necessary wasn't something I thought I should do. Gram was in jail, and though her freedom was on the line, I had no sense that she was in imminent danger. In fact, her being in jail might be the safest place for her.

A sound popped through the air and then something pinged. It was a familiar noise, but I didn't place it right away.

"What was that?" I said.

"That couldn't have been what I thought it was," Jake said as he turned and looked down the alley. "It sounded like a gunshot. Like a bullet ricocheting off something metal."

The sound came again. This time it was more a boom than a pop, but it was still followed by a *p-ting.*

"Isabelle, you and your friend need to stop sticking your heads up in the air like fools on a Sunday. You're being shot at." Jerome was suddenly standing next to me. The scent of wood smoke filled the air, and though I had plenty of questions for him, I figured now wasn't the time.

"Get down, Jake," I said as I pulled on his shoulders.

From the ground and to the side of a storage shed, we both looked up at the spot where the next bullet landed. It broke a pane of glass in the door, right about where his head had just been.

Jake and I looked at each other and then back at the broken glass.

"Where's the shooting coming from?" I said to Jerome, who'd crouched next to us.

Both Jake and Jerome said, "I don't know." Jake's voice was tinged with more panic than Jerome's smooth calm drawl. But Jerome was already dead, I supposed.

Even in all the years I'd lived in Broken Rope, even with all the guns (loaded with blanks though they might have been) everywhere, I'd never been shot at either in real life or pretend. It was horrifying. The sense of fear and feeling of being trapped muddled whatever good sense I might have left. The fear was real and deep and yet detached from me in a way that seemed like an out-of-body experience.

"You two need to get out of here — out

of behind the buildings. You're trapped."

"What do you suggest?" I said.

"We have to get out of here," Jake said.

"Jake, Jerome's here. He's trying to help," I said.

Another shot boomed and then tinged.

"Where are the police? How do they not hear that?" Jake said, either ignoring what I'd said about Jerome or choosing not to comment.

"Sound is a funny thing," Jerome said. "Anyone in front of these buildings might not hear one thing that's going on behind them. But I think I know where the shooting's coming from."

"Hang on, Jake. Jerome's trying to figure it out."

"Betts, you know I love you and you know I believe every word you say because I love you, but telling me that a ghost — one I'm not privileged to see — is trying to help is not easing my stress."

"I know. Just a second," I said to Jake. "Jerome, what are you thinking?"

"The shots are coming from up high, maybe on the roof to the south. Run the other direction you came from and then hurry out to the front of the buildings. Once you start, run your as . . . run really fast. I'm going to see if I can spot who's pulling the trigger. Ready?"

"Can't you just pop up there?"

"I'm going to try, but I'm not sure exactly where they are. I can't do anything to them anyway, and . . . We're wasting time."

"Hang on." I told Jake what we needed to do. He agreed with the plan. "Okay, we're ready, Jerome."

"Wait. There might be another shot. As soon as that happens, get your bu . . . Run! Give it a second."

True to his prediction, another shot rang through the air, this bullet hitting the side of the shed we were using for protection.

"Go!" Jerome said.

Jake and I stood and scurried. Since the area between the back of the building and the storage sheds wasn't big, I felt like a pinball that had just been propelled into the gauntlet with a weak spring mechanism; we couldn't run fast enough to outrun speeding bullets, could we?

Another shot was fired, but I didn't hear the resulting ping. Of course that could have been because I was screaming. Or was that Jake?

The distance from the spot behind the Jasper to the other end of the block was twice what we'd taken coming in the other direction, but it felt at least a hundred times farther.

Along with the bullets, we dodged two plastic buckets, someone's old worn and discarded boots, and a huge wooden box that must have been used for ballots or raffle tickets — my shin got a corner of it, but Jake grabbed my arm before I could tumble to the ground.

Finally, we reached the spot where we could turn and get out in front of the buildings and into the street. Instead of stopping, though, we ran down the walkway, our footfalls rattling the planks and building windows. There were no other people out on the street. In two days, we would have run into hundreds of people, but currently Broken Rope resembled a ghost town more than a tourist town.

I pushed on the door of the jail with such vigor that it slammed open and rattled the handcuffs.

Jim and Cliff jumped up from their chairs and put their hands on their weapons. Mom, Dad, Teddy, Gram, and Verna looked at us like we'd either lost our minds or they weren't sure who we were.

"Betts, Jake, what's up?" Jim asked.

"Someone was shooting at us," I said.

Jim and Cliff moved quickly around

176

chairs, people, and wastebaskets. They told us to close the door and stay in the office until they came back. We did as they commanded.

At first, no one said anything. It was as if my words hadn't registered with them.

Finally, my brother, Teddy, spoke, "Hey, sis, did you notice Cliff's back in town? Whoop, whoop."

Yes, my brother, not a bad guy but a goofball of the highest extreme, actually put his hands up and pumped the air.

Much to Teddy's dismay, no one laughed.

CHAPTER 11

The truth was, I had forgotten about Cliff again. Well, maybe not all the way, but I'd certainly put him to the back of my mind.

Gram's getting officially arrested and my having conversations with a ghost and getting shot at had moved Cliff way down my priority list.

That didn't stop me, however, from being impressed with his police officer skills. Even though he and Jim couldn't find the shooter, they found evidence of the shoot-out in the form of expended bullets. Without my help or Jerome's, they estimated that whoever was shooting at us was on top of one of the buildings to the south of the theater. That meant that someone was on top of the pool hall, the barber shop, or Broken Crumbs, or perhaps had traveled down the entire row.

The only person they could immediately find to question was Miles, who, they said, told them we stopped by the pool hall. If he told them what he shared with us about Gram and Everett and their secret papers, Jim and Cliff didn't let on.

Miles had heard something, but he had been in his basement and the shots had been muffled. He thought someone was practicing a fake gunfight somewhere. Even though it's Broken Rope law that all rehearsals that include gunfire are to be posted on the board outside the jail, he thought he'd missed a post. The shots had been background noise to him.

Jim and Cliff also said they'd talked to Mabel and Amy who said they hadn't heard anything at all. But there was something about the way Jim and Cliff acted when they spoke about Mabel and her granddaughter. Something bothered them, I could tell, but they certainly weren't going to tell me what it was.

I had a brief moment where I thought I should tell them what Jake and I had seen through the window but thought better of it because I truly didn't know what had been going on, and I didn't want to make something of nothing. If they thought something was wrong, I trusted that they'd investigate it fully.

There were no other witnesses to be found. Jenna wasn't in the saloon, and even though Stuart had been working in his shop, it was located on the other side of the theater, and like Mabel and Amy he claimed not to have heard anything at all.

Fortunately, the only injury sustained by either of us was the bloody gash on my leg. Everyone concluded that I didn't need stitches, but the sooner I could get it cleaned out and bandaged, the better. I cleaned it in the bathroom, but I wasn't leaving the jail until I had a few moments to talk to Gram alone.

My goal wasn't easily achieved. Jim and Cliff did work there, so I tried to cut them some slack for hanging around in my way. Verna left shortly after the shoot-out but not before again commanding Gram not to talk to anyone without her attorney present. Teddy thought the whole day might end up ranking as one of his top ten because of the numerous adventures, including the one where his grandmother had been arrested for murder. I wasn't sure if he'd ever grasp the seriousness of the situation. He tried to console me by telling me to look at the positive side, which he claimed was that everything would work out. Gram would be found innocent because she couldn't possibly kill anyone. And he mentioned quietly so only I could hear that Gram's time away would give me a chance to take a leadership role at the school.

"Teddy, I don't want a leadership role. I love working for Gram," I told him.

"Shoot, a person can always build their leadership skills. Hey, did you know Cliff was back in town? I mean, before you were shot at and barreled into the jail?" Teddy leaned back in his chair and smiled the smile that frequently got him in too much trouble.

I refused to talk to him further and he left when he thought the excitement had come to an end.

Thankfully, my parents both had to get to work. High school students don't care much about family emergencies even if they are about murder. They couldn't do much for Gram as she sat in jail.

I was able to convince Jake to leave after he gave a full statement to Jim and Cliff. I told him we'd meet later.

I wished Jerome were around, but he'd already told me he couldn't make his ghostly way into the jail. I didn't know how to call him or ask him to appear, but I thought that might be a useful skill to learn.

As Jim worked on his computer, I sat on the outside of the cell and leaned in toward Gram.

"Gram, I don't think we have time to discuss the disruptive nature of learning that ghosts are not only real, but now I'm able to communicate with one, so I'm just going to ignore that and ask you more important things. I need you to trust me and talk to me. No more elusiveness, okay?"

Gram paused a moment but finally said, "Okay, Betts, what's on your mind?" She scooted forward on the lower bunk. Except for Teddy, she was the one most taking her arrest in stride. She knew she was innocent and that even if there wasn't a good explanation why her fingerprints were on the bag, she believed Verna would come up with one.

I looked at Jim to make sure he wasn't listening. He didn't seem to be, but he was probably well practiced at looking like he wasn't listening. I kept my voice low.

"What's the best way to get hold of Jerome? Can I call out to him or twitch my nose or something?"

Gram laughed. "Oh, Betts, don't be ridiculous."

"Okay," I said with exaggerated patience. "Help me understand that part better."

"Jerome is around. Sometimes he can communicate, sometimes he can't. It's like he's a blip in the system."

"A blip?"

Gram's mouth pinched briefly before she spoke. "Dead people are supposed to be dead, Betts."

"I'm in agreement on that one, Gram."

"But there's something about this place, something about Broken Rope that keeps its citizens around sometimes, especially those who did something special or outrageous. And we've got plenty of those characters, let me tell you."

"This is about Broken Rope? Are you telling me that you see, communicate with, talk to, more ghosts than just Jerome?" Again, I wondered if I really wanted to hear the answer.

"That's not what's important right now. What you need to understand is that Jerome, as much of a ghost as he is, is just a piece of him, something left over from his life. Something left over from the impact of his life here in Broken Rope. We've always known we are part of a different community, a strange one at that. We've had so many odd things happen that odd has become the norm. Ghosts — but let's just talk about Jerome specifically — shouldn't be too much of a surprise. There's something here, something that holds on to our past, some of our people, but that something isn't strong enough to hold on to the whole taco platter plus the guacamole, so to speak. If I understand it correctly, and I've had a lot of time to ponder it, Jerome's ghost is bits and pieces of energy, energy that is fairly random, although my connection to him has been happening for so long that I can, in a way, bring that energy to me. You won't be able to, not yet, but maybe someday."

"If you get a chance to rattle his energy, would you please let him know I'd like to spend a good amount of time talking to him," I said.

"Sure, but he won't be able to come to me in here. Don't know why, but this place is off-limits to him."

"He mentioned that."

"Oh, good, you've spoken to him some more."

I sighed. "Tell me more about Everett."

"Like what?"

I could see the wall build in her wary eyes. She was more willing to talk about ghost energy than the other dead person.

"You hung out with him quite a bit apparently."

"What does that matter, Betts?"

"He was married, Gram."

"Oh, pshaw, Betts. You're assuming our relationship was more than a friendship."

"That's because that's what you made me assume. You made lots of people assume that. I would love to know if it was different."

Gram eyed Jim. "I'm not supposed to talk about it without Verna present."

"And that's good advice. But she didn't mean you shouldn't talk to me. You can talk about it with me, Gram, all you want, or are willing to." In truth, Verna had meant that Gram shouldn't talk to me either, but I was desperate enough to lie.

"Okay. This is what you need to know, Betts. Everett and I were friends, just friends. I knew he was married. I hadn't met his wife, but I hoped to someday. I overheard Jim and Cliff talk about her timing. She came to Broken Rope last night because she found my business card on his nightstand and wanted to know what was going on with her husband. Even though I knew Everett was married, what I overheard gave me the impression that his wife didn't know why he was away from home so much 'working.' "

"Do they think she could have killed him?"

Gram shook her head. "She has a pretty strong alibi apparently."

"What were the papers you and he looked at when you ate at the pool hall?"

Gram's eyes opened wide. "How did you . . . ? Oh, Miles."

"Yes, Miles, but he didn't know what the papers were about. What were you looking at?"

"I'm not telling you that, Betts. No way, no how."

"Why not?"

"None of your business."

"Were you searching for the treasure that Jerome allegedly hid?"

"How do you know about the treasure?"

"Gram, you're in jail for murder. Of course, I'm going to try to figure out who the real killer is, but you have to help me. Or Jerome has to help me. I need to know what was going on. It was an assumption because of some things Jake and I found, one of them being a gold piece on Jerome's tombstone."

Gram's eyes got big but she said, "Well, I'm not going to tell you what I know about the treasure, Betts."

"Why not? Do you want it for yourself?"

"No! Give me more credit than that. I'm not greedy — you know that. Listen, Betts, this has nothing to do with any silly treasure stuff. Get over that right now."

Jim shot us a look. I turned so my back was even more in his way.

"Well, at least I know for sure there's a treasure," I said.

Gram's big eyes went into a squint. "I think I'm done talking to you, Betts." She sat back on the bunk.

"Come on, Gram, give me something else to go on. Make this easier for all of us. If you won't tell me, you need to at least tell Verna where the pieces of paper are that you and Everett were looking at."

Gram nodded stiffly. She didn't like being told what to do. No one did, but she had been infused with an extra dose of stubborn. The nod wasn't to let me know she would talk to Verna. The nod was to get me off the subject, probably tell me again that she was done with me.

"Were they some sort of treasure maps?" I asked.

Gram suddenly sat forward again and put her mouth close to my ear. "Isabelle Anna Winston, I'm not going to tell you anything about any treasure, and I want you to stop whatever it is you think you're doing. Clearly, it isn't a safe way to live, and as I said I'm sure it has nothing to do with Everett's murder."

"You're not telling me because you are trying to keep me safe?"

Gram sat back again and quit looking at me.

By nature, Missouri Anna Winston wasn't a liar. She was honest to a fault sometimes. Even when truth might not be the best thing to share, she always would. It wasn't in her to lie. The reason I hadn't known about Jerome's existence before now was because I'd never asked her about him, I'd never even considered the existence of a ghost. If I had, she would have told me what she knew no matter how strange, weird, or disturbing it was. If she was forced into lying, it was for a very good reason.

"Gram, I'm going to be fine. I'll be careful."

"You were shot at, Betts. You were shot at." She still wasn't looking at me.

She wasn't going to say any more, and I suddenly understood why, though her silence still irritated me. I'd have to find the information another way.

"I gotta go, Gram," I said. "Think about what I said. Think about talking to me or to Verna more. We're both on your side, you know."

Gram nodded as I stood.

There wasn't much more to say.

Jim turned and watched me as I walked

away from the cell and toward the front door.

"We'll make it a good search for whoever was shooting at you and Jake, I promise," he said.

"I know, Jim."

"You be careful out there," he said. "I've got Cliff posted right outside the front door, but watch yourself. We'll take good care of Miz."

"Good. And I will be careful." I wasn't in the mood to say thank you. "She's innocent, you know that."

"I don't know that, but I hope it's so."

"She's not young. Her arrest could cause her too much stress. You need to be aware of that," I said.

Jim nodded.

"Oh, for giblet gravy's sake, I'm right here. I can hear you both and I'm fine. I'm innocent but I'm fine. You two don't need to treat me like I'm going to wither with the wind. Stop it," Gram said from the cell.

Jim smiled at me and I hesitantly smiled back.

"Between you and Verna, I'm sure my treatment of the prisoner will be closely observed and evaluated," Jim said.

I stepped outside to warm sunshine and Cliff leaning against a post at the front of

189

the boardwalk. Even though it had been only moments since Jim had told me where Cliff was, I'd again pushed him to that place in my mind that didn't want to be aware he was around. Another thread of surprise ran through me when he turned and watched me come out of the jail.

"Betts, you doing okay?"

"Fine," I said. Even I didn't like the tone of my voice.

"We'll figure out who shot at you and Jake," Cliff repeated Jim's claim.

"I know," I said. I wasn't in the mood for a longer conversation so I stepped off the boardwalk and toward the Volvo.

"Betts," Cliff said.

Damn, just about got away. I pulled the door open but didn't get in the car.

"Yep?"

"I know you have a lot going on, but I was wondering if you'd be available for dinner this evening."

Dear God, the man was inviting me to dinner at his house. His wife was going to cook, and I was going to have to act friendly and actually welcome her to town or something else equally as horrible.

"I have plans," I lied, anger and bitterness lining the words so much that I embarrassed myself.

"I understand. Would you be able to meet for coffee, then? Later? How about coffee and pie at Bunny's? Say about eight o'clock? I could pick you up or just meet you there."

I, not *we*, not *my wife and I*. Although that didn't necessarily mean anything.

I wanted to tell him that I didn't ever see us being able to have coffee and pie together at Bunny's. I wanted to tell him that I didn't need the conversation that he wanted to have. The conversation that would go something like "I'd love for you to get to know my wife, Betts. She's really a wonderful person and you and she would be great friends. I know you'll get along. Of course, you and I have both moved on from our past."

I kind of wanted to punch him in the stomach for coming back to Broken Rope and ruining my perfectly mediocre life.

But then I saw that dimple and those eyes, and I realized he wasn't trying to pull one over on me. He wanted to talk, and we did need to establish whatever it was we were going to become. I'd grit my teeth and get through it because it was bound to happen sometime. Might as well get it over with.

"Sure. I'll see you at eight."

He blinked as though he was surprised I'd agreed. "See you then."

I got in the Volvo, turned down Toby Keith, and called my brother.

"I need you, Teddy. Get to the school."

He hesitated only a second. "I'm on my way. This is about Cliff, right? He looks good, doesn't he?"

"Get to the school, Teddy."

I hung up the phone and turned Toby to extra loud. He was proclaiming his love for a bar, and at the moment that seemed like a much better option than loving any silly human.

The smell of wood smoke filled the car so quickly that I had to roll down the window.

"I think that fella's got eyes for you," Jerome said as he looked at me from the passenger's seat.

"Jerome, your timing is . . . interesting," I said.

"I've got some news for you — it's about who was shooting at you."

"Tell me." I turned Toby off.

"You're not going to like it," he said.

"Seems like one of those days."

"Oh, gotta go," Jerome said. "I'll be back shortly, though." And then he disappeared, the scent going with him.

"Oy," I said as I steered me, the Volvo, and Toby back to the school.

CHAPTER 12

I had no idea where my brother had gone after visiting Gram, but he managed to beat me to the school. He was leaning against his new truck and looking at his cell phone. He was still in the jeans and T-shirt he'd worn to the jail, and as usual, his hair was messy.

"Thanks for being here, Teddy," I said as I got out of the Volvo and walked toward the school.

"No prob. What's up, sis? You sounded major stressed on the phone."

I unlocked the door and led the way inside. Teddy followed behind as we pushed through the swinging doors and into the kitchen.

"Whoa, what happened here?" Teddy said.

"No one told you about the fire?"

"No. I know about the murder. Maybe that trumped the fire. Holy smokes — uh, I didn't mean to say that."

"I know. It wasn't good, but it could have been much worse. Even though Gram and I put it out, we should have called the fire department sooner."

"Sparks?" Teddy said as he looked up at the ceiling.

"Yes," I said.

My brother was a continually frustrating mix of contradictions. He was wild — he was a heartbreaker; the trail he left in his wake was baffling. He was also intelligent, though you'd never know it by the slow drawl he sometimes forced when he spoke. I could see the wheels turning behind his bright blue eyes. He was "seeing" what had happened in the ceiling, and he was silently calculating how bad it could have been. But despite whatever horror those thoughts might bring to mind, he'd look at the positive "fun" side. As I watched him I waited for the comment that was sure to be irreverent or silly.

"Gives a whole new meaning to cooking in the kitchen, huh?" he said, smiling.

He didn't disappoint.

"Teddy, I need your help. I need you to get this cleaned up and then I have to ask for something else. I might need a few days of your time, starting today."

"I don't mind getting this put back together. I was already off today. I can take the rest of the week . . . well, I should ask what for though. For what?"

"You're not going to like it," I said.

"Well, then, let me commit right away. Tell me, Betts."

"I need you to teach."

"Oh, hell no," Teddy said. "Not my thing, you know that." He started looking for an escape, but I put my hand on his arm.

"Come on, Teddy, I really need your help. It's Gram's champagne cookies recipe tomorrow and between that and the cook-off, I just can't do it all." I didn't mention the research and the conversations with a ghost that I felt I needed to have. I didn't think he'd be quick enough to see that I was hiding these other activities.

"Why not? Gram might be in the hoosegow, but she won't be there long. I'll get this cleaned up, but other than a meeting or two about the cook-off, all you'll have to do is teach. Not my thing, Betts. Not my thing."

He hadn't fallen for my trickery.

I didn't notice the smoke smell this time, probably because Teddy and I were standing next to the stinky fire damage when Jerome appeared.

"Ah, your brother, I see," he said.

I shot Jerome a quick look. "Teddy, there's

more to it than that. Jake's helping me research some things and I need to be able to devote myself to that."

"You're researching something now? Can't that wait until after the cook-off? Priorities, Betts."

"Tell him about me," Jerome said.

"I will not," I said.

"You will not prioritize? Boy, that doesn't sound like you," Teddy said as he leaned against the butcher block. At least he wasn't attempting to flee anymore.

"No. Teddy, I'm researching stuff about Jerome Cowbender. I think his . . . well, his history has something to do with the murder."

Teddy laughed. "The bank robber who couldn't shoot a refrigerator at two feet?"

"He has a point, but there really is more to the story, I think," Jerome said as he rearranged his hat. "Tell him about me. You told Jake. You might as well tell Teddy. Maybe he can help."

I ignored Jerome. "Yes, that one. It's a long story, but I really need to give this attention. I can't do that if I have to teach, too. You're one of the best bakers in town and you make Gram's cookies like a pro."

Teddy's culinary talents were yet another one of his contradictions. He was a natural in the kitchen. He was almost as instinctual as Gram, but even though he enjoyed cooking he had no passion for it. Even when we were kids, he'd whip up some amazing cookies that everyone would love but when we all asked him for the recipe, he'd just shrug and say he didn't really remember it.

"Yeah, maybe, but I don't like teaching. Those people drive me crazy. They ask questions and stuff."

"There are a couple cute girls," I said.

"I know. I've already . . . oh, never mind," Teddy said.

"He's dating someone. Got his heart in a little knot for her, too," Jerome said.

"Who?" I said.

"Just never mind, okay?" Teddy said.

"Someone named Opie of all things," Jerome said.

"What? No!" I couldn't stop the words from coming out in time.

"Betts, what's wrong with you? What does it matter who I . . . oh, all right, I might have had a small fling with that girl named Susan, but that was last fall and it's long over," Teddy said.

Jerome laughed.

"Teddy, I don't care, really I don't." Except that I did if he was dating Opie, but I wasn't prepared to fight that battle. "I just need you to teach. Please."

He looked at me and then I thought he looked directly at Jerome. His eyes landed exactly where Jerome's eyes were.

"Son?" Jerome said softly.

But Teddy turned away quickly and looked back at me. "You owe me big. In ways you might never have owed me before. Big."

"I get it, Teddy, and I will find a way to sell my soul and repay you in whatever way you command. I promise." I stepped forward and hugged him, which caught him off guard. He let me hug him but barely.

"Fine, fine. Get out of my way now. I need to get to work so I can have this finished for *my* students tomorrow," he said with a sigh.

I eyebrow signaled Jerome that he was to follow me outside. I wanted to talk to him, but I didn't want Teddy to overhear.

Just as we reached the swinging doors, Teddy said, "Hey, sis. I saw Cliff looking at you're a —"

"Don't! Even! Go! There!" I said.

Teddy and Jerome both laughed.

I pushed through the door, not holding it for the ghost behind me.

I hurried outside and toward the cemetery. Jerome followed dutifully, even though I couldn't hear his movements. His feet didn't make a sound as they hit the ground. His clothes didn't rustle. The only ways I knew he was following were by catching sight of him out of the corner of my eye or hearing him clear his throat or make a noise that told me that climbing over the rope taxed some part of his dead legs.

I stopped directly in front of his tombstone and pointed at the coin. "What's that?"

Jerome peered at the coin. "I do believe that's a gold piece."

"Why's it on your tombstone?"

"I don't know, darlin'. I truly don't. Like I already told you, I didn't put it there." Whatever amusement twinkled in his eyes dimmed when he saw how serious I was.

"I guess what I want to know is was this the sort of thing that was in your buried treasure?"

"I don't rightly know." Jerome lifted his hat and swiped back his hair. "I don't remember, Isabelle. That's the problem. If I remembered any of it clearly, I would have told Miz where I put things. As I said, I don't remember much of my life. I lived a long time ago. Even if my memory weren't spotty, I might have forgotten anyway."

I caught myself looking at his jawline and the stubborn strength in his chin. I suddenly saw clearly how he had a crooked set to his mouth. I looked away and silently chastised myself. Was I under so much stress that I was noticing things like chins and jawlines on a dead man? What was wrong with me?

I cleared my throat. "I doubt you would have forgotten where you put a treasure, though."

"Miz said it was like when she bought birthday cards early and hid them and then forgot where."

A treasure was different than misplaced cards, but there was no point in arguing.

"Gram and Everett were out here the day he was killed. Were they talking to you?"

"No, I talked to Missouri in the morning, in her office, but she told me that she was busy with the cook-off for the next few days, so I roamed around town and tried to remember things. Miz says that's what I usually do when I first arrive. I didn't even know about the fire or her arrest until after she'd been taken to the jail that night."

Maybe she hadn't been talking to herself. Maybe I'd heard her talking to Jerome, though at the time I hadn't seen or heard him.

"Have you talked to her much since you got here this time around?"

Jerome nodded. "At her house, but her son, your father, was watching her so closely, that she didn't say much. She asked if I

200

knew where the treasure was or if I knew who else might be looking for it."

"And you still don't?"

"No."

"There was something taken from the historical archives. Jake isn't sure what it was. It must have been something very important. It might have been the paper you said you saw in Everett's office. Can you think of any documents that you created, maybe a map or a diary, that might have given clues as to where you put the treasure?"

"I'm sorry, Isabelle," Jerome said as he ran his hand through his hair again. "I just don't know. Ever' now and then something comes into my mind and I'm trying hard to remember. I'll let you know the second I do."

"That has to be frustrating," I said.

Jerome put his hat back on and shrugged. "It's what I know. I'm happy to be here, even if 'here' is a little less here than the rest of you. I'm always happy to talk to Miz, and now you."

"Earlier, you said you had some information about who shot Jake and me?" I said.

"Yep. I walked around on top of those buildings and found a little drop of blood. See, it's not much, but it's something. If you can find someone with a cut or a scratch, you might find the shooter."

"Blood? That's a good clue, Jerome. You might be right. DNA's an amazing tool."

"DNA?"

Of course, he wouldn't know a thing about DNA. I searched for a way to summarize the last hundred years or so of scientific advancements. "Yes, it's what we're made up of. We can match blood to people by testing the DNA. We can tell who the blood came from just by learning its DNA." It was an awkward explanation but the best I could do.

Jerome whistled. "I'll be. That's something. I bet no one gets away with anything anymore."

"Sadly, no, people still get away with lots, but DNA testing is changing the world."

"I expect so."

"Where was the blood?"

"On top of the pool hall, but I think the shooter was moving. They might have started at the end of the block which is the cookie shop, I believe. There could be more blood, but I only saw the one drop."

"Where exactly?"

"Right on the northwest corner, on the ledge, about a hand's width from the corner and to the south."

"Got it. Now I just have to figure out a way to let the police know about it, unless they saw it already."

"I don't think they did. I watched that young fella, the one that's got eyes for you, looking around and I don't think he saw it."

"I'll have to find a way to point it out."

My cell phone buzzed. It was a blocked private number but I answered it anyway. "Isabelle Winston," I said as I flipped it open.

"Betts, it's Cliff. You need to come back down to the jail. Right away."

"What's wrong? Did something happen to Gram?" My heart leapt to my throat.

"No, it's Jake. He's fine, but he's been hurt. He requested that I call you."

"Jake? What happened, Cliff?"

"Just come on down. Like I said, he's fine. Drive carefully, but we'll see you in a minute."

"On my way." I put the phone back into my pocket. "I gotta go. Talk to you later, Jerome. See what you can remember. Come see me this evening if you can."

"Yes, ma'am. Be careful in that automobile," Jerome said before he disappeared again.

I ran into the school and told Teddy where I was going. He'd already cleaned up the first layer of gunk in the kitchen. He'd have it spotless in only a few hours. I'd put the right man on the job.

The drive back to town was never long or taxing, and though traffic was light, it felt like this trip took forever. I wouldn't remember turning off the car or my sprint into the jail. But I'd forever remember the sight of my best friend as he sat on a chair next to Cliff.

Jake pulled a soda can away from his blackened eye and said, "This might be the only safe place, Betts. I thought you should get down here quickly."

Chapter 13

"Jake, what happened?" I said as I gently touched the puffy skin to the side of his eye.

"I was accosted. Trust me, if I wasn't so scrappy, it would have been much worse."

I looked at Cliff whose tight face showed he was just as concerned as I was.

"He wouldn't let me call the doctor. He just wanted you," Cliff said.

"Tell her the details," Gram said from the cell.

"When I went back to my office, I headed directly to the archives," he began. "Betts, I've been locking the door obsessively for many years. Particularly now, when there's been a murder. Maybe getting shot at shook me up more than I thought, but I must have forgotten about locking them. I came out of the archives and suddenly the world went bright and then black and then my eye and head hurt. I was on the ground, kind of on my hands and knees, trying to figure out what was going on when whoever hit me in the eye, kicked me in my side."

"Oh, Jake," I said.

"The side is fine, believe it or not. I'll probably be bruised, but not badly."

"How did you get out of there?"

"My horse," Jake said.

"Your horse?" I asked. Jake didn't own a live horse, but Patches was his one and only Palomino stick horse. "Patches?"

"Yeah, somehow I ended up in the corner where she's always tethered." Jake smiled, his black eye puffing bigger. "I grabbed her and started swinging with all my might. I couldn't see right, black spots everywhere, but I kept getting pumped with more adrenaline whenever the stick landed on something solid."

"So you hit your attacker?"

"A couple times at least, but then . . ."

"Uh-oh, what?"

"He or she seemed to disappear. I thought I heard a commotion in the back room, so I crawled toward the door that leads to the archives. I still wasn't seeing right, but I know they left out the back door and once I could see better I realized they took Jerome's files with them. They're gone, probably never to be seen again."

"Could you make out the person at all?

Did you get an idea of who it might be?" I asked.

"No. When they were hitting me or when I was hitting at them, I never got a good look, my vision was messed up. When they were in the back room I was on my hands and knees and the table was mostly in the way, but I think I saw long black pants."

"Tell her what else you saw, Jake," Gram said.

"Oh yeah. When they were hitting me, I thought I might have seen red spots on the shoes — random spots and only a few of them. I thought they were just more spots like the black ones in my vision, but Miz, Cliff, and Jim don't think so."

"Told ya," Gram said. She seemed perfectly comfortable in the cell.

"Men or women's?" I asked.

"I have no idea," Jake said.

"Well, those shoes and those archives are somewhere. We just need to find them. When we do, everything else will surely be solved," I said, but I knew nothing was that easy. I also wasn't sure he'd seen real red spots despite how much we all wanted a solid clue to the identity of his attacker.

"Jim's looking for evidence over at Jake's building," Cliff said.

I hadn't known Cliff as a police officer for

very long, but what I'd seen so far made me think he might be pretty good at his job. But his concern for Jake, and perhaps the rest of us, was showing a potential chink in the armor he probably hoped he'd created. Though he and Jake hadn't kept in touch, they had once been pretty good friends. He was concerned and might not be able to keep a professional distance in this case. I was glad Jim was the one looking for evidence.

"Betts, you need to be careful," Jake said. "You've been looking into the treasure, too. Someone might think you know more than you do."

"Treasure? What treasure?" Cliff said.

"I'm sorry, Betts, it might be rotten of me to do it this way but the police need to know. I wanted to know you were safe and I wanted us both to tell them. I don't know if Everett was looking for the treasure, Cliff, but he'd been researching Jerome Cowbender," Jake said as he put the soda can back to his eye.

"What's going on?" Cliff said.

"Gram, you want to tell him?" I asked.

"I have nothing to say."

"I don't know much, but I have my own suspicions," I began.

"I'm all ears," Cliff said.

Without Gram's corroborating what I said and without Jerome Cowbender's presence, the story sounded weak and potentially made-up. There was the coin on the tombstone and the fact that Gram had only implied that she and Everett "might" have been looking for the treasure. I couldn't say anything about Jerome or Jerome's conversation with Gram or the fact that he himself didn't remember — not yet, anyway — where he'd hidden it. As I told Cliff what I was able to, I sensed his doubt, but at least he tried to act interested.

"Is the coin still on the tombstone?"

"It was a little bit ago," I said.

"I'll let Jim know."

"Thanks."

"Am I done here, Cliff?" Jake asked.

"I have your statement, but where do you want to go?"

"I want to go home."

"Will you feel safe there, Jake?" I asked. "Do you want to stay with me?"

"I doubt I'll feel safe anywhere for a while, but I want to go home. I want my own bed. I'll take precautions." He stood, his legs steadier than I would have predicted. "You be safe, too, Betts. You might want to consider staying with your parents or . . ." He looked at Cliff briefly. "Well, just be careful."

"I will."

Jim pushed through the front doors. He glanced at the group and nodded at Jake. "I didn't find much of anything, but I might have gotten a fingerprint."

"I'm going home, Jim. I'd like to get some rest."

"I'll take you. Come on, we'll get your bike."

Jake sighed but didn't argue further. When they left, the office felt a lot emptier. Jake wasn't a big man, but his personality tended to take up a lot of space.

"I'm about done here, Betts. Can I help you get home? Are we still on for eight?" Cliff asked quietly.

My wide eyes probably didn't hide the fact that he'd surprised me with the reminder. We were going to have coffee and pie at Bunny's. Suddenly, that seemed like the wrong thing to do. It seemed too jovial for the serious turn of events. But it was something that we needed to get out of the way. Besides, maybe I could use the opportunity to get some information out of him. Maybe he and Jim knew more than they were sharing.

"I can get home. Thanks. Sure. Absolutely. I'll be at Bunny's."

"Good."

"You two making a date?" Gram said with a smile to her voice. She was having far too much fun for someone behind bars.

"Gram," I said.

Cliff said nothing.

Despite her teasing, it wasn't easy to leave with Gram still locked up. After Cliff confirmed our meeting (I wasn't going to call it a date), I checked on Teddy at the school and left him with the order to keep the doors locked. It was starting to get dark, but I made sure the gold coin was still on the tombstone — it was — and drove back to Bunny's.

I parked in front of the 1950s retro-style diner. It was the one building in Broken Rope that didn't hearken back to the Old West. Bunny's parents had built the diner in 1954. Broken Rope's tourist-destination status didn't hit until the 1970s. Now there were specific building ordinances that had to be followed if you wanted to build something new or remodel something within the town limits. Structures had to meet current safety standards while at the same time keeping the Old West theme. Since Gram's school was right outside the town's historic border, she wasn't required to follow the ordinances, but she had made sure that the only modern touches in her building were on the inside in the form of the appliances.

The outside of Bunny's was done in alternating chrome and big windows. Inside, booths filled the areas next to the windows, a half-circle bar counter sat in the middle of the eating area, and extra tables and chairs filled both sides. Chrome and pink were the colors of choice.

Bunny was almost sixty, and had been almost sixty ever since I could remember. She was stocky with short, straight, unruly gray hair and a mustache that could rival Tom Selleck's when she forgot to shave. When her mouth was closed, her lips were pinched tightly. But when she was talking, the world forgot about the mustache and the unruly hair because she was friendly, funny, and had a laugh that sounded like the boom of a gun. The diner was her life, so much so that she lived in a trailer set up behind it. She never acted as though she disliked what she did. In fact, she acted as though she thought she was the luckiest person alive to be able to work ungodly hours and never be too far from having to wait on a customer.

"Betts, come on in. Sit anywhere," she said as I entered the diner. There was a small spattering of customers throughout the restaurant. That would change in two short days. Tourists would fill the place very soon.

I'd already seen Cliff sitting in a booth next to the window. He had changed back into civilian clothes and was already sipping from a mug of coffee. I'd arrived at exactly eight o'clock. I wondered how long he'd been there.

He waved me over.

A pretty brunette exited the bathroom and seemed to be walking directly to Cliff's table.

She was pretty, just in case I hadn't mentioned that yet.

Damn.

She didn't even look at Cliff as she walked past him and toward the far end of the diner where she took a seat at a table with two other women.

I tried to hide the sigh of relief.

I'm being ridiculous, I told myself.

"Hi," I said as I sat across from Cliff.

"Thanks for coming, Betts," Cliff said. "Coffee?"

"Well, lookee here, it's just like the old days." Bunny was at the table, coffeepot in hand, before I could nod in the affirmative. "You two an item again?"

213

"I'd love a cup, thank you, Bunny," I said as I held up the blue plastic diner-issue mug.

Bunny's laugh boomed. "Sure, honey. The more things change, the more they stay the same," she muttered as she filled the mug. "Anything else? Pie?"

"I bet you haven't had dinner either," Cliff said to me.

"I, uh. No," I said.

"Burgers?"

"Yeah, okay, burgers." I turned to Bunny.

"I remember: both well done, both with extra cheese, and both with a side order of sour cream."

I smiled and nodded. Actually, I'd cut back on the cheese and sour cream, but she was having so much fun reliving the past that I didn't want to spoil it.

Coffee poured and dinner ordered, I looked at Cliff. I didn't know who was supposed to go first. Though I hadn't acknowledged it, Bunny had a point. Sometimes the more things did change, the more they stayed the same. Sort of. Cliff and I had probably sat in this booth or another one hundreds of times. We were certainly two different people than we were years earlier, but we still went by the same names.

"Betts, I'm sorry I didn't let you know I was coming back to town," Cliff began.

"You didn't owe me any explanation." Maybe he didn't, but I was pleased he thought he might have.

"No, but it would have been polite. So many things happened at once that I became selfish and did what I needed to do to get through."

I nodded, but I wasn't sure what I was nodding about or how much I should ask. I sighed. I was tired of being concerned I would do or say something wrong.

"Cliff, I have no idea what you're talking about. You quit your job and moved back to Broken Rope and became a police officer. Were there other things to go along with the 'so many things'?"

"Well, yes, the career change, but there was also the divorce. Leaving the life I'd built wasn't easy even if it was something I wanted to do."

"Divorce? You're divorced?" I asked not because I wanted to date Cliff again. I might have, but I couldn't be sure of that until all the haze of seeing him again cleared. I asked because the best news I'd received in a couple days would be if I didn't have to pretend to be friendly to someone I didn't want to be friendly to. I wanted to make sure I'd heard him right.

"Yes. I thought you knew that."

"How would I? You're wearing a wedding band."

Cliff looked at the ring on his finger. "I know. It's like I have to get used to one thing at a time."

"You're still not over your wife?"

His eyes pinched but not in pain, in thought. Finally he said, "No, I've been over my wife for a long time. I'm not over the fact that I couldn't help create a successful marriage. I'll take the ring off soon, just not yet."

"No kids, right?" I took a gulp of coffee.

"No. Two golden retrievers, though. I miss them."

"More than you miss your ex-wife?" It was a nasty question.

I was surprised when Cliff laughed. "Lots more, Betts, lots more. Do you want me to tell you about my marriage?"

"No," I said too quickly. Oh God, no! I wasn't prepared to have that personal a conversation with him, though I was now warming to the thought that he wasn't married. "Instead, tell me why you had coffee with Opie yesterday morning."

He looked genuinely surprised. "I didn't . . . Oh, she was here the other morning when I was having breakfast. We said hi to each other, but we didn't sit together or talk about my golden retrievers or anything. I didn't tell her I was divorced."

Bunny brought us the burgers and we both dug in. It didn't take long before almost all resentment from whatever each of us thought we needed to be resentful about began to dissipate. We weren't back to our old selves, but that would be impossible anyway. Thankfully.

We talked about family and what everyone was doing now. We talked about the upcoming cook-off. We talked about the wonderful job Jake had done with the archives and the Historical Society. We talked about how brave and amazing he'd been during the attack.

Finally, the conversation came around to the shooting.

"You're okay, really?" Cliff asked.

"I am. I've concluded that the shooter wasn't seriously intent on harming Jake or me. I think he or she was just trying to scare us away."

"Scare you away from what, the treasure you and Jake talked about?"

I used my fingertip to pick up a few crust crumbs on my plate. "Actually, more the Jasper," I said.

"Everett's place of business? Why?"

I shrugged. I couldn't tell him the real

217

reason. "Did you and Jim search it?"

"Sure."

"What did you find?"

"Nothing at all. In fact, we were talking about how important it is to get it open before the cook-off. There'll be lots of people looking for something to do in the evenings very soon around here. We need to find someone to run it before the day after tomorrow."

"How would you feel about searching it again? Want to — unofficially, of course?"

"Clearly you do. What're you looking for?"

I'd like to point out the blood on the roof, I thought. "Nothing, I just want to look around."

"I suppose one dinner isn't going to make you trust that I can do this job."

"You're a police officer, Cliff. I trust you to protect and serve. I even trust you to find Everett's killer, unless you think it's Gram. Then I don't trust you as much. I'm just curious. Really."

"I don't think Miz killed anyone. You know that don't you?"

"Not fully until this second, but I'm happy to hear it."

Cliff looked doubtful a moment. I thought I'd lost him, but then he said, "The theater isn't a crime scene. Jim and I have already searched it. I have access to the keys. I suppose it wouldn't be illegal, though I don't think it's a good decision."

"It's *not* illegal," I said.

It wasn't, technically. I was counting on our newfound friendliness toward each other to make him bend to my wish. Old times' sake and stuff. And I really hoped the urge I felt to touch his hair would go away. I swallowed and silently told myself to shape up.

"I suppose, but I don't believe you're just curious. Something to do with the treasure? If you find what you're looking for, will you point it out to me?"

"Sure," I said. I'd planned on pointing out the blood, but I'd never admit that's what I was looking for.

"Let's go."

"Really? Great."

As we stood and he dropped some bills on the table, his phone buzzed. He answered it and his face sobered quickly. "I'll be right there."

"Change of plans, B," he said. "I'm sorry. I have an urgent matter."

"Something to do with Everett's murder?" I asked hopefully.

"Dunno," Cliff said unconvincingly. "Tomorrow mid-morning, say, ten o'clock, I'll meet you at the Jasper, okay?"

"Sure, yeah. Great," I said. I had the cook-off meeting tomorrow morning, but it wouldn't take long and Teddy had already committed to teaching.

Cliff left with a distracted wave. I sat down in the booth again and held the cup up for Bunny to refill.

"Duty calls, right, honey?" Bunny said as she poured.

I nodded.

As Bunny walked away, another figure slid into the booth across from me.

"Hello, Isabelle," Jerome said.

"Jerome," I said quietly. No one was paying me a bit of attention. We could converse without hiding if I kept it quiet. "Anything new?"

"I heard you talking to the young man. I'll go with you into the Jasper tomorrow. I can point out the blood and the piece of paper and there's something . . . well, there's something else there. I keep looking around and it's like I almost remember something but never quite do."

"Maybe it's just because Everett owned it? Could you be — I don't know — sensing him because he's dead now, too?"

"I don't think that's it. Maybe Everett purchased the Jasper because of me, something that had to do with me."

"Like what? The treasure?"

"Maybe. I just don't know, but I feel like I'm close to remembering."

I tried to think of something to push his memory. "Did you work there? Did you own it?"

"I don't think so. That sounds like too big a commitment for the fella I was. I was a loner, that much I'm pretty certain of."

"You left Boston because you thought you would be convicted of murder. Do you remember that?"

"I remember Miz telling me about it one time."

"Did you know you were cleared?"

"I don't know. I don't think so. I was cleared?"

"Yes, totally. I don't have the details but if we round up the stuff that was taken from Jake, I bet I can tell you exactly what happened."

"What happened to that fella, Jake?"

I told him about the attack and Jake's insistence that he'd be fine at his own home.

"What about you, Isabelle?"

"What do you mean?"

"Where will you stay tonight? You should stay with your parents or your brother. Or even stay with Jake."

"I'm not concerned."

"You were shot at, too. Perhaps you should remember that."

I ignored his comment as something else occurred to me. "Oh! Jerome!" I said. "Go to Cliff. Go see what he's doing. You could spy on him. He might be doing something that has to do with the murder."

"Where did he go?"

"I don't know."

Jerome laughed. "It doesn't work that way, Isabelle. I can't just wish my way to someone. I have to have a destination, a place not a person, in mind."

"I should have had you follow him. Shoot."

"I bet he'll give you more details tomorrow. Come on, let's go to your house. I'm not much protection, but you can hear me, so if someone tries anything I can at least wake you up."

"You're staying at my house?"

"Unless you go to your parents' or your brother's."

Like Jake, I didn't want to go anywhere but my own home. I shrugged and said, "Come on, then. When I was a kid, we used to try to summon ghosts at slumber parties, but this will be the real deal."

"I remember when you did that," Jerome said.

"Uh, you do?"

Jerome laughed. "No, I'm pulling your leg, but the look on your face was worth it."

A ghost with a bad memory and a slightly twisted sense of humor. Lucky me.

CHAPTER 14

I wasn't used to much company at night. I thought it would be strange to have Jerome in the house, but by the time we got there I was so exhausted I fell into bed and into one of the deepest sleeps I'd ever experienced. Having a watch-ghost made me relax completely. If someone tried to break in or anything else suspicious occurred, Jerome would wake me and I would call 911.

I slept like the dead while the dead watched over me.

I woke extra-early the next morning, right before 6:00 A.M., refreshed and more than ready for whatever the day had in store. The cook-off and opening of the tourist season was only a day away and suddenly the excitement of the coming events overshadowed everything else.

Jerome said that no one attempted to disturb me or the house. This only added to my positive attitude. My car was still at the school, so we took Gram's Volvo and parked it just as the sun was coming up. Teddy's truck was there, parked in a different spot than the day before, so I knew he'd left for at least a little while.

The mess had been cleaned up. Other than two missing ceiling tiles, a small amount of leftover stink, and a slightly darkened worktable and stove, no one would know the school had recently seen a fire.

But more impressive than the cleanup of the school was the cleanup of my brother.

"Sis, you're here," he said as he entered the kitchen through the far doors.

"Teddy?" I said. His hair was brushed, his face was shaved, he wore pants that weren't made of denim, and his shirt actually had a collar. "Is that you?"

"Who else would it be?"

"You look so . . . so put together."

"Well, I'll be tethered. He sure does," Jerome added.

If I hadn't known that he wasn't prone to blushing, I would have sworn Teddy's cheeks got pink.

"If I'm going to teach, I have to command respect, don't I?"

"Yes." I wanted to tell him he'd done a good job and I was proud of him, but there was no surer way to get him to do the opposite of what I wanted him to do.

"Why are you here so early?" Teddy asked.

"Judges' meeting. Before school for Amy and hopefully not interrupting everyone else's work. Hey, Teddy, has Jim or Cliff been out here this morning?"

"No."

I looked at my watch. The judges would be arriving soon. I only had a few minutes. "I'll be right back in."

"No hurry."

I wondered if the coin had been removed yet. Had Cliff forgotten to tell Jim?

"It's still there," I said as Jerome and I looked at his tombstone again. "I thought Cliff was going to tell Jim."

"Call him. He had the emergency. Maybe he forgot."

I didn't have Cliff's number, but I knew the number to the jail. Jim answered on the first ring.

"Betts, everything okay?" he said. Caller ID still frequently caught me off guard.

"Fine, fine," I said. "Jim, did Cliff . . . I mean, there's a coin . . ."

"Yes, on the tombstone. Cliff told me last night. We were busy. I'll be out at the school today. Do you know if the coin is still there?"

"Yes, I'm looking at it."

"Good. I'll be out."

"Thanks." I hung up the phone.

"Hey, what's going on, Betts? Why are you out there?" a voice said from the parking lot.

Miles Street and Jenna Hopper were standing next to Gram's Volvo.

"That's the pool hall owner, right? And the woman who works in the ice-cream saloon?" Jerome asked.

"Yes, they're both here for the judges' meeting," I said without moving my lips too much.

"What're you doing, Betts?" Jenna added her own question.

Jenna was pretty in a slightly rough way. She didn't look completely rode hard and put away wet, just damp maybe. Her blond hair was almost not too blond, and her eye makeup was almost not too thick. She'd done a good job of keeping Teddy's liquor consumption under control, so I liked her.

"Just going for a walk," I said.

"Through the cemetery?" Miles asked.

"Yes."

Jerome laughed.

Miles and Jenna climbed over the low rope and trudged their way toward me.

"Jerome Cowbender. Wasn't he the bank robber who couldn't land a bullet anywhere in the general vicinity of his target?" Miles said.

"That's me," Jerome said.

"I think so, yes. Do you know anything else about him?" I said.

"Not much." Miles shook his head.

"There are so many great characters from Broken Rope's past," Jenna began. "I don't know a lot about him, but he was one of the interesting ones. He was so handsome!"

Jerome might have been a ghost, but he still knew how to puff up at a female's compliment. He tipped his hat and said, "Thank you kindly, miss."

I tried not to roll my eyes.

"What's that?" Miles said as he crouched and pointed.

We all, including Jerome, joined him and looked at the side of the tombstone. At first I didn't see anything unusual, but Miles reached for what looked like a rut in the stone, something naturally made and not out of place or unusual. But when he pushed on it with his thumb, a piece of the stone fell to the ground and revealed a hole.

"I'll be," Jerome said from behind me.

"What's in there?" Jenna asked.

The only person who was at a good angle to see anything was Miles so he moved closer and said, "Coins maybe?" He reached for the hole but I grabbed his hand.

"Stop, Miles."

"Why?"

"Well, there was a murder here yesterday and this is weird. Don't you think?" I said.

"How would one thing have something to do with the other?" Miles asked.

"I dunno. I just think we should let Jim know before we touch anything."

"Okay." Miles hesitated, but then pulled his hand back.

I leaned forward and twisted my neck just enough to look into the cubbyhole. It was only a few inches deep and the diameter of a Ping-Pong ball. There were coins inside. They looked exactly like the gold one that was still on the top of the tombstone — the one that Miles and Jenna hadn't noticed. Yet.

But there was something else, too: a small piece of paper mostly hidden underneath one of the coins and dingy enough to stand out against the shiny bright of the gold. I didn't mention that I saw it. No one else said a word about it either, including Jerome, but I wasn't sure if they saw it.

Two cars pulled into the parking lot. Stuart and Mabel and Amy were arriving. It was time for the meeting and I didn't want the crowd in the cemetery growing.

"Miles, my brother, Teddy, is inside. Would you run in and ask him to come out here, please? Thanks. And Jenna, would you mind greeting the others and grabbing some treats out of a fridge? I'll be right in after I talk to Teddy."

Hesitantly, they both did as I asked. Gold coins in a secret hole in a tombstone were much more interesting than setting up for a meeting.

"You see that piece of paper, Jerome?" I asked without moving my lips. I acted casual.

"I do. Can you get it?"

"I'll try." Miles was already inside. As Jenna directed Mabel and Amy through the front door, I crouched again. "Tell me when you see Teddy."

My finger could fit easily into the hole, but I didn't want to get my prints on any of the coins. I used one of my short but just long enough fingernails to flip at the corner of the piece of paper.

I didn't ever call myself "almost a lawyer." I used that title for those who had finished law school and were either preparing to take the bar exam or were waiting for their results. A dropout is nothing more than a dropout, plain and simple. But I'd had enough schooling to know I was tampering with things I shouldn't be tampering with. I didn't even need school to know that much. I could have learned that from TV. I should leave everything exactly as we found it.

But I couldn't. I needed some answers and something told me there might be at least something on the piece of paper that would help. Gram wasn't talking, and the ghost that I'd become acquainted with had memory issues and couldn't get into the one place where he could further discuss things with Gram. I doubted that Gram had anything to do with Everett's death, but if she did, I wanted to either be aware of the facts or find a way to help hide the crime.

It was probably a good thing I'd dropped out. At least I wasn't risking being disbarred.

My nail tipped the corner of the paper but didn't make it any easier to get a hold of. I didn't have enough time to be as careful as I wanted to be. I turned my finger upside down so that any fingerprints I might leave wouldn't be on the coins but the top part of the hole. Without being able to see my own maneuverings, I pushed at the coins with my nail and the very tip of my finger and exposed what I thought was the paper. I used my nail again to try to lift it up.

"Teddy's out the door," Jerome said.

Teddy could see me crouching, but he

wouldn't be able to tell what I was doing until he was a good ten feet into the cemetery.

I could still lift a corner but it felt as though it was stuck.

"He's stepping over the rope," Jerome said.

I had two choices. I could abandon the mission or I could turn my finger over, put pressure on the piece of paper, and try to scoop it out that way.

I chose the riskier method. There was a chance I'd get a print on one of the coins but I'd have to deal with that later.

The paper was stuck, as though it had gotten wet and dried to the stone.

"Isabelle, finish it up," Jerome said.

I pushed with lots of pressure and then pulled. The paper broke free and came out with my finger. And fell to the ground.

"What's up?" Teddy said as he came up behind me.

I stayed in the crouch but moved my knee over the paper.

"Look." I pointed to the hole.

"Whoa. Money. Lucky find. How much is in there? Split it with me?" Teddy asked.

"I don't think it's money necessarily," I said. "I think it's gold or something."

"Like a doubloon?"

"Exactly." I smiled.

"Doubloon?" Jerome said. "That's strange."

"Anyway," I said. "I need you to stand guard. I've already called the police and I need to start the meeting. But someone needs to be out here until Jim gets here."

"Or Cliff. Cliff might come out."

"All right. Whatever. Don't touch anything. I'd hate for your prints to be on anything."

Teddy's face fell a little. He'd hoped to grab a couple of whatever was in the hole, but I'd dashed his hopes.

"Please," I said. "They'll be right out, I'm sure."

Teddy sat and leaned against the back of the tombstone. Though he was taking his teaching job seriously, he'd enjoy a short nap.

"I suppose," he said. "But you're beginning to owe me even bigger than big."

"I know. I appreciate it."

Somehow and without Teddy's noticing, I lifted my knees as I pushed off the ground with my hands. I pulled my right hand back and grabbed onto the small piece of paper and stood. It wasn't the smoothest move, but it wasn't awkward enough to gain anything more than a questioning squint

233

from my brother.

"Thanks," I said as I turned.

"Good job, Isabelle. What's on it?" Jerome asked.

As I walked quickly toward the building, I unfolded the old yellowed piece of paper. Surprisingly, it was still somewhat substantial and didn't fall apart. I didn't know if that proved it wasn't old or that it had been well preserved inside the tombstone.

"Does it say anything?" Jerome asked again.

"Hang on," I said. The piece of paper was only about half an inch by about two inches. There was something on it but it was hard to tell what it was. "I can't read it. Can you?"

We were right outside the doors to the school. I peered back at Teddy whose eyes were closed as he leaned against the tombstone.

"Well, I'll be," Jerome said.

"What?"

"If you turn it this way, I can read it." He pointed.

"What's it say?"

"It says 'Jasper.'"

"Like the theater?"

"Darlin', I don't know, but I'm thinkin' so."

When he pointed it out, I could see the word even though the ink was faint. The handwriting was long, slanted heavily to the right, and the *J* had a flourish to its top.

"I'd be willing to bet that's exactly what it is. Maybe your Jasper instincts are right on," I said.

"I think we should find out."

"Betts, what're you doing?" Teddy yelled from the tombstone.

"Nothing," I said.

"Let's get this over with," I said as Jerome and I went back into the school.

CHAPTER 15

"You found a treasure?" Amy said, her fourteen-year-old eyes wide and intrigued.

"Not exactly," I said. I hadn't mentioned to Miles and Jenna that they shouldn't share the details of what we'd found, so they had done what any of us would do: share enthusiastically. I'd called Jim again and knew he would be there any minute, but I also knew I should keep the cook-off judges/nighters in their seats until after the police arrived and investigated whatever they needed to investigate. Jerome had wanted to go back to the Jasper so he'd disappeared again.

"Tell us what it was, then," Mabel said as she put her hand on her granddaughter's arm and guided her back to the stool. There was nothing violent about the gesture, and Amy didn't flinch at her grandmother's touch.

"Well, there were some coins in a hole in a tombstone, but certainly not enough to be called a treasure."

"Whose tombstone?" Stuart asked, his eyes as wide as Amy's but magnified bigger by his thick glasses.

"Jerome Cowbender's," I said.

"The bank robber?" Stuart said. "I'd heard he'd hid a treasure. Do you suppose you found it?"

"No. Where did you hear about the treasure, Stuart?"

He blinked and then said, "Well, I guess I'm not sure. I thought it was a well-known fact."

Murmurs from the others told me it wasn't a well-known fact to them. Stuart's face turned red and he scooted back on his bench. "Maybe Jake told me. You know how he goes around telling everyone about the history of our little town. Yes, I bet that was it. Jake must have told me."

Stuart wasn't outspoken. In fact, he was shy to the point of painful at times, but I wanted to push him to tell me more. Unfortunately, Mabel interrupted.

"How's the search for that horrible man's killer going?" Mabel asked.

It was my turn to blink. "Do you mean Everett?"

"Yes, of course."

"Mabel, I've never heard him described

that way. I've only heard good and nice things about him. Why was he horrible?"

It was Amy's turn to put her hand on her grandmother's arm. Amy's skin turned gray, and her eyes came together in concern. She shook her head ever so slightly.

"Never mind," Mabel said.

Everyone was looking at Mabel with questioning curiosity.

"Mabel, I hope you've told the police why he was horrible. For the rest of us, well, it's none of our business, I suppose."

Unlike Stuart, Mabel wasn't shy in the least. She was one of the town's busybodies, but she was always friendly so no one minded her nosy ways. I wouldn't have been surprised if she knew something about Everett that the rest of us didn't. I was dying to know what that something was, but her mouth was now pinched tightly shut. She put her arm around her granddaughter and hugged her tightly. Amy leaned into the hug.

Of course, the worst possible thoughts ran through my mind, but that was bad form. It was wrong to assume the worst, no matter what. Maybe Gram would know something.

"Okay, then, shall we talk about the cook-off?"

The cook-off was held at the south end of

Broken Rope's downtown Main Street, which was right at the intersection in between Mabel's cookie shop and the saloon, the same spot Jake and I had walked around to sneak behind the buildings. The cooks created their meals in the school's kitchen and then took aluminum-foil-covered pans to the event. Mabel allowed the students to use her cookie shop ovens to keep things warm, and Miles would allow them to use his refrigerators. An old-fashioned hanging platform would be set up before tomorrow morning, and the judges would be seated on the platform as they sampled the dishes. It was tradition that whoever won the contest got to climb the stairs up to the platform, grab the noose, and ceremoniously cut it off, effectively beginning the Broken Rope tourist season. It was all very morbid but had become tradition, and the tourists looked forward to it, cheering and booing through the entire event.

Other people were in charge of setting up the tables and the hanging platform. We were only responsible for explaining to the judges what we were looking for from them, which was an honest and fair judgment based on their trying every single item that was put in front of them. We always screened for food allergies and always had a doctor on the premises just in case someone was allergic to something they weren't aware of, but we hadn't had any problems in the past.

Gram usually led these meetings, but I'd have to take over. I was up to the task. I knew the menus for each of the four students who had entered. I wouldn't share specifically who was bringing what, but I did list off some of the items just to see if I got a sour reaction from anyone. It was a sour reaction that Gram looked for each year and used to emphasize how the judges must be fair.

There would be fried chicken, roast beef, pot roast, pork chops, collard greens, mashed potatoes, vegetable dishes that made vegetables taste like the most delicious foods ever created, and so much more.

The fried chicken was always a big hit. We'd thought of not allowing the contestants to add it to their menus because it was next to impossible to beat Gram's recipe, but the mere mention of disqualifying it sent the students into loud vocal protest. And it had turned out to be a good thing that we kept it qualified. Sometimes students would try to perfect the simple recipe. They thought they'd found a way to make it better. They soon learned that messing with the simplicity was a bad plan. It was a good lesson for them to learn.

"Any questions?" I finally said after covering all that I thought needed to be covered.

"Can we discuss the food while we're sitting at the judges' table?" Mabel asked.

"Oh no. You can't even discuss it with Amy. We want you to fill out the form using your opinion only," I said.

"What if we really, really hate something?" Jenna asked.

"Then write that on the form along with a zero or whatever number you'd like to give the dish. We don't show the forms to the students, but we do use the information to help them learn. We're not going to hurt their feelings — at this point we have total confidence in their cooking skills. If you don't like something, Gram and I would like to know. But give us specifics. Too salty, too bland, et cetera."

"Will Miz be able to help this year?" Mabel asked.

Despite the fact that I'd led the meeting. Despite the shooting and visiting Gram in jail. Despite everything, I hadn't accepted that Gram wouldn't be helping with the cook-off. The judges faced me. I realized they'd been wondering about Gram's status the entire time. Mabel had just been the first one brave enough to ask.

"You bet your sweet bippy I'm going to be able to help!" Gram burst through the swinging doors as if she'd been waiting for her cue. She'd somehow made it home and changed into a USC long-sleeved cotton shirt before her arrival.

"Gram!"

"Miz, you've been sprung," Stuart said with a smile.

"Good to see you," the others joined in.

"Good to be back. Now, I imagine Betts has covered everything, but are there any other questions?"

"How did you get out of jail?" I asked.

"Not enough evidence or some such thing that Verna beat into Jim. I'm not to leave town, though, and Jim threatened to put one of those ankle-cuff things on me that would make his computer beep if I took one step too many outside the town limits. If they find more evidence against me, I'm back in the slammer." Gram waved away the thought.

Jim followed directly behind Gram. He gave us a few minutes to greet her and then signaled that he'd like me to join him outside.

"Not enough evidence?" I asked as I shaded my eyes from the warming sun.

"Just fingerprints on the bag. Since the bag was in a place that Missouri owns and we couldn't find any other evidence, we thought it would be okay to release her on her own recognizance."

"Verna worked her magic."

"That part doesn't matter right now, Betts." Jim had been well handled by Verna, but he wouldn't have released Gram if he thought she was guilty. He knew how important the cook-off was. "What's with the coins?"

Teddy was still sitting beside the tombstone. He was either texting or playing a game on his cell phone.

"Right," I said. "Over here."

At first glance it didn't look like Teddy had stolen anything.

"Do I have to teach since Gram is free?" he asked as we approached.

"Yes, she'll need your help."

"I'm at your beck and call," he muttered as he stood and swiped grass pieces off his pants and sauntered back inside. There was a hint of delight in the tone of his voice.

"That certainly is interesting," Jim said as he peered into the hole and at the coin on the top of the tombstone. "I think you *might* have found something of value, but I'm not sure it has anything to do with the murder.

Cliff told me what you and Jake said about Jerome Cowbender's treasure and that there might be a connection, but I just don't know. Someone could have just put these here for the tourists. Sometimes, Betts, when we want to help a person we love, we make something out of nothing, you know what I mean?"

"I dunno, Jim. It's all strange and unusual: Everett is murdered, Jake and I get shot at, Jake is attacked, his archives are stolen, and now this. Everett had been looking at Jerome's archives. I think it's worth looking at. Maybe fingerprints? What would it hurt? I'm glad Gram's out of jail, but you still don't have the real killer. I'd hate for this to go to trial and the only evidence you end up with is Gram's fingerprints no matter how coincidental they might be."

Jim inspected me from behind his glasses. "You have some good points, but you're not telling me something, Isabelle Winston. I suspect it's for a good reason. You're protecting someone, probably your gram, but I understand that. I'll tell you what, I'll take these and find out what they are and have them fingerprinted. I doubt they'll tell us much, but I guess I'm curious enough to want to know what they are anyway."

"Thank you." He was sort of right. I was

protecting Gram. She wouldn't admit that she and Everett had been looking for the treasure. He might already know that but if I reinforced it he might arrest her again, or at least call her back in for questioning. I'd work on getting her to talk to him but I didn't want him to try to force her.

"Anything else that might help with the case, Isabelle?" Jim asked as we stood.

"What do you mean?"

"Just curious if there's anything else you think you should share with me that might help. Nothing's too small."

"No, nothing else."

"Be sure and let me know if that changes."

"Will do."

At first I thought he was being sarcastic, but I quickly realized he wasn't. He was truly curious about what else I knew, or thought I knew. Unfortunately, all I was really sure of was that my world had grown to include a ghost, the ghost of an outlaw at that. I couldn't tell him, or anyone but Jake, that bit of news. I nodded agreeably, but I still had a bad feeling. It seemed I was having lots of those lately.

CHAPTER 16

Jim left with the coins, and Gram sent the judges away right before the daytimers showed up. We didn't have any time to discuss anything between the two of us. And we were caught off guard when the daytimers proved to be an unhappy bunch.

The class was made up of fifteen students — fifteen wonderful and unique personalities. Gram knew how to teach. She knew how to read her students and get the most out of each and every one. Each student required something different; some were self-motivated, others needed a metaphorical kick in the butt. The daytimers had missed only one day of class, but it was an important day. They should have been taught the champagne cookie recipe yesterday and spent today practicing for tomorrow's cook-off. Now they were going to have to combine the days.

The champagne cookies were more than

just the ingredients they were made of; they were a symbol. When the students began their nine-month journey at Gram's Country Cooking School, the cookies were the promise that was given. Complete the course and she'll show you how to make her famous champagne cookies, cookies that, in some form or another, were served all over the country by cooks and chefs who'd worked hard to learn Gram's ways. The congratulatory clinking of champagne glasses was replaced by the hum of mixers at work.

There was a general sense of crankiness throughout the kitchen, though no one would come out and say they were angry or irritated. Instead, they just acted it, which was worse.

I planned on meeting Cliff and hopefully Jerome at ten o'clock. Teddy was there to help Gram but since I still had an hour or so I stuck around to see if there was any way I could help.

Gram, aware of the discontent, began the meeting with an apology — she was sorry about the previous day's cancellation, she was sorry about Everett, she was sorry she'd been thrown in jail, she was sorry that Jim and Cliff had contacted most of the students for a statement regarding the day of Everett's death. She was actually more patient than I would have expected. I wanted to tell the students that it was normal for people to be questioned when a crime had been committed. They should have nothing to worry about if they were innocent.

The age range of the class was twenty-one to thirty-seven. This was one of the younger groups we'd taught, and they meshed pretty well, but Gram and I hadn't thought about the fact that not only would the students feel inconvenienced, they might be scared, too.

"They don't have any clues at all?" Marie asked. She was tiny with closely cropped brown hair and big green eyes.

"Nothing substantial," Gram said.

"Are you okay, Miz?" Myron Dillon asked. It was the first nonheated question. Myron was tall, thin, dark-skinned, and bald. He was planning on opening a restaurant in his hometown of New Orleans, which wouldn't necessarily serve the type of food that Gram had taught him to cook, but Myron was a big believer in learning everything one could learn about preparing and cooking food. His wife and young daughter had come to Broken Rope with him, and we'd all fallen a little in love with Myron's Creole accent and the way he worshiped his little girl.

"I'm fine," Gram said.

"Should we arm ourselves, carry weapons, maybe?" Missy Landon asked. Missy had proved to be Gram's biggest challenge this year. She'd received her PhD in economics from Georgetown and then immediately signed up to take Gram's class. Previous professional baking or cooking experience wasn't a prerequisite to be accepted into the class, but a passion for such things helped. Gram admitted that she'd mistaken Missy's desire to put off joining the real world for a true passion. Frequently, Missy would complain about something and literally throw up her hands in defeat. Giving up wasn't something Gram subscribed to and more than once I thought Missy might have pushed her too far. But Gram stuck with her, saying this class might end up being the best thing for Missy.

"I want everyone to feel safe, but I don't allow guns in the school. We'll watch out for each other, Missy. And you'll notice that I locked the doors after everyone got here today. Jim — the police — will be stopping by frequently to check on us."

"Huh," Missy sighed. She pulled at one of her tight blond curls. When she first arrived, I thought she was adorable. It didn't take long for her attitude to change my mind.

"Miz, do they think one of us could have killed Mr. Morningside?" Jordan Kingsley asked. Jordan was the quietest person I'd ever met. He was from Connecticut and had signed up for classes mostly to learn how to be a better baker. He and his brother owned a small coffee shop in Wolcott and wanted to start adding their own baked items, instead of ordering them from elsewhere, to their menu. He dressed like Mr. Rogers but looked like Mr. Magoo. I thought I liked him, but it was hard to tell because he was so difficult to talk to. It was as if it was painful for him to have a conversation with anyone — except Myron. The two of them had hit it off and spent lots of time together at the school and with Myron's family.

"I think you'd be arrested by now if they thought that, Jordan. They locked me up so fast I didn't have time to plan an escape," Gram said.

The class laughed, a little, but it was enough to be encouraging.

"Well, there's a lot to do today. I think we should get started on the cookies. Ready? Okay," Teddy said, sounding like the cheerleader he never was.

"Who would like to pop the corks?" Gram added cheerily.

It was the slight nudge the students

needed. Once one of them volunteered, others seemed to think it was okay to jump in, too.

As the bottles of pink champagne were opened and other ingredients passed around and smelled, I secretly gave my brother a thumbs-up and made a quick exit out the front doors. He would be fine. Gram would be fine. And the students were in good hands.

I glanced at my watch as I pulled out of the parking lot. I was going to be a few minutes late, but at least I was back in my own car.

As it was with every year, suddenly things were picking up in Broken Rope. RVs and other vehicles were snaking down the state highway, causing my trip to be at least three minutes longer than it was the day before. Foot traffic had picked up, too, and where there had been no one the day before, there were suddenly pockets of people peering in windows or taking pictures.

Cliff was waiting outside the theater, but I didn't see Jerome anywhere.

"Sorry I'm late. Had to help Gram."

"No problem. I'm glad Jim set her free." Cliff unlocked one of the front doors and held it open. "It'll be dark, no windows past the entrance. The main lights are off, but there are a couple emergency lights in the lobby. Go on in and wait for me while I go back and flip the breaker."

I'd spent many evenings at the Jasper when I was younger and still attended a few movies. But I was too busy anymore for it to be more than an infrequent visit. I didn't know how authentic the items in the lobby were, but I knew the pictures on the wall were of real performers from the past.

The emergency lights were dim. As I waited for Cliff, I stepped close enough to the pictures so I could see some of the details. Elsa McMacenroe, with a tall blond wig and heavily made-up eyes, teased the camera with discreetly placed large feathers. Just the scandalous parts were covered, but everything else was well-exposed, proving that curvy women were once thought of as sexy. I'd stared at this picture when I was younger, wondering if I'd have such a body when I grew up. It didn't look like it was ever going to happen. I still found Elsa beautiful, though, and loved thinking of her on the stage, teasing the audience with her fanning feathers.

"Ah, Elsa. Sweet, sweet Elsa," Jerome said from beside me.

I jumped a little, but I was beginning to get used to his sudden appearances. "You knew her?"

"Everyone knew Elsa. She was famous and people would come from all over Missouri to see her perform. She was amazing on stage but as quiet as quiet could be when she was off stage. She liked to perform but I don't think she liked people all that much."

"You remember her?"

"Yes, clearly for some reason, but she *was* famous. I'm always surprised when a clear memory comes."

"Did she have a family?" I asked. I wondered if Jake or Verna had found any descendants.

"I don't think so. It wouldn't have been respectable for her to have a family and do what she did. I know, I know, that's not the way it is nowadays. I suppose I think that's a good thing. The times have changed since Elsa was dancing on that stage."

"That's very true."

I moved to the next picture. Orville and Coco were the human/puppet ventriloquism team that had worked at the Jasper the same time Elsa had. Jerome said he didn't remember them or the Siamese twins who'd been joined at their hips.

He did think he had some memories of Belinda, the human contortionist, who'd died in one of Broken Rope's freak accidents. The details were quite gory, but the gist was that one of her tricks went wrong and she somehow fell off the stage, breaking her neck and dying instantly.

"I look at the picture and I sense that I was fond of her, but I can't be sure. I'm drawn to it, though," Jerome said.

"Fond of her? In what way? More than friends?"

In the picture, Belinda faced forward and so did the bottoms of her feet that were riding on the top of her shoulders. She was an exotic brunette, with a heart-shaped face and big dark eyes.

"Maybe."

"Keep trying to remember, Jerome."

"I will."

I looked at him, and my breath suddenly caught in my throat.

"What is it, Isabelle?"

In the dark and with only the emergency lights, Jerome looked different. He looked almost real in a glowing sort of way. Though he'd seemed three-dimensional before, he was more so now. His face was both fuller and lined more heavily. The hair on his head and mustache seemed more textured, as though it could move better.

"You look so different," I said. I couldn't help myself as I reached forward to touch him. He seemed so substantial. But just as my finger almost reached his arm, the lights came on and Jerome went back to his dimmer, less-detailed self. My finger went right through his elbow.

"Sorry," I said, but I wasn't sure why.

"No need to be."

The rest of the lobby was filled with typical movie theater paraphernalia; a counter displayed candy and an old cash register. The wall behind the counter was mirrored, and a chill took my breath for an instant when I realized I was the only person reflected in the murky light of the lobby. I wondered curiously if he'd had a reflection in the dark. The big popcorn machine was off, but the scent of butter still hung in the air.

"Does it look anything like it used to?" I asked.

"I doubt it, but I'm not sure. I do remember that it was rough-and-tumble in here. Lots of drinking, lots of cigar smoke, lots of fights, particularly when it came to the ladies. We were a much rowdier bunch. The more time I spend in here, the more images come back to me."

"Maybe Everett was onto something. Maybe you were tied to something here."

Jerome turned and looked at the picture

of Belinda. "Maybe."

"Do you want to start in here or behind the stage? Everett had an office back there," Cliff said as he came through the old doors that separated the lobby from the auditorium.

"Let's start back there, I guess," I said. I ventured a look at Jerome who nodded and shrugged.

I knew the mosaics on the auditorium walls were original. The town had spent a fortune keeping the tiles in reasonably good condition. The mosaics were elaborate, detailed, and abstract designs. The mostly warm-toned art was an important part of the town's history.

The chairs looked old-fashioned but were in pretty good condition, and I thought I remembered hearing that the previous owner had replaced all the seating with designs approved by the Historical Society. They were covered in red velvet, reclined a little, and were wider and softer than the previous versions.

The seating area swooped slightly downhill toward the stage, and the two aisles in between the three sections of seats were carpeted in a red color that matched the seats.

"We turned off the heating and air-conditioning, but I'm wondering if we should turn it back on. It isn't uncomfortable in here, but it is kind of stuffy," Cliff said.

"Who's going to run it?" I asked.

"We're not sure, yet. Evan, the new fire marshal, has expressed interest, but we're still not sure who're the bad guys and who're the good guys. Evan called us the day after the murder saying he'd like to consider buying it. We were curious about his motives for wanting to volunteer so quickly."

"Does he seem suspicious?" I asked.

"Not in the least. He lost his family in a terrible tragedy. We can't find anything suspicious, but we just have to make sure."

Cliff gave me a hand as we climbed up to the stage. It was larger than any recent audiences would ever know. The movie screen had been installed for many years and sat more toward the front than the back of the large area.

Cliff guided us behind the screen. Our new view revealed the real stuff of the theater, the inner workings, the guts. Ropes, pulleys, and levers were everywhere. If I looked closely I could see that very little was probably in working order but instead frozen, suspended in time. It was as if the theater ran one last burlesque show and then tied the ropes, secured the pulleys, and left the levers where they were before they turned out the lights one last time and went home.

There was also a distinct smell at the back of the stage. It was the same smell that I noticed in many Broken Rope locations. I also smelled it in Gram's house. I always referred to it as "antique stink." It didn't smell bad; it was just the smell of time, perhaps moisture that had been trapped in old wood crevices, perhaps dust that hadn't been swept away. I always found it comforting and a reminder of the history I constantly lived around.

"Look at this," Cliff said as he pointed at the floor.

The stage floor was made of old wood planks that had stood the test of time. Amid the planks and in a space well behind the screen and in the smack-dab center of everything was an ornate *J* done in lighter wood than the rest of the floor. It was as artistic as the mosaics but not nearly as well taken care of. The entire stage floor could have used a sanding and new varnish coating. But, nonetheless, it was still beautiful.

"Has the Jasper always been the Jasper?" I asked.

"I don't have any idea, Betts. You should ask Jake," Cliff said.

"I will," I said, but I looked at Jerome who suddenly seemed lost in thought as he walked around the *J* and rubbed at his chin. I wanted to ask what was on his mind. I cleared my throat to get his attention.

"You okay?" Cliff asked.

"Fine."

Jerome looked at me and his eyebrows came together. He shook his head as if to tell me that he couldn't quite capture the memory that seemed to be teasing him.

"Everett's office is back this way." Cliff turned and stepped around two pulley ropes. I didn't watch what Jerome did but followed Cliff. He had his hand on a door-knob. "There are a whole bunch of rooms back here. They must have been dressing rooms in the old days, but this one — the one with the big gold star — is the one Everett used as an office. I'd be happy to show you all the rooms, but I promise they're empty."

Everett's office was large and cluttered. It looked just like a movie theater manager's office should look. Movie posters, stacks of paperwork, even a couple rolls of "admit one" tickets.

I put my hands on my hips. "You okay if I

look through things?"

Cliff didn't want to tell me yes, but technically the office wasn't a crime scene. Everett had been killed at the school.

"We've gone through everything," Cliff said. "There's nothing here."

"Good. You've gone through it. What would it hurt if I looked, too? I won't make a mess, well, not a bigger mess than it already is."

Cliff's cell phone buzzed. He grabbed it from his pocket, looked at it and said, "I need to take this. I'll be out here."

Code for "go ahead, but don't disturb anything too much." That was convenient.

As Cliff left the office, Jerome joined me in it.

"Point me a direction, Jerome. Where's the paper? What should I look for?"

I hurried to the other side of the desk and started opening drawers. Pens, pencils, Sharpies, staples, files, none of which were interesting.

"It was on top of everything. I don't see it now. Maybe it fell or got moved. Look for anything, though."

I was disappointed there was no paper mentioning Jerome and the treasure, but I didn't want to miss the opportunity to search for other things, so I trudged forward.

Nothing grabbed my attention. Additionally, there wasn't anything personal in the office. There were no pictures, crayon drawings, greeting cards. Even I had a funny birthday card from Teddy in my office, a space I rarely visited. Everett had spent more time in his office in one day than I probably did in a week.

Out of frustration, I opened the wide-top pens-and-pencils drawer again. The muscle I put into the maneuver shifted the drawer's contents my direction. If it hadn't been so lightweight, I doubt the small piece of paper would have come into view. I didn't think it was much of anything anyway, but since I hadn't found anything else, I plucked it from in between a No. 2 pencil and a blue ink pen. It was about two inches by two inches, roughly bordered as if it had been torn from a larger piece of paper and folded in half. I unfolded it.

"This might be something," I said.

I'd hidden the piece of paper I found in the tombstone in the glove box of my car so I couldn't compare side by side, but from what I remembered, this new find looked like a copy of the first find. A copy made from a copy machine. The paper said *Jasper.*

"Hmm," Jerome said.

"What?"

"It seems so . . ."

"Convenient?"

"Something like that. In the tombstone and now in the desk drawer. We found them both within just a few hours. Where else should we look? If we find another one, I might think we're being set up."

I got what Jerome was saying. It was strange to find two of the same thing, two pieces of paper with the same word in such different places. Were they metaphorical bread crumbs? Was someone leading us a certain direction? Was it the right direction or was someone trying to throw us off?

I stared at the piece of paper and hoped my brain would grab onto something that told me what I'd found.

My brain got nothing.

Finally I did exactly what I'd done with the first Jasper I'd found; I put it in my pocket.

"Yeah, if we find one on my porch, I'll wonder, too. For now, we'll keep them both and compare," I said.

All I knew was at the moment the small pieces of paper meant absolutely nothing.

"Anything good?" Cliff peered into the office.

"Not a thing," I said.

"Want to look around some more?"

"Actually, I'd like to go onto the roof."

"Uh, well . . ."

"Is it easy to get to?"

"Not bad. Why do you want to go up there?"

"Jake and I were shot at from someone up there." I pointed. "I'd like to look around."

Cliff thought a moment and then said, "Sure. It's not too precarious. This way."

Cliff led the way down the back hallway, past the old empty dressing rooms.

"Hang on tight. The stairs aren't bad, but they're a little wobbly," he said as we approached a set of thin, short steel stairs. They were steep and seemed more precarious to me than they were to Cliff, but I was curious enough to make the climb.

"Careful there, Isabelle," Jerome said from behind me.

I nodded.

"A little wobbly" was an understatement, but we made it to the top of the twenty (I counted) steps and Cliff opened a door which took us directly to the roof.

The view from the roof was great. I could see all the way past Bunny's and to the RV park where traffic was still building. I could also see that the hanging platform was beginning to be assembled.

The roof's floor was made of rocky asphalt and was warm enough that I felt a little heat through my shoes. There was a large HVAC unit to one side of the space, but nothing else anywhere.

Jerome stood in the corner he spoke about and said, "It's still here, Isabelle."

I nodded. "Well, there's not much to see up here, is there?" I said to Cliff.

"Nice view," he said.

"Maybe I'll just walk up and down the back ledge." My words sounded too forced.

I started in the opposite corner from Jerome. "Interesting view from this side, too."

The alley, with props, Dumpsters, and storage sheds backed up to Missouri woods. I could see trees that seemed to go on forever, but there wasn't time to enjoy all the greenery. I turned my attention to the banister around the ledge. As I made my way toward Jerome, he kept saying, "Right here, right here." I looked up quickly to let him know that I knew, but he didn't get the hint and kept repeating himself.

Cliff followed behind me. He looked at the ledge, too. Finally, I reached Jerome and studied his discovery.

There was something on the ledge that looked like a couple drips of something. The spots were more brown than red and blended in with all the other pocks in the concrete banister, even though a close look showed they were different. Jerome must have good eyes.

"Cliff, what do you think this is?" I asked as I pointed.

"Good job," Jerome said.

Cliff crouched and looked at the spots. "Huh." He pulled out what looked like a pocketknife and extended a small magnifying glass and held it over the spots. "I'm not sure, but it might be blood."

"That could be important, right?"

Jerome nodded.

"Sure. It could be very important. The shooter could have cut him- or herself. I don't remember seeing it before, but maybe I missed it. I need to process it, but I didn't bring the equipment in."

Cliff's phone buzzed again. He folded the magnifying glass into the case and put it in his pocket.

"Gotta take this, too. Sorry, Betts." He walked to the other side of the roof and talked quietly into the phone.

"I took my time because I thought it

might be kind of fishy to walk directly to the blood," I said to Jerome.

"I just didn't want you to miss it." He smiled.

Were ghosts capable of teasing?

"No chance of that."

Jerome smiled again.

"Betts, we gotta go," Cliff said as he hurried to the door to the stairs.

"What's going on?" I asked as I joined him.

"Just police stuff."

Jerome didn't walk behind me but popped himself down to the stage while we took the wobbly steps.

"I'll get the drops processed quickly, but I have to get somewhere else first. Good catch, Betts," Cliff said when we reached the stage.

Fortunately it didn't look like it was going to rain. I hoped the spots stayed where they were until Cliff could get back to them.

"The breaker board is back here. I'm going to switch off the lights, and we'll use my flashlight to guide us out," Cliff said.

Cliff turned on the flashlight and flipped some switches on a breaker board that was on the stage left wall, next to a podium. The theater fell into thick darkness, dotted only by the flashlight.

If I thought Jerome looked lifelike before, the deeper darkness caused him to reach a whole new level of reality.

He wore a ratty cowboy hat that suddenly seemed rattier with worn spots and tears here and there. I thought his eyes were dark, but now that they were clear, I saw they were a deep blue. I could see the laugh lines that framed them. I could see some hair on his chest peek out from the collar of his shirt. I hadn't noticed any hair before. My eyes were drawn to his hands that were defined by calluses and straight, rough fingernails. As a ghost, I'd already decided he must have been a handsome man, but with the lack of light I could see how he was not only handsome but handsome in a rugged-I-could-maybe-pull-down-a-big-tree-with-just-my-thumb way. I couldn't stop staring.

"Betts?" Cliff said as he extended a hand to me. "You okay?" He looked in the direction of Jerome.

"Miss, you're making me blush," Jerome said as he did exactly that.

I shook my head slightly but didn't take my eyes off of him as I gave Cliff my hand.

"I've never seen anything like it," I muttered.

"Like what?" they both said.

"So real, so real."

"Let's get out of here," Cliff said as he guided me off the stage and into the theater's side aisle. Jerome followed.

Once we were outside in the bright sun, Jerome took on his previous less-than-stellar ambience as he tipped his hat and told me he'd see me later. And then he disappeared.

Cliff, with a confused look and without many words of good-bye, left, too.

I stood in front of the theater, alone but for a young couple walking directly to me with a camera and big smiles. They would want their picture taken. I was happy to oblige.

As I snapped the picture I thought about the two men who'd just departed. One I'd suspended in my mind as the picture of perfection for almost fifteen years.

And the other one was a ghost.

And there was something about both of them that caused something to stir in my chest, something that hadn't stirred in a long time. It had been so long, in fact, that I wasn't sure what it was right away, but it didn't take too long to remember.

All the years that had passed since Cliff and I broke up, I'd been waiting for something that made me feel the way I'd felt with him. Here he was again, and here *it* was again. I just wasn't sure if it was stronger for him or the ghost.

I was worse off than I'd previously thought.

CHAPTER 17

"That really doesn't look good at all," I said when Jake opened the door. His eye was swollen all the way shut and black puffy skin surrounded it. It looked less fresh but worse.

"It only hurts when I touch it, or hold my head up, or walk, though, so no big deal." Jake smiled. "Oh, and when I smile, too, so I won't be doing any of that either."

"Maybe you should have stayed home today."

"Not a chance. Tomorrow's the big day. I'm not allowing anyone to scare me away from missing all the fun."

"I didn't think you were scared. You could use the rest."

"I'm fine. How are you?"

"I have some archival questions."

"You've come to the right place. Come in. I'm locking the door and Patches will hang with us. I'm not scared, though, just being cautious." Jake held up the stick horse.

I petted its head. "Patches, thank you for saving Jake yesterday. I hope we don't need your brute strength again."

"What's your archival issue?" Jake asked as he and Patches escorted me to the back room.

I'd run home for a couple of small plastic sandwich bags to hold the small pieces of paper. I reached into my pocket and pulled them out. I explained where I'd found them and under what circumstances.

"Fascinating. You found the first piece of paper in the tombstone and only hours later found something almost identical in the office?"

"Sounds like a setup, doesn't it?"

"I don't know, Betts, let's think about it. Who would have known you would look inside a hole in a tombstone, of all places? And then of that group, who would know you would be looking in the desk in the theater. To me it sounds like more a coincidence than a setup. Weird, sure, but planted 'bread crumbs' — I think that would be hard to pull off."

He had a point. "What do you think they are?"

"I'm pretty sure they're both copies, of what, I'm not sure. The thief took my Jerome stuff, but I can probably still round up some Jasper stuff."

"What makes you think they're copies?"

"The paper. Both of these are in pretty good shape. Paper from that time would be more disintegrated. I do think someone made copies of something and placed these pieces of paper where you found them, but I have my doubts that they were for you to find."

"Who should have found them?"

"It seems pretty clear to me that Everett was searching for the treasure. Perhaps they were bread crumbs for him or even for Miz. They were at the tombstone and this was in Everett's desk. Maybe he found it some-where. You need to show them to Miz and see what she says. Does she know about the coins in the tombstone?"

"If she didn't already know, I didn't tell her. Everything was too crazy today."

"Well, you're looking at an authentic Broken Rope treasure."

"The papers are a treasure?"

"No, I'm the treasure."

"Of course."

Jake set Patches against the table and reached for a file on the end of the shelves.

"These are some old flyers from the Jas-per, back in the day of live performances. Let's take a gander and see if anything matches."

Jake flung the large plastic folder onto the table and pulled out a stack of its contents. There were mostly papers, each piece also individually wrapped in plastic. He spread them on the table. There were notices of shows, even a couple WANTED posters, neither of which had Jerome's face. One talked about Elsa and her fanning feathers. And the last one, the one that Jake pulled from the pile and examined more closely, began with "Tonight!"

"What is it?" I asked.

"Lookee here," Jake said as he slowly and dramatically took the two small pieces of paper and held them to the bottom of an advertisement to compare. The very last line, written with letters the same size and the same kind as my finds said: *Jasper Theater, Broken Rope, Missouri, Proprietor Belinda Jasper, daughter of recently murdered Homer Jasper.* "The 'Jaspers' are an exact match."

"They sure are. What a strange thing to put on an ad, though. And I thought they were handwritten."

"Not too odd. The original proprietor was a man. If his daughter, a woman, took over, the public would want some explanation. Plus don't forget, we're Broken Rope, and we make a big part of our living based upon strange or horrible deaths. As for the handwriting, you were just fooled by the fancy letters. The original was most definitely made using a printing press, but remember, letters for presses were just individual blocks and weren't lined up all the time and sometimes ink didn't cover them completely."

I looked closely at the picture. The woman was the same woman with dark hair and dark eyes who'd been forever immortalized in a picture on the Jasper's wall. Belinda Jasper was the contortionist and the woman Jerome felt certain he had somehow been close to.

"She's the contortionist from the picture in the Jasper," I said.

"Oh. Yes, she is. I hadn't thought much about it, but you're right."

"How did you find this so quickly?"

"I've spent the entire morning looking through these archives. I know that Everett spent time looking at the Jerome and Jasper stuff, so I spent a lot of time memorizing it. When I saw your pieces of paper, I thought I might have a match. Everett must have made many copies of many things, Betts. I bet that what you found today are parts of the copies he made. One in his office would be normal. Maybe he planted one in the tombstone. Remember, we didn't know the man that well. Do you suppose he was trying to set Miz up for something, maybe taking her on a wild-goose chase instead of a treasure hunt?"

I thought about Mabel and Amy's behavior earlier, what they'd said about him being horrible.

"None of us knew he had a wife, Betts," Jake continued. "I hope the police are looking at her or someone from his past as suspects, too. To me, all this only makes Everett look suspicious of doing something he should not have been doing. Maybe someone got mad enough at him for whatever shenanigans he was up to and decided to kill him."

"In the cooking school."

"In the cooking school," Jake repeated.

"That information might make Gram look guilty again."

"It's not really information as much as speculation."

Jerome appeared on the other side of the table. "Isabelle," he said. "Sorry to interrupt."

"Jerome's here, Jake."

"Where?"

"Right there."

"Hi, Jerome."

"He says hi back," I said.

"Isabelle, I have some news to share," Jerome said.

"He has some news, Jake."

"Tell her and then she'll summarize it for me," Jake said as he looked slightly to the left of where Jerome stood.

"I rushed off earlier, so I could go with Cliff. He seemed to have an urgent situation and you'd mentioned that you'd like for me to spy."

"Good job. What did you find out?"

"Mabel Randall," he said. "Well, Mabel and Amy."

"What about them?"

"The best I could tell was that last night, Mabel told the other officer, Jim, something bad about Everett. She told him — and others — that Everett had done something terrible to her granddaughter, Amy."

"Oh no," I said, my mind conjuring the worst possible thing again.

"Here's the rub. He didn't. Amy lied to Mabel. That's what was being straightened out today."

"Did Mabel kill Everett because of what she thought he did to Amy?"

"Jim and Cliff think it's possible, but there's not a scrap of evidence."

I thought about how the small pieces of paper and the treasure hunt might work in conjunction with Mabel or Amy potentially contributing to Everett's death. It didn't work. None of those thoughts fit together at all. Maybe I was placing importance on things that weren't important in my desperate attempt to prove that Gram didn't kill Everett.

I made some sort of frustrated gurgle at the back of my throat.

"What? Tell me what he said," Jake said.

"We have a whole other angle," I began.

While I told Jake what Jerome had said, Jerome moved to the side of the table and looked closely at the advertisement Jake had found. He studied it with full attention.

"That *is* a whole new angle," Jake said. "And how horrible to have blamed Everett for doing something he didn't do, something that was probably terrible. Mabel's got her hands full."

"I think I've figured something out, Isabelle," Jerome said.

I held up a finger to Jake: *Hang on a second.*

"Remember how I'm so certain that I knew this woman, Belinda Jasper?"

"Yes."

"I'm becoming more and more certain,

but there's something else. Look at her closely. She resembles someone else you know."

I did as he instructed but couldn't see a resemblance to anyone.

"What if her hair were blond?" Jerome said. "She'd look like the woman who works in the saloon. What's her name? Jenna?"

It occurred to me that maybe Jerome was just as desperate as I was when it came to proving that Gram wasn't a killer. The advertisement was old and I thought that the picture might either resemble no one or everyone; it seemed impossible that the person in the picture, a person long dead, would resemble someone alive today. But I looked closely and realized that Jerome was right — there was something about Belinda that reminded me of Jenna. There was something similar about their heart-shaped faces and thin but straight lips and their wide-set eyes.

"Jake, does this woman look like a brunet version of Jenna?" I asked as I moved the picture in front of him.

Jake looked at the picture even more closely than Jerome and I had. The same thoughts must have occurred to him, too, because I saw the look on his face transform from doubt to curiosity to a surprised discovery.

"I'll be . . . Well, I'll be . . . Betts, Jerome, I think you might have just found yet *another* angle," he said.

CHAPTER 18

"Do you suppose they're related?" Jake asked.

"The resemblance is kind of uncanny, except for the hair, but I'm sure Jenna dyes her hair," I said.

"And what would it mean if they were related? Does this have something to do with . . . You're sure he left?" Jake said. I nodded. Jerome, looking as though more memories were coming back to him, disappeared again with a quick good-bye. "What does this have to do with Jerome?"

"Just when I think we're onto something, something else happens."

Jake laughed. "I'm not sure we're very good at investigating crimes."

"Probably not, but still . . . it's all so . . ."

"Interesting, strange, odd?"

"Yeah, but mostly interesting. No matter what, all of these things are interesting. Ghosts, coins in tombstones, bartenders who resemble dead contortionists. Interesting."

"That's Broken Rope, sweetie. We're nothing if not interesting. In fact, I found a few more interesting things, things I'm not sure Jerome should see yet. We still have *The Noose* files. As frustrated as I am about not having this place as organized as I'd like, I'm glad I hadn't filed all the newspaper articles with their respective citizens yet. I know a little more about Jerome just from some of these articles that weren't with his stolen files. *The Noose,* though a semi-respectable newspaper, spent a good amount of space telling gossipy stories about locals."

"Tell me more."

"Jerome started off his life in Broken Rope as a loner. He lived out in the woods and came into town infrequently, but something happened toward the end of his life that caused him to not only spend more time in town but to start thieving."

"Right. You kind of told me that before."

"But why, why did he turn into a criminal?"

"Maybe he ran out of money?" I said.

"I don't think so. I don't know for sure but from all I can glean he was a big strappin' guy."

"He was."

"Those were valued qualities back then. Life wasn't easy; big and strappin' could get you a job. He could figure out how to make a living. He didn't need to steal."

"Why did he, then?"

"Dunno. Read this. You'll see why I didn't want him to see it."

It was another copy of something old. This time it was a newspaper article from *The Noose*. It was dated July 23, 1918. I read aloud.

Local citizen and wanted bank robber Jerome Cowbender was shot and killed dead today by Sheriff Earp. Wanted for stealing a treasure of gold from the Broken Rope Bank a month ago, Jerome was shot down after robbing the bank of a parcel of cash today. Before he was killed, he left a poorly aimed storm of bullets in his wake. It seems the man was not good with a gun.

The dead criminal had mostly worked a herd of cattle on his land outside of town. No one had claimed to have seen him since the gold robbery and since he'd been posted as a wanted man.

As he rode his horse down Main Street, he was approached by Sheriff Earp. No one heard the words they exchanged, but the sheriff pursued Mr. Cowbender on horseback. Witnesses say that Mr. Cowbender fired all the bullets in his gun but didn't hit more than a building or a post. The sheriff took three well-aimed shots, two of them finding their target and killing Mr. Cowbender dead. He'll be buried in the outlaw cemetery beside the church. Word has it that an anonymous person has purchased a tombstone so his grave will not be unmarked.

A lump formed in the back of my throat. It was as if I were reading about the killing of a friend, not someone I hadn't known and who was a ghost. I knew the ways of the Old West. I knew guns ruled the day and bank robbers and horse thieves usually weren't treated to a jury of their peers. Shoot-outs occurred all the time. They still did, but blanks and fake blood were used.

"You okay?" Jake asked.

"Fine," I said, swallowing the ridiculous emotions.

"I hadn't thought this might be too sad for you. You like him, don't you?"

"He's a nice . . . ghost," I said.

"Good, I'm glad to hear that, Betts. You need more people, even dead ones, in your life that you think are nice."

My cell phone buzzed.

"Hello," I said.

"It's Jim, Betts. I see your car across the street. Stop by my office when you can. I have something I want to tell you."

"I'm on my way," I said. I hung up the phone and told Jake we'd meet again later. If Jim wanted to tell me something, I wasn't going to miss the opportunity. Jake and Patches walked me to the door, watched me cross the street, and then locked the door again.

"I barely hung up the phone," Jim said as I came through the jail's front doors.

"Jake and I were done," I said. I swiped a piece of hair off my forehead as casually as possible. I should have waited a minute but I was not good at containing my enthusiasm.

"Hey, Betts," Cliff said. He was sitting at his desk with his hands over his keyboard. Suddenly it seemed normal and right with the universe that Cliff Sebastian, former architect, former married guy, and my first love, had abandoned his previous life and was a police officer in our hometown. Whatever crazy puzzle of events ruled our lives seemed to come together, everything fitting as it should.

"Hey, Cliff," I said.

"Come on over and sit down," Jim said.

"I've got something I'd like to talk to you about."

He waited until I took a seat in the same chair I'd been in the night of the murder before he sat down, too. He looked at me a long moment, pushed up his glasses, and opened a file on the desk.

"Something's going on, Betts. I need you to be as honest with me as you possibly can, do you understand?"

"Am I being questioned formally regarding the murder of Everett Morningside? If so, I'd like to request an attorney." I couldn't help myself.

"No, Betts, you aren't being questioned regarding the murder, well, not in a legal manner of speaking. I don't think you killed anyone, but if I find evidence that you did I will arrest you. You're more than welcome to an attorney. In fact, you didn't even need to come over here, but here you are. Shall we continue?"

I nodded. I'd have a friendly conversation with Jim, but I'd be on the phone to Verna if he acted like I or Gram was a prime suspect.

"Good. Fine. Thank you." Jim peered at the open file. "I think someone's playing a trick on all of us."

"A trick?"

"Yes. I just got the results on the 'coins' you found in Jerome Cowbender's tombstone."

"And?"

"They're worthless. Fake. Something kids might give away as birthday party favors. They aren't even old. According to the lab guy who tested them, the gold paint on their outsides chips and flakes quickly. They haven't even been out of whatever container or package they were in for very long."

"Someone planted them? *In* the tombstone?" I said. Who? I went through the list of possible suspects in my mind, but the list seemed to only grow more.

"That's what it seems like," Jim said. "Now, I don't know who would do this and why they would do it, but I'd like to know if you know anything more about the coins."

"Nothing. I found them and I called you."

"Right." Jim leaned back in his chair and looked at me again. "Betts, are you one hundred percent sure you didn't have anything to do with putting the coins in the tombstone?"

Now would have been a good time to call my attorney. Jim wasn't questioning me directly about Everett's murder, but he was questioning me around something that might have something to do with Everett's murder. It was murky and it wasn't. I knew what was going on, but I decided to throw caution to the wind, like any good dropout would do.

"No, Jim, I didn't. Why would I?"

"A diversion."

"A . . . ? You mean from investigating the murder? No, and I'm trying not to be offended at your accusation."

Jim put his hands up. "Hey, I'm not accusing. I'm just asking."

I looked at Cliff whose focus was intently on his computer screen. "Okay, well, the answer again is that I didn't have a thing to do with the fake coins. I don't know who would plant them, but perhaps it was a joke of some sort or perhaps it was something someone did for the tourists like you said," I cleared my throat. "Maybe they do have something to do with the real treasure."

"These were fake coins. These weren't part of any valuable treasure," Jim said.

Maybe Everett's murder had nothing to do with the treasure. Maybe Everett had been killed because of some false accusations from a teenager. Maybe his wife — the one no one in Broken Rope seemed to have known about — had something to do with his death. But even if Gram was involved with the search, the treasure was still an avenue I thought Jim should look at closely.

Did I think that the coins were the result of someone boosting the appeal for tourists? Not really. It was possible but not likely since I didn't know anything about them beforehand. The cemetery was a tourist destination, but it was right next to the cooking school. If someone had hidden the coins for something fun, they would have told me and Gram about them. Additionally, they'd been well hidden. We didn't make things that hard for the tourists.

I shrugged and tried to sound doubtful. "Maybe someone *did* put them there for the tourists."

"But the more I think about it, who would have done that?" Jim asked. "Sounds like something Jake might do but not without telling you, Miz, and maybe the rest of the world, too. Jake likes to share his good ideas."

I shook my head. "I'm certain that Jake didn't."

"And how would these coins have something to do with Everett's murder?" Jim asked. Cliff scooted his chair over a couple inches.

"I don't know." I didn't. "But it's weird isn't it? Coincidental, maybe, but the coins were found shortly after the murder. I'm not saying that I know for certain that the real treasure has anything to do with Everett's murder, but it might be something you should look at more closely." I couldn't be more direct than that.

Jim bit at his bottom lip for a moment. Finally, he surprised me and said, "I think so, too."

"You do?"

"Yes, I just wanted to see how you'd try to persuade me. I might have a small hunch that everything's connected, but I have no real idea how, Betts. I hoped you'd say something that made me put it all together. You didn't."

"Sorry. Did your guy find any fingerprints on the coins?"

Jim's eyebrows rose. "Actually, yes, it looks like he did. But just on one of the coins. The one that was on top of the tombstone. Unfortunately, that doesn't help us much. The coin was out in the open. Any number of people could have touched it. Well, any number of people who happened to be looking at the tombstone lately."

"Did you identify the fingerprint?"

"Maybe."

"I see."

The three of us looked at each other for a

moment. It was as if we were creating some invisible triangle with our laser vision. The cuckoo chirped and I resisted the urge to grab one of their guns and shoot it.

"I processed the drops on the roof. They were blood. Good work, Betts," Cliff finally said. "I admitted that I missed them."

"Yes, he did, and he's not fired yet. That was a good catch, Betts. Again, I don't know where it will take us, but it's another piece. Somehow the pieces fit together to form the picture, but I'm not seeing anything clearly. I'm almost positive you are, though. If something happens and you finally think you can share your information with me, will you call me right away?" Jim said.

"Of course," I said. "But I'm not connecting the dots either. At this point, I'd tell you if I was."

Jim nodded slowly and doubtfully. "And you'll continue to be careful and make sure Miz is careful, too?"

"Yes."

"Thank you for coming in, Betts," Jim finally said.

"I'll walk you out," Cliff said.

The growing crowd had grown some more. People were everywhere now. There wasn't much to see yet, but sometimes that was the best part of the day before the opening. It was easier to walk casually around town and peek into windows to see the beginning, the preparation.

The hanging platform was almost a quarter finished. The saloon and the pool hall were open and I could see customers file in and out of each business.

"Well, thanks for dinner last night and for taking me into the theater today," I said.

"You're welcome. It's been good to see you again."

"You, too," I said. It was, but I felt like my words rang false. I hadn't meant for them to.

Cliff looked at me with a sideways smile. "Betts, I'm new at this job, but I think I have pretty good instincts — plus I think I know you pretty well — and it's obvious there's something you're keeping to yourself."

"Hang on!" I said. "You don't know me! You know the young teenager high school me. You don't know the me I am today. Don't presume that our past gives you immediate knowledge of the person I've become."

The anger that lit through me like the kitchen fire was as big as an ocean. It was okay for Jim to think I was hiding something but not for Cliff to. But even I knew it

291

wasn't all about Cliff's innocent assumption. It was about the other things that had happened in between our past and our present, that gap, that defined who we were at that exact moment as we stood on the boardwalk outside the jail. I'd let him go, pushed him away, in fact. He'd gotten married and started a life I wasn't going to be a part of. And then he'd come home, though not back to me, a single man who hadn't shed his wedding band. Other things like my new acquaintance, the ghost, and Everett's murder were swirling in that ocean of anger, too, but mostly it was full of me and Cliff and our choices and mistakes. I put my hand on my chest and took a deep breath. I didn't like feeling that angry and I didn't understand it.

"I get that, Betts. I apologize if I sounded presumptuous. All I wanted to say was this — I'd be happy if we could be friends again, but you probably shouldn't share things with me that you don't also want shared with Jim. I'm taking this job seriously, but I don't ever want you to think I'm not on your side. If you tell me things that you shouldn't, I'm going to have to make some pretty tough decisions. So, as a favor to me," he put his hand on his chest, "please keep secrets."

And he smiled — just a little, but enough to form that stupid dimple.

And I wanted to touch his hair.

I wondered if I had some new weird hair fetish happening or if I was just being nostalgic. Either way, Cliff's return to Broken Rope was going to be something really wonderful or something really awful. And it might end up being my own outlook that would be the determining factor.

The ocean calmed somewhat and was replaced with deep embarrassment. I'd reacted too quickly and to something that probably hadn't been there in the first place, but I wasn't going to apologize. I nodded and looked down the street at an elderly couple going into Broken Crumbs.

"Something tells me there are more things you'd like to say to me, perhaps unpleasant things. Feel free to anytime, Betts. I'd like for us to get our pasts out of our systems, if that's possible."

I didn't mean to. In fact, it was almost an involuntary action. My eyes went directly to the wedding band.

"Good point," Cliff said as he tracked my line of vision. He took off the band and put it in his pocket. "Better?"

"Only if you were really ready."

Cliff nodded and smiled. "We'll see."

I nodded, too, and smiled, but only a little. There was more to discuss and I hoped we could become friends again. But only time would tell.

"See you later, Betts."

Cliff went back into the jail as I stood on the boardwalk and contemplated my next move. I could go back and talk to Jake again, but I didn't think that would lead to knowing much more than I already did. I knew I was going to owe Teddy even more, but I pulled out my cell phone and called Gram.

"Meet me at Verna's office," I said.

"Isabelle Winston, what makes you think I have time to meet at Verna's office? Tomorrow is the cook-off."

"Teddy can take care of things there, Gram. We need to talk. It's important. And bring Jerome if he's with you."

She muttered unpleasant things that weren't fit for fine conversation but then agreed to meet me. As she hung up her phone, I heard her say, "Teddy, come here, sweetie, I've got to go. Your sister's in a mood."

CHAPTER 19

"Everything you say in here is protected by attorney-client privilege," Verna said as she reached for a piece of candy in a bowl on the corner of her desk, unwrapped it, and popped it into her mouth. "You've already told me that you didn't kill Mr. Morningside. We are sticking with that being the current story, right?"

"Of course I didn't kill Everett," Gram said. "But I do have a cooking school to attend to, so if you wouldn't mind, Betts, telling me why you demanded this meeting."

"I'm curious, too," Jerome said from where he leaned against the wall in the corner of Verna's small office. He had been back at the theater when he saw me talking to Cliff and then on the phone with Gram, so he'd come with me to Verna's. He'd wanted to talk about Cliff and then the reason for the meeting, but I hadn't. I did tell him that he had indeed found blood on the roof and that it just might help solve the crime.

I turned my head and peered at him over my shoulder. How was he able to lean or sit, but when I touched him, there was nothing there? Verna probably wondered what I was looking at but she didn't ask.

Verna's office was in her home, at the back of it, to be specific. Her husband, Ben, had built on the addition some ten years earlier. There was no separate entrance so to get to it you had to come into the front door of the house, step over and around things in the front room, walk down a hallway and through the kitchen. The other option was to enter through the kitchen, but that meant going into the backyard, which was a dangerous maneuver. Verna and Ben had dogs that were trained to scare the "guilty right out of a person." Bo and Peep were both big and quick with loud barks and teeth that could intimidate from a good block away. They were Verna's protection for her country home. And protection was something she often noted that attorneys needed.

The walls of Verna's office were decorated in anything that had anything to do with fishing. Pictures, posters, magazine covers, hooks, flies, taxidermy fish, and even a couple of poles covered the walls. Her desk was also well covered but with files and paperwork. I knew some of the files were for her law practice and some were for her genealogy work but it was difficult to tell which was which. Some were manila folders and others were a bright purple. If I had to guess, I'd say the purple ones were for the genealogy.

"I need some answers, Gram," I said as I peered again at Jerome, who tipped his hat agreeably. "I thought I should ask you in front of Verna, so you won't feel like you're going around your attorney."

Gram looked at Verna who leaned back in her chair and nodded. "Go ahead."

"All right then, Betts, ask away," Gram said. "I suppose it's time to answer a few things anyway. If Verna doesn't stop me, I'll try to be cooperative."

"Were you and Everett romantically involved?"

"No. We were friends. I told you that when I was in jail. I also already told Verna."

"Did you know he was married?" I was just revving the engine. The bigger question was coming in a second.

"Yes, and I told you that already, too, but his wife didn't know he and I had become such good friends. He didn't want her to become suspicious of the time we were spending together."

"That didn't work," I said. "Why the secrecy? Why were you and Everett so close? Why didn't you just invite Mrs. Morningside over for dinner and we could have all been friends?"

Verna sat forward. "Hang on a second, Miz. Why do you need to know this, Betts?"

"I've come upon some information that might help with the case but only if I have all the pieces."

"What's the information?" Verna asked.

"I can't tell you," I said, "but I assure you I'm doing everything in my power to find someone other than Gram as the killer."

Verna laughed. "Why can't you tell me?"

I hesitated for dramatic effect. I'd said what I'd said to get her to say what she said. Verna was smarter than most people I knew, and I didn't think I'd be able to lead her down any path. I was going to act coy for a moment to see if she'd bargain. If I held out a little and then finally offered the information I had, she'd be more willing to allow Gram to share her information. I didn't have that much to reveal anyway.

"I just can't," I said.

"Quid pro quo, sweetie. You remember what that means?"

"Of course."

"Then you share and maybe we'll share, too."

Jerome laughed. "I think I like her."

I tried to look defeated, but I wasn't sure if I pulled it off. I hoped so. "Fine. Gram, were you and Everett looking for a buried treasure? The buried treasure that outlaw Jerome Cowbender left behind? That's what the information I have is about: Jerome's buried treasure. I'm pretty sure it existed." She wouldn't allow me to ask her questions about the treasure when she was in the jail. I was putting money on the fact that she also hadn't told Verna about it, and I thought that Verna would think it was important. Gram might have said she'd try to be cooperative, but she also probably thought I'd given up on the "silly treasure stuff." It was all a guess and rotten manipulation on my part, but it needed to work.

Verna looked at Gram. "Miz, you didn't tell me anything about this. Is this what you and Everett were doing, looking for a buried treasure?"

And I'd been right. Gram hadn't told Verna.

"What of it?" Gram said, scooting herself taller in the chair.

"This would be pretty important information," Verna said. "If you were onto something, someone might have killed Everett so he didn't get to the treasure first. You might be in danger, too." Verna looked at me and then back at Gram. "I need you to tell me. You don't need to answer in front of Betts. I can ask her to leave."

"That doesn't seem fair at this point," I said, crossing my arms in front of my chest. Jerome laughed again, and I shot him another look.

"What in the Sam Hill do you keep looking at, Betts?" Verna asked.

"Nothing."

"Miz, what do you want to do?" Verna said.

Gram paused and then turned to look at Jerome. She must have communicated some question to him with her eyes, because he pulled himself away from the wall and took the short two steps to her side. He crouched down and said, "Miz, if anyone found the treasure, I would want it to be you." He glanced at me and back to Gram. "My memory's starting to come back, but I still don't remember it all yet. I would love nothing more than for you to find it. Look, if Everett was killed because of it, the authorities need to know. You have to tell the truth now. Someone already thinks Betts and Jake know something they shouldn't. Maybe that 'something' has to do with the treasure, maybe not, but you need to tell Mrs. Oldenmeyer what you know. She'll help."

I'd never seen anyone talk to my gram the way Jerome just had. There was something between the two of them that must have been formed over the many years they'd known each other. I wasn't jealous, but a part of me wanted to hug Gram and tell her that Jerome was right and more than anything I hoped to someday be as trustful a companion to her as he seemed to be.

"Miz?" Verna said. "What's going on?"

Gram turned to Verna. "Yes, we were searching for the treasure the legend says Jerome Cowbender hid all those years ago. It's why Everett moved here. It's why he bought the Jasper. We didn't tell his wife because she would have thought he was on one of his foolish quests. He wanted to find the treasure and surprise her. I didn't want to talk to Betts or you about it because I was concerned someone else would get hurt."

"Do you have any idea who killed Everett?" I asked. "Was someone onto you two?

"Not really," Gram said after a long pause.

Verna and I were suddenly on the same team. We looked at each other with matching raised eyebrows. Jerome straightened.

"Gram," I said.

"Miz," Jerome and Verna said together.

"Gram," I repeated, "if you know something, you have to tell us. Or tell Verna or the police. You can't keep a murderer's identity to yourself." I turned to Verna. "She still thinks she's protecting us."

"I don't actually know who the killer is. I might have some ideas as to who it might be, but I truly don't know."

"Who?" Verna said.

Gram thought about it a long minute and then said, "It's not much of anything. I promise I will tell you and tell Jim if I think I know for sure. I promise."

We were silent. I looked at Verna and Jerome. Jerome looked at me. Verna looked at me and the general direction of Jerome. She grumbled something but didn't again ask what I was looking at.

Finally, Verna spoke. "As your attorney, I must advise you against keeping anything to yourself, Miz. I don't even care if you choose not to tell me. Tell Jim. Tell the authorities so they may protect you if they feel you need it."

"Pish. I don't need protection. I'm fine. I'm safe. I would speak up if I felt like I should. Don't worry. I'm sorry I didn't mention the treasure and Everett's real reason for moving to Broken Rope before today. I didn't mean to worry any of you. It seemed like I should keep it to myself, that's all."

"Gram . . ."

"Isabelle, enough," Gram said.

Gram wasn't stern very often, and when she was it was rarely directed at me. A sudden rush of concern rocked my gut. I didn't want her either hurt by or angry with me. It was a childish response, but I couldn't help it.

"I guess we're done, then," Verna said, an edge of irritation to her voice. Verna wasn't known for her patience or love for suffering fools.

"Good. I've got to get back to the school. In case everyone has forgotten, there's an important event tomorrow that my school is a pretty big part of."

"I'll be there later, Gram," I said.

"Fine." She stood and left Verna's office.

I sat still for a moment.

"I'll find you later, Isabelle," Jerome said, and he was gone, too.

"Betts, I'd appreciate it if you told me what's going on, if you know," Verna said. "I'm here to protect your grandmother and I promise you that it does no good to keep secrets from your attorney. She didn't tell me about the treasure. Those types of things can be quite dangerous. Greed is a wicked master."

"I know that. I wish I knew what else Gram claims to know, but I don't. I will, however, continue to try to figure it out."

"Call me if you do."

We confirmed that we had each other's cell phone number, but I didn't think I'd learn any more from Gram, not tonight. Maybe after tomorrow, after the winner was declared and the hanging platform cleared away, Gram would give up the rest of her secrets. Until then, I just had to hope something else would appear in front of me, but the likelihood of that happening seemed pretty small.

I had to remember, however, that this was Broken Rope. Unlikely stuff happened all the time.

CHAPTER 20

"I don't like the look of these tomatoes. Do we have time to run to Springfield?" Teddy asked.

It was 9:45 P.M., and we were in the one and only Broken Rope full-service grocery store. As with previous years, we hadn't ordered enough food for the cook-off. Usually, though, we had a good half day to round up what we'd missed, but since Gram and Teddy had had to teach champagne cookies *and* allow the students to ready themselves for the big day tomorrow, we got to the last-minute shopping extra last-minute. The grocery store was only open another fifteen minutes and we had a half-full cart. We still needed several more items.

"No, we don't," I said.

Teddy had fought his role as Gram's assistant, but at some point during the day, he'd taken over, and now he suddenly felt responsible for the cook-off's success. It was rare that Teddy felt responsible for anything, so I let him roll with it.

"Then these will have to do." Teddy bagged the tomatoes and put them in the cart.

"Well, well, well, if it isn't Teddy Winston," a voice I knew very well said from behind us. "And, Betts, of course."

"Of course, Opie," I said. "Hello."

Opie wasn't in her Sally Swarthmore getup but instead was wearing an old T-shirt and some faded and tightly fitting jeans. Everything she owned fit her just a little more tightly than my clothes fit me. I had to admit, though, she pulled off the look well. She was always on the verge of slutty but never quite there. Tonight she was more subdued than usual, her face mostly devoid of makeup. Her toes were her most colorful part. They were painted a bright red and matched her flip-flops.

"Hello." Opie gave me a brief nod and then pasted her eyes back on my brother. "You get better and better looking all the time, Teddy."

"Thanks, Ophelia. You're looking pretty good yourself." His tone was far too smooth.

Ugh, I thought. This was not something I wanted to witness, but there was nowhere to go. We had only a few more minutes before the store closed.

"Well, excuse us, Opie, but we've got lots more to get before we're kicked out of here." I pulled on the cart. Teddy pushed it and smiled apologetically at my rival.

"No problem. I'll walk with you."

Seriously? "Sure," I said.

"You know, I don't think Missouri killed that man," Opie said. She gave her full attention to Teddy, but something told me she wanted me to hear the words, too. I was suddenly baffled. The only time Opie had cared what I thought was when she wanted to make me angry about something. I pretended not to be too interested.

"Of course not," Teddy said. "Gram would only kill if someone deserved it. I can't imagine Everett's death was justified."

I stopped the cart and looked at him. If Gram was put on trial for murder, I hoped he'd never be called to testify on her behalf.

Without warning, Jerome appeared directly in the path of the moving cart. Even though it wouldn't have hurt him, I stopped it abruptly.

"Ask her about the woman named Jenna," Jerome said.

"Ask what?" I said.

"What's that?" Opie said.

"Who're you talking to?" Teddy said.

307

"Ask her if she knows about Jenna being related to Everett."

I blinked. Jenna? Related to Everett?

"Opie, do you know Jenna Hopper?" I asked.

"The bartender? Sure."

"Do you know anything about her maybe being related to Everett?" I asked, suspicious of my own question.

Opie's eyes got big. "Oh my, I had no idea it was common knowledge. You already know?"

I could pretend that I knew what we were talking about and hope Opie gave me more than the nothing I really did know. But even though Opie had been a pain in my backside for all our lives, she wasn't stupid. Honesty was the best way to go about it.

I sighed. "I don't know anything, Opie. I just heard their names mentioned together in conversation and I think there's more to it. What's it about?"

"Oh, Isabelle, I can't tell you. That would be the wrong thing for me to do."

I'd chosen wrong. I wouldn't say "please" to Opie no matter how much I needed information from her. I bit at my lip as I thought about what else I could say to get her to give up what she knew. I had nothing.

"Okay," I said, defeated. I looked at Jerome.

"Sorry about that, Betts, but it's pretty typical that you're the last to know. Look at Cliff. He's back and you didn't even know he was divorced. I suppose if you two had any chance of becoming an item again, he would have let you know first thing," Opie said.

I didn't think I could ever truly kill someone unless it was in self-defense or in defense of someone I loved, but Opie certainly gave me homicidal thoughts. Fortunately, Jerome distracted me.

"She's a fine jug of rum," he said as he ran his thumb and finger over his long mustache. "She was just talking to Jake. That's how I know she knows something. I didn't catch their whole conversation but enough to know that Jake will tell you if she won't. Jake was too talkative and I could tell he wished he hadn't told her as much as he did."

"Betts?" Teddy said. I'd been silent as I listened to Jerome.

"Oh, sorry. Whatever you say, Opie," I said as I pulled the cart again, this time with more vigor. I wished Jerome had mentioned that he'd overheard Jake and Opie talking before he'd had me ask her anything.

Teddy and Opie froze in place and watched as I turned the corner around end shelves that were full of green beans. They both probably expected Opie and me to get into a verbal battle. We'd been known to do as much a time or two before. But if Jake had some new information, I'd find out shortly.

"I'll catch up in just a second," Teddy said.

"Fine. Whatever," I said, and then I lowered my voice and said to Jerome, "What's up?"

"I only happened upon Jake and that woman. I don't know exactly, but it has something to do with Jenna and Everett."

Again and despite the fact that Jerome had mentioned "related," my mind grabbed on to the most extreme idea, the most salacious. Was there something romantic going on between Everett and Jenna? Besides the fact that he was significantly older than she was, from first glance neither of them seemed to be the other's type. Jenna was a partier/bartender. She was gruff and kind of tough when she had to be. Everett had been quiet, most likely a shy gentleman from what I could tell.

"Hey, I got the info," Teddy said as he came up behind me.

"You . . . ? Oh, you took her number or

something," I said, meaning to sound more sarcastic than serious.

"No, I have her number. I just asked nicely."

"Right."

"She's not all bad, and she's looking pretty good."

I put my fingers in my ears. "La, la, la, la." I took my fingers out. "Teddy, I will hurt you if you attempt to give me details about any sort of . . . thing you have with Opie. Got it?"

"Sure."

"So what'd she say?" I asked.

"It's good."

"Teddy."

"Jenna is Everett's daughter."

"What?" I practically shrieked. I looked at Jerome who shrugged.

"I know. Far out, huh?" Teddy said.

"Way. Far. Out. I don't understand."

"That's all I know. That's all she told me."

I'd have to get the rest from Jake. Suddenly, out of the corner of my vision I noticed the security mirror at the end of the aisle. Both Teddy and I were reflected in its convex curve, but we were the only two. Jerome stood in front of me but he was noticeably absent in the reflection. And when I turned to look at him again, he was gone. I had an urge to call out for him, but I held back.

"Come on, let's get this done," I said, telling myself to worry about one mystery at a time.

We rolled through the aisles and checked out only five minutes after the store was supposed to close. The clerk wasn't happy at having to stay one second longer than she was supposed to, but Teddy helped her bag, which seemed to lessen our rudeness.

We hurried back to the school and put the groceries away. Gram was still there, too. As distracted as I was, for an hour we focused on the one thing we were supposed to focus on: the cook-off. This was our students' chance to shine. It was our responsibility to do whatever we could to make sure they were given the tools, the knowledge, and the best ingredients to perform. Gram and I both felt like we'd neglected our responsibility. And Teddy, somehow having magically matured without us noticing, took on the cause with enthusiasm and excitement.

I made a deal with Teddy that we wouldn't mention Jenna and Everett to Gram. I wanted to talk to Jake before I believed anything Opie said. If Jenna was Everett's daughter, it was the biggest twist since the last twist. It must mean something, if it was true.

But for that hour, I tried to focus on chicken, pork chops, potatoes, bacon, cream, sugar, and the other ingredients that would bring the town together to kick off the tourist season.

The students weren't allowed in the school until tomorrow morning at 8:00 A.M., but I knew that none of them were sleeping or at least sleeping well. Most of them were still up, working on something as simple as boiling an egg or as complicated as one of Gram's creams.

One of the students had signed up to cook Gram's fried chicken, using her original recipe. It was a great recipe but it was a risky move. Everyone knew Gram's chicken, and even though we instructed them not to be, sometimes the judges were harder on the students who thought they were good enough to fry like Gram. We always encouraged the students to prepare whatever they wanted, though.

Gram's school was not only the place to learn, but it was the place to make the mistakes that every cook inevitably made. Cooking mistakes were some of the easiest mistakes to correct, though. Usually it took only one disaster to become experienced enough to avoid that specific disaster the next time. Watching the students grow and learn was satisfying in many ways.

I'd only been working with Gram for a month when I'd suddenly felt more complete, satisfied, and comfortable in my own skin than I ever had. There was no doubt in my mind that I'd made the right choice when dropping out of law school, but that still didn't change the fact that I'd quit something I'd started with such passion.

I would never have thought myself a quitter. I would never want the students to think they hadn't gotten a hundred percent of my attention and effort. I was more worried about them thinking that than I was about anything else. I triple-counted and triple-shelved everything.

I knew it wouldn't — couldn't; genetics win out — last, but I was also grateful that my brother had chosen to straighten up for the big event. We'd need him and he was a good help. I hoped he hadn't planned a date later; the likelihood of him being just as wonderful tomorrow was in inverse proportion to how attracted he was to whomever he might see this evening.

Finally, when we thought we couldn't be any more thorough, we closed the school. Teddy went one direction, again, hopefully not on a date.

"I'm going home, Betts," Gram said as we stood by her Volvo. "Even though I usually fall asleep easily, I don't sleep well the night before the cook-off, and I'm exhausted. Even if I just relax, the rest will be good. Give me tomorrow, sweetheart. No talk about treasures and killers and the like. Give me tomorrow."

"I will. You should rest. Tomorrow will be a big day."

She pulled on the handle of the driver's door and then looked at me again. "But, Betts, we do need to be careful."

"Careful how? Because there's a killer on the loose?"

"Yes."

I sighed. "Okay, Gram." I wanted to go back on my word and push her for more, but I didn't.

"Don't forget to look for red-spotted shoes."

"I think everyone will be looking for them."

"I hope so."

"You need some rest," I said again.

"That's the plan," she said cheerily as she got into the Volvo and drove away, Toby's voice was turned up loud enough that I was fully aware that he thought he should have been a cowboy.

And speaking of cowboys . . .

"There you are," I said to Jerome. "Where did you go?"

"I wanted to check on Jake again. He was fine. And Miz told me to let you all work on cook-off duties."

"And you listened? What could she possibly do to harm you?"

Jerome crossed arms in front of his chest as he leaned against my car. "Good point."

It was dark, but the parking lot was well lit by the outside floodlight. There was something about the darkness, though, that did something to the ghost. As in the theater, it was almost as if he came to life. The light hit about half of him — his left side — but his right side was more in shadows than in light. His right side looked almost, but not quite, real, and his left side seemed flat as if the colors were duller and less dimensional.

"What?" he asked.

I'd been studying him.

"Sorry, it's just that . . ." I couldn't bring myself to describe what I was seeing.

He pulled himself away from the car. "What?"

"Nothing. It's all just a little strange — meeting a ghost, wondering where he'd been, and thinking of him as a new friend."

"I like the idea of us being friends," he said as he peered at me from under his hat. His eyes were in the shadows, but again I could see them better because it was dark. "Are you flirting with this old rundown ghost?"

"No! I mean, did that sound like I was flirting?"

"A little."

"I'm out of practice. Maybe I was. Sorry."

"Don't be sorry. I like it, but . . ."

I laughed. "I know there's no future for us, Jerome. Don't worry."

He lifted one eyebrow, which caused his hat and one ear to lift a little higher. "Yes, that is too bad, but what I wanted to say was that you might want to concentrate on the living. That young man, Cliff, is so head over heels for your affections that I'm almost uncomfortable being around the two of you."

"Cliff and I were high school sweethearts. That's all you're picking up on."

"Hmmm." This time he tipped his hat so it sat farther back on his head, and he suddenly looked very young and very real. "Well, keep it in mind. And Isabelle, there's something else." He leaned against the car again. "I explained to you how I show up in times of crisis, specifically times that include fire . . ."

"Yes."

"I also leave spontaneously, too. I could go at any time and I usually sense when that's coming — I'm sensing it now."

"You just leave? Where do you go?"

"I don't know."

"What if I set something on fire? Will you come back?"

No matter what we were — friends, flirtatious friends, whatever, I didn't want Jerome to leave. I hadn't known that's what would happen, but I should have thought it through. He'd appeared because of the fire. It made sense that he only got a limited amount of time. But there was no rule book for this.

"I don't think that's a good idea. But I'm sure I'll be back to haunt you in the future, just don't reckon I know when. But what's important here is that we try to get a few things figured out before I leave. Do you suppose we could go talk to Jake about Jenna and Everett?"

"Sure. Sure," I said. "I was going to call him anyway. He'll meet us at the archives. Should I meet you there?"

"I'll go in the automobile with you. I could just pop myself in there, but if you open the door, I'll try to slide in like I was alive or something this time."

I reached for the knob and accidentally grazed one of his hands; a part that was in the dark. It felt real, skinlike and human. I gasped and pulled my hand away.

"What's wrong?"

"Nothing," I said. I reached for the handle, opened the door, and watched him make his way into the passenger's seat.

I was both thrilled and horrified that I'd felt what I thought was skin. It wasn't possible anyway, but it had been interesting.

It would be just like me to develop a crush on the ghost of a bank robber. Not since I'd been a teenager and Cliff and I had been in the thick of our relationship had touching someone else made my skin tingle. But I had to remember, his wasn't skin at all. It couldn't be. That only made it worse.

I was pathetic.

Fortunately, we had something to do. I called Jake who was waiting to hear from me, hoping I'd call, in fact. It was late and we all had a big day set to begin in about six hours, but between needing to know more about Jenna and Everett and Jerome's imminent departure, I couldn't just go home.

He'd driven his VW into town. He greeted

us at the door of his sheriff's office and then closed and locked it behind us. Patches had been retethered in the corner so Jake must have been feeling more secure. His black eye was still as awful as it had been earlier.

"Jerome here?" Jake asked.

"Yes, but he's not sure for how much longer."

"Really? Is he fading?" Jake asked, his eyes wide and somewhat wild.

"No, not that. He's just here for a limited amount of time until the next crisis. It's difficult to explain," I said.

"Let's get to work. I was going to call you but I didn't want to be a nuisance the night before everything. I'm so glad you called me. I've happened upon some things that I'm certain were supposed to remain secrets. It's big, perhaps bigger than anything Broken Rope has seen and that's saying something," Jake said as we marched the now-familiar path back to the archives.

The table was clear this time except for a few pieces of paper.

"Okay, I wish I could take credit for finding this stuff, but I can't. Wait, where is Jerome?"

I pointed to my left.

"You're part of this, buddy," Jake said as he looked in the vicinity of Jerome's shoulders. He looked at me and said, "You know how Verna is into genealogy stuff?"

"Of course. I know all about Verna and her genealogy."

"Exactly. Well, this was in a file she brought me about a week ago. Only a few hours ago she called and told me I should maybe look at it. Soon, she emphasized." He pointed to one of the pieces of paper. "And this" — he held up another piece of paper — "is something I got in the mail slot. Shortly after her phone call. It's anonymous. Which would you like to look at first?"

I took the paper he held and read quickly. Everett Morningside was a direct descendant of Belinda Jasper. So was Jenna Hopper.

My thoughts started to turn and percolate. We'd just met with Verna earlier that day and somehow she must have thought this information was important. I was one hundred percent certain that this note came from her. It just fit. Verna followed the letter of the law, but I always thought there was something about her that would make her do something extreme if she felt it was necessary. I was suddenly grateful for her probably illegal meddling and I'd never tell on her, but I still didn't know why it was important.

"Here." He picked up the other piece of paper and handed it to me. "Look at this. There's something missing, but the possibilities open things up."

I'd seen the family trees before — boxes with names of couples, lines leading to other boxes with couples' children's names and their spouses, et cetera. This page was full of the boxes. It was handwritten, which made it very difficult to follow.

"Look at the top one."

"Belinda Jasper."

"Now," Jake continued, "while it might be fun to read all the old names, don't do that now. Just look at this one." Jake moved his finger to a box at the bottom of the grid: *Everett Morningside m. Susan Orion.* Two lines were drawn out from that box. One of the boxes listed the name of a Morningside son, coincidentally Jasper. The other box said: *Morningside daughter, name and whereabouts unknown. Assumed adoption.*

It didn't take long to connect the dots. "And you assume that this daughter that was put up for adoption is Jenna? I don't know. That seems like a pretty big stretch." I looked at Jerome who combined a shrug and a shake of his head.

"Hang on, here's the pièce de résistance." Jake flipped the family tree piece of paper.

322

"Read this."

In Verna's bold but tight handwriting, there was a note on the back of the paper: *Jake — You'll notice that Belinda doesn't have a husband or a father's name listed for her child. I do know this, there was rumor that famous-but-bad-with-guns robber Jerome Cowbender was the father of Belinda's child. I believe there was a huge scandal regarding their affair. I also know that after Belinda died from the fall, the child was cared for by one of Belinda's cousins who moved to Broken Rope. I don't know more than that.*

I looked at Jerome.

Jake nudged my arm. "What's he saying?"

"Nothing yet. Jerome?"

Jerome looked off in the distance, his eyes and mouth tight. "There's something to that. I seem to remember something, but not much. Ask Miz."

I didn't hesitate but pulled out my phone that instant. She might have needed the rest, but I knew she'd still be up and I didn't care if I woke her anyway. I needed answers.

"Betts?" she answered on the second ring.

"Gram, what do you remember about Jerome and Belinda the contortionist at the Jasper? Did they have an affair? Did they have a baby?"

"Oh dear, Betts. I don't remember him

ever mentioning anything like that. I think I heard rumors as I grew up but I can't be sure. I didn't pay much attention to rumors. Jerome's with you?"

"Yes."

"What's he say?"

"He's not remembering much."

She was silent a long moment. "Yes, the curse and the blessing, I suppose. I do know this: Jerome's demise was legendary — at the time. As the years have passed and Broken Rope legends have piled up, Jerome's blaze of glory has fizzled somewhat. After all, he didn't kill anyone — he was just a thief. Maybe ghosts don't have a good memory of their lives because some things are too awful to remember."

Of course, her comment begged the question, "Ghosts, as in plural?" but we didn't have time to chitchat. I cleared my throat.

"There's more. Everett was a descendant of Belinda, which means he might be a descendant of Jerome — if the story is true."

"Oh my, that most definitely is more," Gram said. "I had no idea. Everett never told me. Everett and Jerome related. Interesting."

"There's something else, too. It's being surmised that Jenna is Everett's daughter, a daughter that was given up for adoption."

Gram was silent again. She probably didn't want to deal with all this news the night before the cook-off, but time was ticking. The ghost — okay, maybe ghosts — that had been haunting her all these years might have seemed like a natural part of her life, but I didn't think she'd ever given them serious credence. They were there and maybe even friends, but from what I'd recently learned their disappearance followed their appearance pretty closely. It would have been wise not to get too attached. I felt my chest clinch at this idea. Had I already become too attached? I swallowed and told myself not to think about it.

Finally Gram said, "That's the thing I wouldn't mention to you and Verna today, Betts. I suspected it because of some of Everett's actions, but I wasn't sure. Do you suppose Jenna killed Everett because he and his wife gave her up for adoption?"

"I don't know," I said.

"This is information that needs to get to the police, Betts. Right away. I think you need to tell Jim about the possible connection. I could but it doesn't matter who tells at this point. Perhaps he can find out more from Everett's widow. Oh dear, oh dear. I had no idea this was so deep. I thought Everett was just having fun searching for a treasure that he wanted to surprise his wife with. I thought there might be something with Jenna but I was doubtful. I had no idea about the Jerome connection, no idea. Maybe Jerome showed up because one of his descendants was killed not because of the fire."

My own mind suddenly shifted into overdrive. "But that wouldn't explain why I see him."

"Genetics from me, maybe. I don't know. Call Jim. Call me back if he wants me to come into town. I promise you I didn't know about the possible connection between Jenna and Everett *and* Jerome. I promise, Betts."

"I know. I will." I hung up. "You okay, Jerome?"

"Fine, I'm just trying to remember. You think I'd remember something like that."

I didn't remember a lot of things and I was only twenty-nine. Maybe Gram was right; perhaps it was a blessing that he didn't remember the details of his life.

"What'd he say? What did Miz say?" Jake nudged me again.

"Gram says to tell Jim. And Jerome is trying to remember."

"What a story this is," Jake said. "This all has to have something to do with Everett's murder."

"I'm going to call Jim and have him meet us," I said. "Jerome won't be able to go with us. He can't get into the jail."

"I'll be at the theater," he said, and then he disappeared.

"Jerome, try your best to remember," Jake said.

"He's gone," I said.

"Have I mentioned how jealous I am of you seeing him while I can't?"

I pulled out my cell phone.

Getting a hold of Jim wasn't as easy as it should have been. The jail was shut down for the night and the only person on duty was a woman who answered the phone. I didn't know who she was or where she was located but similar to what Gram had felt the night of the murder, I was less than pleased with her communication skills. Finally, she said she'd call Jim and have him meet us at the jail. Once that was established, Jake and I loaded up with information, locked the sheriff's office, and hurried across the street. We sat on the boardwalk and waited.

"Normally, my night shift crew doesn't begin working until after the cook-off," Jim said as he got out of his car. "Sorry it took me a few extra minutes."

Jim was in jeans and a T-shirt. I couldn't remember him in such casual dress but I knew we must have attended some of the same barbecues when he wasn't on duty.

Jake and I had brought Verna's genealogy chart and the "anonymous" note. Neither of us would say a word about who we thought dropped off the note. I didn't think we needed to, and I didn't think Jim would use it against her.

The night was warm and well lit by two large spotlights at the end of the street. Evan, the new fire marshal, and a few of his volunteers had been recruited to set up the hanging platform. Evan, his hands on his hips in supervisory mode, looked our direction as we stood and waited for Jim to let us into the jail. He seemed to pause and stare at us curiously. Once he knew who we were, he waved and then turned back to his crew.

We were mere hours away from the biggest day of the year as Jim unlocked the door and we followed him into the jail.

We showed him what we had, we tried to connect imaginary dots with imaginary lines because, after all, it *must* all mean something.

"That's not enough for us to arrest Jenna for anything," Jim said. "I mean, I can ask her some questions but not officially. I could use more evidence than this."

"Maybe she has a gun," Jake said. "Maybe it's been fired recently."

"I can ask her, but I've got no legal reason to get a search warrant," Jim said. "We're having the blood from the roof tested, but unless her DNA is in our system for something else, we can't just ask her for a sample. We could, I guess, but I'd be surprised if she'd give it to us."

"We could try the drink cup trick they do on television all the time. Make her take a drink of something and then steal the cup," Jake said.

"Inadmissible, probably," I said, though I wasn't totally sure.

"It's okay on TV," Jake said.

"That's television," I said. "However, and though it still might be inadmissible in court, Jenna's a smoker. She can't smoke in the bar, but I've often seen her go out back on her breaks. I'll bet we could find a butt we could use. Still maybe not admissible, but at least we might know."

Jim sat forward in his chair. "Betts, Jake, thanks for the information and the ideas, but leave the police work and evidence gathering to us, please. You've already had too much drama out in that alley. We will look into this, but you have to remember to be careful. Got it?"

Jake and I looked at each other, silently wondering what else we could say. Suddenly, the jail door opened again and Cliff walked in. He nodded but didn't say anything.

"We're taking this seriously," Jim said. "I promise that I have listened to every word you've said and we will look into it. We're on board now with the theory that Everett's murder might have something to do with an old outlaw's hidden treasure and I might buy into something about his adopted daughter being involved — if Jenna is his daughter."

I looked at Cliff as he pulled up a chair and sat next to Jake. He was probably curious about the middle-of-the-night emergency but he didn't interrupt. Jim would fill him in later.

"Thank you for bringing this to us," Jim said.

Something suddenly felt off. It took me a second, but I realized why.

Jim still thought we were here only to turn the glaring light of guilt away from Gram. He didn't think we were lying, but he probably thought Jake and I had spent hours poring over documents in the archives, trying to come up with something that would make someone else look guilty. We'd searched for some little thread and built it into something we thought was substantial.

I fought an urge to stomp my foot and exclaim that we weren't just trying to throw them off the killer's scent but instead get them headed toward the real killer. I could see the look in Jim's eyes. He would look at what we'd brought, but I didn't think he'd take it seriously.

And maybe I wouldn't either if I were in his shoes.

Old treasures, dead bank robbers, contortionists, fake gold coins hidden in a tombstone, potential descendants who might not know about their ancestors anyway. It was only getting more outrageous, not less.

It was outrageous, but it was also connected — I was sure of that. As sure as I was of anything.

"Thanks, Jim, Cliff," I said as I stood. I encouraged Jake to stand with me. He did, but only hesitantly. As he reached for the jail's doorknob, a pair of handcuffs fell to the floor, the same pair that had fallen the night Gram was arrested.

I turned and looked at Jim. "See, we didn't touch them."

They didn't say a thing as we left.

"That wasn't as satisfying as I thought it would be," Jake said as we walked across the street again.

"No, but maybe they'll give it some consideration," I said. "Maybe they'll find something."

"Should we go search for a cigarette butt?" Jake asked with half enthusiasm.

"Nah, I do think they were right about us having experienced too much drama. I don't have much desire to hang out in the alley again especially at night."

I looked at the goings-on at the end of the street once more. Though it was lit, the alley would still be shadowed and mostly silent. Tomorrow — no this — evening now, the entire town would be hopping, including the alley. People ventured back there all the time, mostly just out of curiosity.

"Maybe later, tonight — it's that late, or early, I suppose — after everything's over for the day," I said as I peered at the theater. It looked like the doors were open.

"Betts." Jake waved his hand in front of my face. "Where did you go?"

"Sorry. I think we should be done for now. Have you written your poem for opening day festivities yet?"

Jake laughed. "I've written a number of versions. Need to finish it up when I get home. I think it'll mention ghosts and treasures, though. Write what you know and all."

"Go home. Write, get some rest, and I'll see you later."

"You're going home, too?" Jake asked as he followed the line of my vision and looked at the theater.

"Absolutely."

And to prove it further, I let him walk me to my car. I got in and drove toward home. I pulled off on a side street and waited five minutes until he drove by going in the direction of his house. And then I went back into town.

CHAPTER 21

Jerome had said he'd be in the theater. I figured the doors had been opened to prepare for the big day. Maybe live people were inside cleaning, maybe Jim found someone to run it.

Whatever. It looked like I could get in, and for a reason I wasn't sure I understood, I wanted to be there.

I parked in front of the theater, which was about a half block from the hanging platform in one direction and a half block to the jail in the other direction. It looked like Jim and Cliff had left, too, but anyone who happened to look this way would see my car.

"Isabelle, right?" Evan approached. His shaggy blond hair glowed with the artificial light and I remembered how he'd looked with his head in the school's ceiling: like he had a halo.

"Most everyone calls me Betts."

"Everything okay after the fire?"

"Yes. My brother got everything cleaned up. We have a couple missing ceiling tiles, but he said he'd have those replaced soon."

"Good to hear." Evan looked around. "We've got a pretty big day ahead of us, huh?"

I laughed. "Yes, as quiet as it is at this moment, you'll be shocked at the amount of people we'll see soon. It's very fun, really."

"I'm looking forward to it. I've never had the duty of putting up a hanging platform. So far, Broken Rope has been full of surprises."

"And it will continue to be, I'm sure."

Evan laughed, but it was a sad laugh. I remembered his history and was suddenly sorry for him.

"So, what're you doing down here this time of night?" he asked.

"I never sleep well before the cook-off. I saw the theater doors were open. I'd like to take a look around. Have you seen anyone coming or going?"

"I don't think so but I haven't been paying attention. The doors are open though, so someone might be doing something."

"Evan, we could use a hand," one of the workmen called from the other side of the street.

"Nice to see you, Betts. Tell Missouri hello for me," he said before he turned and hurried to the platform.

The light from inside the theater seemed to beckon me inside. I looked around to see if anyone else was watching me and then went to look for Jerome.

He was right inside the door, looking at the pictures, Belinda's picture to be exact.

"Jerome?" I said quietly as I approached.

"Isabelle, hello." He tipped his hat, but his eyes went quickly back to the picture. I suddenly wondered why I'd never told him to call me Betts, like I did the rest of the world.

"What's going on?" I asked because I had no idea what other question to ask.

"I remember her," he said, a smile tugging at his mouth but not making it to his eyes. "We were in love, deeply."

"Go on." A thrill zipped through my system. Were we finally going to learn that final piece of the puzzle? I looked at the picture and the impossible pose. She was lovely and didn't have Jenna's rough edge. Belinda and Jenna were a couple generations apart, but the genetics had carried well.

"I was dying."

"What?" The zip fizzled. This was sad

news even if it wasn't timely.

"I was dying. The doctor told me I had the cancer. Belinda and I were together, but we kept it a secret. She owned this place. She'd run out on her mean SOB of a husband, run from back east, just like I had. She was legally married and worked with her father until he died. We couldn't get married. Shoot, we couldn't even let on that we were together. When she told me she was with babe, I begged her to run away with me, told her we'd go somewhere where no one could ever find us again. Maybe there'd be an ocean, maybe there'd be a desert, but we'd be together. I almost had her convinced when the doctor told me I didn't have much longer to live."

"Oh, Jerome, that's so sad."

"It's why I robbed the bank. It's why I stole the money and then the gold. It was a lot of gold, Isabelle. I knew I was going to die and she'd be left with a young'un. She didn't know what having the baby would do to her body, do to her reputation, but she wouldn't be able to do this for a while. I was going to die, there was no doubt. She'd be left alone with the babe." He nodded at the picture. "She owned the Jasper but mostly made money on her own act. I had to do something to make sure they would be provided for. I ended up dying much more quickly and with less suffering than the cancer would have brought."

"Oh, Jerome, Gram told me it might be a blessing that you didn't remember. I'm sorry if anything Jake or I did forced you into reliving these things."

Jerome was genuinely surprised. "Isabelle, no, it's a blessing *to* remember. I don't have much of anything in this existence. Mostly it's bits and pieces of things and not remembering much of anything from one visit to the next one. This is real, a real memory and something that makes me think my life might have actually been worth something. A man — a dead man — doesn't need much more than that, even when he was alive maybe. I thank you."

I nodded. Belinda must have died after she had the baby. According to the note, the baby had been adopted by a cousin.

"I'm trying hard to remember where we hid the treasure. We hid it together, Belinda and I. She wasn't happy with my thieving ways, but she would have done anything to protect the future of that child." He laughed. "She was all for hiding a treasure for its future."

"It was a boy, you know," I said. "I at least paid attention to that part of the family tree.

She had a boy. It looked like there were no other children and he grew, married, and had a family of his own. I'll have Jake and Verna investigate it closer. Maybe there are pictures somewhere."

Jerome shook his head slowly. "I don't think there's much time left, Isabelle, and I don't know if or when I'll come back. If you find something, hang on to it and maybe some day . . ."

"Sure, of course."

Jerome turned his attention back to the picture.

"Hey, you want to come with me? I can take you to Gram's, or you can come to my house again," I said, but the offer felt strange and uncomfortable. He was capable of getting himself anywhere he wanted to be, but it didn't seem right just to leave without offering.

"Thank you, Isabelle, but I think I'll stay right here. I might remember more."

"I understand," I said after a moment. "I'll see you later." *I hope.*

There was no one else in the theater. I still didn't know why the front doors were open and the lights were on. I peered into the auditorium but had no desire to search it alone. If someone was inside, they were being very quiet.

Jerome's story had left me sad and spooked. I wanted nothing more than to go home, go to bed, and not think about the previously unknown tragedy of Jerome Cowbender's life. He really had been misunderstood. I stepped back out into the night. The hanging platform was almost in place, and I had a sudden vision of older times, when the platform was used for what it was meant to be, not a place for cook-off judges to sit and sample the labors of cooking students.

I could "see" the throng gathered to watch the horrible deadly punishment. I could see the women in their dresses and cloaks and the men in their dusty clothes. I could hear the sounds and even imagine some of the smells. Broken Rope was an odd place to live, but it was home and for the first time in a long time I was glad to be there; sad and spooked though I might have been, I suddenly appreciated the history that was all around.

I ventured one last glance back into the theater before heading home.

Too bad I didn't notice the shoes that had been left beside the old front counter. They were just canvas tennis shoes, but they had some red spots on them.

It might have saved us all a lot of trouble.

CHAPTER 22

I ended up with about three hours of sleep. The adrenaline from the excitement of the cook-off and a pot of coffee would get me through at least most of the day. I'd be fine.

My dreams had been haunted by stories of Jerome, but by the time I got out of bed I had to switch my complete focus to the cook-off. I hoped Jerome hadn't left, but I'd have to worry about that later. I'd meet Gram at the school at seven, so I had some time.

From all indications, it was going to be perfect weather — sunny and warm but not too hot. On my way to the school, I took the long way around town to the outskirts to inspect the RV park. As I suspected, it was full to overflowing with one fifth-wheel parked on the road waiting for either a space or help with maneuvering into a spot. I'd forgotten that it was my yearly ritual to check it every night before the cook-off.

Late the previous evening, it would have had only a few vehicles but it always sprouted exponentially overnight. The fact that I'd forgotten the tradition left an uncomfortable whoosh in my gut. I wasn't superstitious about many things, but this ritual had become important. Finally, I forced myself to shrug it off and not think about any possible blips I'd put into the universe.

Before the road was closed to motor traffic, I drove down Main Street toward the hanging platform. Every light was on everywhere, even as the sun rose. The door to Jake's sheriff's office was open, and I thought he was probably rehearsing or sweeping the floor. I could see both Mabel and Amy in the cookie shop. I knew the shop was going to sell cookies, but they were probably making sure their ovens were ready for the contestants.

Miles was sweeping off his pool tables, and Jenna stood behind the bar in the saloon and concentrated on something on the shelf in front of her. They'd all have someone cover for them when they left for judging duty. I admired their dedication to making sure everything was in place before the cook-off. They had probably slept about as much as I had.

I pulled over to the side of the road and stared at Jenna. If she looked out, she'd see me and wonder what I was doing, but it was worth the risk.

I remembered the first time I met her. It was just over a year earlier when she came to town and got a job at the saloon. She'd struck me as almost stereotypical, with her heavy makeup and cigarette-ragged voice. She had a big scratchy laugh that everyone enjoyed and a way with cuss words that made you want to cover children's ears. She was a party girl, but she'd never once struck me as homicidal.

I wondered briefly if I could just ask her. Could I just walk into the saloon and ask her about her relationship with Everett? Did she even know? Did Everett know? Could I go in and search for some sort of gun?

Jerome had been interested in his family tree but not as far as wondering more about Everett and Jenna. He seemed only interested in gaining the memories from his relationship with Belinda. One thing at a time, I supposed.

"Betts," a voice said through the passenger's window.

"Cliff, you're up early."

"Everyone is." He looked toward the saloon. "Trying to figure out if she's Everett's daughter?"

"Actually, yes."

"I might be able to help. Drive me to Bunny's for some coffee? I'd suggest walking, but Jim's going to shut down the street in a minute and you don't want the Nova towed, do you?"

I thought about it a second. Might not be a bad thing. "Maybe not." At least until I knew if I'd be able to afford the Mustang.

I needed to get to the school but it would be okay if I was a little later than everyone else. The students might start working early but things didn't get too crazy until about mid-morning.

"Hop in," I said.

Even Bunny's early crowd had grown. Many of the tourists had marked Bunny's as one of their prime destinations, and it would be packed all day. The early birds seemed to think they'd get the best food.

Cliff and I found places at the counter and had cups of coffee and plates with large sweet rolls in front of us in record time. I knew there were plenty of sweet rolls to last the entire day. Gram had given Bunny her sweet roll recipe about twenty years ago, and they were still one of the most popular items on the menu. Bunny made them by the hundreds.

There was no privacy, but the place buzzed with the hum of the crowd, so we weren't concerned about being overheard.

"What do you know about Jenna?" I asked.

"She was adopted," Cliff began, "by a couple in Kansas. Her birth parents are from Springfield, but we don't have any further information. We suspect that when we get all the pieces of the puzzle put together, we'll find that Everett was her father."

"You took me and Jake seriously?"

"Of course."

"You acted like you thought we might be making things up."

Cliff chewed on the roll for a second and swallowed. "We did, but we thought it might be worth a look. Jim has a cousin who works for Family Services in Topeka. He called his cousin last night, well a few hours ago, and had him go into his office and do some computer snooping."

"That's impressive," I said.

"Just because we're small-town doesn't mean we can't get stuff done."

"Well, good, I suppose. It must mean something. Maybe." There still wasn't any bright light shining on a guilty party. The familial connections were strange, but not yet proven to have created a killer.

"Yes, and Jim is planning on another visit with Everett's widow as soon as he can get out of here for the day, but when that will be is a mystery. It's a pretty big day. Plus someone's got a happy trigger finger. We'll be earning our pay today."

"I know. I thought about that. Do you think there's cause for much concern?" I said.

"We're taking extra precautions."

"How?"

"I can't go into detail, but not all of the fake cops will be fake cops today. We've called in some help from Springfield. We don't want anyone hurt."

"Good plan," I said.

"Jim's been as on top of things as he could be."

"Got it," I said.

Cliff and I were sitting in Bunny's having sweet rolls and coffee — and it was easy. Suddenly it wasn't as if all that time and all that life had passed. For an instant, I forgot that I was a law school dropout. I forgot that Cliff had gone away and lived a whole other life, forgot that he'd been married. And seeing him hadn't surprised me again. I'd accepted that he was back. It was as if the world suddenly righted itself on its axis.

But only for a second, which I realized was a good thing. I had somehow become mature enough that I knew no matter how easy it was between the two of us as we sat at Bunny's counter, there was no going back to the way things had been in high school. My relationship with Cliff, whatever it turned out to be, was going to be new and different, perhaps tainted a little from the past, but the worst thing I could do was hold on to that past. Moving forward was the only healthy path.

Cliff glanced at his watch. "Gotta go, Betts. Jim needs me." He stood and dropped some money on the counter. "Listen, I want you to be aware of everything around you today. Pay attention and listen to your gut. If any place or any situation feels strange, remove yourself from it immediately." Cliff's dimple was always deeper when he smiled or when he was extra concerned.

"I'll be careful. You, too," I said.

Had Cliff been Jake, we might have hugged or even kissed cheeks. There was a clear gap in what was expected. I just smiled and Cliff awkwardly patted me on the arm before hurrying out of the restaurant. I turned back to my mug and caught Bunny looking at me. She rolled her eyes before turning to deliver coffee to a customer on the other side of the counter.

I was tempted to take a dollar out of the amount Cliff had left, but I didn't. Instead, I dropped a couple more. Bunny and the rest of her staff were just about to experience their busiest day of the year. I could forgive the eye roll.

I wanted to check the theater for Jerome, but I'd run out of time so I drove back to the school.

While the rest of the town was preparing for their performances or tours or just question answering, Gram, Teddy, and I would be at the school for the next few hours as our students created their best meals ever — or so they hoped. Sometimes, the stress would get to someone and they'd forget a key ingredient or burn something or mix when they should have folded.

No matter how good they thought they were, there were always challenges.

Things were set up, but not rolling along too quickly when I got to the school. Gram and Teddy greeted me as if they didn't mind I was a little late and the students were too focused on their plans to care. I jumped in, and before long things were moving at a crazy pace. There was something about the cook-off that made the hours seem both long and short. It was a strange anomaly that Gram and I had discussed many times but had never been able to understand. One second it seemed that there were many hours ahead of us, but somehow the next time we looked at the clock, we'd all fallen into a warp and nothing would be able to get done before the deadline.

Marie would be making pot roast with potatoes and carrots, a cucumber salad, and a pumpkin pie, which she claimed was even better than Gram's. I doubted that Gram was worried.

Myron Benson would be making Cajun pork chops, red beans and rice, and something with carrots that included brown sugar. Bananas Foster was his dessert.

Missy Landon had taken on Gram's fried chicken. She was the first student in a long time who wasn't going to change the original recipe even a little. However, she was also making a cheesy potato side dish that would either ruin the meal or make it so incredible that we'd have to ask her to share the recipe with us. And, she claimed that her chocolate cake with peanut butter frosting would put her meal securely in the winner's spot. We'd see.

Jordan Kingsley was making an all-appetizer meal. We didn't put restrictions on the students' choices, so he wouldn't be breaking any rules, but it was a risk. He planned on using mushrooms, potatoes, bacon, liver, jalapeños, carrots, tomatoes, cream cheese, and eggs. We had no idea how it would all turn out, but we were excited to see what he came up with.

It was fun to watch everything, especially my brother. He was excited to be a part of the cook-off, and I observed him talking to and advising the female students without infusing extra Teddy-charm into the conversations. Oh, he was still charming, just not hopelessly so.

Gram and I had never seen him act this way.

"You know," Gram mentioned quietly, "maybe we should give him a job. He's being so responsible."

"Today. I'm all for helping Teddy if he proves he can keep it together for more than just a few days. Let's watch him."

Gram nodded.

"Have you seen Jerome?" I said even more quietly.

"No, I hoped you had."

"Not since last night, well, early this morning, at the theater. Maybe he's gone," I said, swallowing a little sadness.

"He might be. They come and go, Betts. You have to get used to it, and you can't become attached to them."

They? Them? "I understand."

Gram put her hand on my arm. "Oh, no you don't. I'm so sorry, dear, I wish I would have talked to you more about all this ghost goofiness. It's been so crazy. No, you can't become attached. Neither we nor they can control when they're here or when they go. It rattles you the first few times, but you get used to it. I promise."

There was no time to ask the questions I wanted to ask. How many ghosts were there? How often did they show up?

"I'll do my best," I said.

"Good. That's all any of us can do." She pulled a long apron over her Mizzou T-shirt. Today, she was all yellow and black. Today she was all Missouri.

I watched her as she turned to look at the students. She loved this time of year but it was also sad, too.

"A good group," I said.

"Yes, I think we're getting better, Betts. I think we're becoming worth the tuition."

Gram had been worth the tuition for years. I was still catching up, but I got what she was saying. We owed it to our students to teach them to the best of our abilities. We would always strive to improve.

"Let's get to work," she said.

351

We observed, we answered questions but we were careful not to offer too much advice. We didn't want anyone to have an advantage because we told them something, so we were equally coy with everyone. We weren't allowed to touch anything unless human blood dripped from someone as the result of some accident. Even if we saw part of an eggshell in a mixture, we had to resist both pointing it out and reaching in for it ourselves.

The students were magnificent. Even Missy Landon, whom we'd often wished we hadn't allowed into the program, cooked up a storm. Only Jordan seemed to burn something, but it turned out that was how his stuffed mushroom appetizers were supposed to look.

Though we'd said something similar every year, it seemed that our students had outdone themselves and all those who came before them. I was glad I wouldn't have to judge.

As Teddy and the students were loading the van with supplies and food, Gram pulled me aside and said, "Betts, you need to look for red shoes, got it?"

"I haven't forgotten."

"Good girl."

I took a deep breath. I didn't want to have

to think about red-spotted shoes, but I would.

"Just be on your toes, Betts," Gram said.

"You, too."

So, other than the fact that there was a killer on the loose, delivery and setup went as expected. Around 11:30 A.M., Teddy drove the van around the closed and now-crowded Main Street and parked on the other side of the hanging platform. The rest of us piled into Gram's Volvo. She parked on a street a block away from Main Street, and we hurried down the boardwalk to help Teddy unload.

I peered into Jake's sheriff's office just as he was entertaining a decent-sized crowd. The black eye worked well with his costume, and I wondered what story he was telling about how he received it. I bet it had something to do with an unruly criminal that he finally managed to subdue. I wanted to hear his poem, but there was no time. I waved, but he didn't see me.

The street was too crowded to keep my eyes lowered, but I tried to look at feet as I zigzagged around people. I was surprised by how few people really wore red shoes. And no one had red-spotted shoes.

Red food-coloring-stained shoes seemed like such a silly clue, a long shot at the very best. But there was nothing else. Jim and Cliff received a report on the blood, but the person who lost it wasn't showing up in any DNA databases anywhere. Besides, whoever shot at Jake and me still might not be Everett's killer. It seemed unlikely that they weren't one and the same, but anything was possible.

I looked up and around — really looked closely. I didn't see Jim or Cliff, but I saw others who could have been there to observe and catch any potential violent moments. Standing on the perimeter of the action were men and women I didn't recognize. They weren't wearing costumes or any sort of uniform but were dressed in civilian clothing. They blended into the crowds well, unless you were specifically looking for them, and they were striking because of how still they stood in one place, looking around constantly.

A sudden sense of security calmed my nerves. I knew that if someone really wanted to hurt someone, they'd find a way to do it. Maybe with so many people on the lookout, though, we'd catch on to something before disaster struck.

Setting up the food for the cook-off was more difficult than preparing it. The students had prepared enough food for each of the five judges to have a full taste of each meal, but those plates of food had to be delivered at the same time. The covered plates were put on a cart and then transported up to the hanging platform on a ramp. In years past, we'd mostly filled the cart in the saloon and then stored the remaining food — because there was always extra food, just in case — in coolers in the saloon or in an oven in Mabel's cookie shop. We'd still use Mabel's ovens, but this year we'd decided to use the coolers in the pool hall. The pool hall's coolers were bigger than the saloon's, and it was more convenient.

We made for a pretty big crowd ourselves, and we got in visitors' way as we placed food and plates here and there. It was a big production, but Gram and I had done it so many times now that we took it in stride. The students, however, weren't so calm. They were concerned about things being put together correctly and not being spilled. They were nervous, and every year about this time I wished they'd just go sit in the saloon and have a beer or two.

I gave Teddy the job of helping the students relax and keep their wits about them. He was glad to have the responsibility.

"Oh, sis," he said. "Someone wanted me

to give you a message. He stopped me just as I got here."

"Who?" I asked as I moved a hot pan into one of Mabel's ovens.

"Didn't tell me his name. I didn't know him either. Must be a new actor or something. He was dressed as a cowboy and he smelled like he'd walked through a campfire."

I juggled the pan, only saving it because a counter was close by.

"Oh?" I said.

"Yes, he said he wanted to meet you in the basement of the pool hall."

"Really?"

"You know the guy?"

"Yes."

"Who is he? Are you dating him or something?"

"A friend, and no." I couldn't believe that he had seen Jerome. Teddy would love knowing that he had seen a ghost, but I wasn't going to be the one to tell him.

"You okay meeting him? You want me to go with you?"

"Oh no, I'm fine," I said with a big smile.

Fortunately, Teddy had to attend to a spat between Marie and Jordan. I could only imagine how nervous they all were.

I couldn't just walk away from the preparations, but I had another idea. Missy's chocolate cake with peanut butter frosting looked like it could use refrigeration. The outside temperature was just hot enough that getting that cake to a cooler could be considered an emergency; maybe. I grabbed it and looked for Gram. She was helping with the table on the hanging platform and wouldn't miss me if I wasn't gone too long.

I ran into Myron as I turned back toward the pool hall.

"Myron, I've got to get this into the cooler. You might want to help with the hot stuff in there." I pointed to the cookie shop.

Myron nodded and hurried away.

The pool hall had only a few customers playing pool, but a few others sat at the bar and enjoyed sodas. Miles had brought in plenty of help so he was moving from area to area, keeping things cleaned up.

"Betts, I've cleared out the first two coolers. You want me to put that in there?"

"I can. You know, it'd be great if you headed out there and helped with some stuff at the cookie shop. They'll need you for judging soon anyway. If you're okay to leave, now would be good."

"I'm on my way. Keep things running smoothly, boys," he said to the two teenagers behind the counter. They nodded.

I joined them and found a good spot for the cake. They didn't pay me any attention.

I had no idea where the stairs to the pool hall basement were located, but I guessed in the back. The teenagers couldn't have cared much less what I did, so I walked boldly through the pool hall, stopping only when I reached the restrooms. Each of those doors was marked, but a third door didn't have a sign. I opened it, reached into mostly darkness, and found a light switch. Old wood stairs led the way into the basement. If I hadn't had a mission in mind, I never would have attempted those stairs. There wasn't even a handrail, but I ventured downward nonetheless.

The basement was both a mess and a disaster. Disorganized stacks of boxes of potato chips, peanuts, and pretzels filled one space. Cleaning supplies were on the opposite side, and there wasn't anything organized about them either. It was as if everything had been moved in a hurry to clear away the space in front of a side wall.

It looked as though the wall had been pounded upon with a sledgehammer, probably the one that was leaning up against it next to where Jerome sat.

"My brother told me to come down here. How did he see you?"

Jerome smiled weakly. "I can make people see me if I really need to. It uses up a lot of my energy, but I couldn't find you and I knew he'd give you the message."

I stepped over a couple boxes and crouched in front of him. "You okay?"

"I'm fine for a dead guy, I suppose." Jerome laughed. "I don't feel weak, Isabelle, I just feel like time's about up. I can't sustain myself much longer. I wanted to make sure I showed you what I found."

I smiled sadly. I would miss him. "What did you find?"

"Last night after you left the theater, Miles came in, picked up those shoes" — he pointed — "and hightailed it back to here. The shoes were in the lobby. They were right in front of us."

On my other side were the red-speckled shoes we'd all been searching for.

"No, not Miles," I said.

"I'm afraid so, or at least I think so. Look behind that stack of boxes." Jerome pointed.

He stood and joined me as I walked over debris and looked on the other side of the boxes.

"Jake's archives?"

"Right here the whole time."

"Miles? I don't understand."

"Here, read that." Jerome pointed to a

single piece of paper that was out of the files. "It's her obituary. Go ahead, read it out loud. I think it was the paper I saw on Everett's desk."

"Belinda Jasper died tragically as she fell through the stage trapdoor of her own theater. During one of her daring performances, the trigger to the trapdoor was somehow flipped and she fell through, breaking her neck and dying immediately. She was performing her most famous pose, where her body seemed to defy all things normal and twist into a backward pretzel-like stance. She is survived by her son, Jeremy, who will be cared for by other family members.

Best known for her performances, it was also thought she had an affair with the infamous outlaw Jerome Cowbender, the affair having produced the child. From the day Jerome died, she wore a pin over her heart in the shape of a *J.* She also reboarded the floor of the Jasper stage with a *J* — never to honor Jasper as the theater was named but to honor Jerome. She died without ever confirming the rumor that she and Jerome had hidden a treasure of gold." I looked at Jerome. "I'm so, so sorry."

"They accepted her, Isabelle. She had the baby, she got to continue her work, she got to stay in Broken Rope. It's okay. Really, it is. I'm happy for the news. But it made me remember what happened to the gold."

"What?"

"It's over there." Jerome signaled with his head. "Under the stage, buried in the ground. Mr. Street must have figured it out. I give him credit — there aren't any good clues. Even with all the records your friend Jake has, not a lot was said about the treasure. Reading about the *J* pin might have done it for him, but he's pretty clever. It's still there. I was over there and saw where it's buried."

"I'd be willing to bet that Miles didn't figure it out. Everett did. Miles just let Everett do the dirty work and then he killed him." I looked at the wall. "But I don't understand why Miles is breaking down the wall to get there. Just go through the trapdoor."

"He spent a lot of time in the theater last night. He can't figure out how to get below the stage. Me neither. I looked around for something that opened the trapdoor, but I couldn't find anything. Maybe they sealed it up, got rid of the switch at some point. The stage is high, Isabelle. From what I remember, nothing ever got built down there. Magicians weren't as popular as other acts, so the trapdoor never really got used. There's probably a fifteen-foot drop to the ground underneath. We used ropes to get us and the gold down there."

I envisioned spiderwebs, rodents, and moist darkness, but it was still a place we were going to have to go.

"Okay." I needed to let everyone know, especially Jim. "Jerome, was Jenna with Miles last night?"

"No, he was alone. In fact, he got a call from her on his phone — I still can't get used to those contraptions — and told her he was going to have to miss some late-night rendezvous because he wasn't feeling well." A smile pulled at one corner of his mouth. "I'm pleased if she didn't know what Miles was up to. If anyone should get the treasure, it should be the descendants of someone I stole it from or my descendants. In a way I stole it for *them*."

"Yes, you did," I said. I didn't bother to point out that it was the treasure that also killed at least one of his descendants. "I guess I'd better go let someone know about the shoes. It's a start at least, right?"

"I have a favor, Isabelle, if you wouldn't mind."

"Okay."

"Will you go over to the theater with me

and see if we can figure out how to get the trapdoor to open or figure out another way to get to the treasure? I suspect the police will destroy the floor and I'd like to find a way that doesn't have to happen."

"It's really there?" I asked.

"I'm certain." Jerome smiled.

"Sure," I said. "But I need to talk to Jim first, let him know. Hopefully the shoes and the mess down here will be enough to arrest Miles. Meet you over there in about a half hour?"

"I'll see you there, Isabelle," he said uncertainly.

"You might not last that long?"

Jerome shrugged. "Doesn't matter now. You know and can handle it from here."

I looked at my watch. I needed to talk to Jim, but I felt an obligation to Jerome. He needed to see this through to the end — whatever that might be.

"I'll be there in ten minutes, I promise," I said.

"Good. I'll see you there," he said more confidently.

I hurried back out into the crowd — the crowd that seemed to have bloomed just in the short time I was in the pool hall basement. Everyone's focus was on the hanging platform, where Gram was introducing both the cook-off students and the judges. I'd been in the pool hall longer than I thought and she probably wondered where I'd gone. Miles stood behind Gram and next to Jenna. He looked harmless.

I didn't see Jim or Cliff anywhere. I still didn't have Cliff's number and when I tried to call back the private numbers they'd called me on and the jail's direct number I got no answer. And, I wasn't totally sure who was undercover and who wasn't. I searched for Teddy, only to see him on the hanging platform, too. He stood behind Gram, the students, and the judges. His arms were crossed in front of his chest and he looked proud. I debated whether I should call him or not. But what would I say — Miles is a killer, and do you, by chance, spot Jim in the crowd anywhere?

Miles wasn't going anywhere any time soon. He had food to eat and judge. The first meals would be brought out shortly and he'd be busy for a while. I also didn't think he'd be shooting at anyone. He'd figured out where the treasure was. He was probably in a hurry to get to it but knew that keeping up a normal appearance was the best way to look innocent.

I turned and stepped to walk toward the jail to see if anyone was there but stopped as I reached the front of the Jasper.

With everyone's attention on the cook-off activities, no one was lingering in the theater. The lobby, at least, would fill up once the eating and judging started, and then empty again when it was time to announce the winner.

I sprinted through the lobby and into the auditorium. Jerome was waiting for me on the stage.

"Isabelle, the door is on a wheel system. There used to be a crank somewhere on the wall, but I can't find where."

"Something over there?" I pointed at the side wall that was covered with switches, small and large.

"Miles tried them all, and I bet it wasn't his first time. Nothing opened the door."

Urgency tingled under my skin. I didn't like that I hadn't talked to Jim yet. I didn't like that Miles was out with the crowd, even though I truly didn't think he would harm anyone. And Jerome could disappear at any moment.

I hurried to the wall and began to try the switches, the levers, everything. Some of them did nothing, but others moved things like curtains or hanging backdrops, and one of them must have been attached to a sound system because when I flipped it the sound of a telephone ringing filled the auditorium.

After I flipped and pulled everything I could see, there was only one switch left; it was the biggest one on the wall. I pulled down hard and suddenly it was totally and utterly dark — except for the glowing ghost. Cliff had used a breaker, but this switch did the same thing.

As I'd noticed before, Jerome transformed in the darkness. When his ghostly presence was lit, he wasn't quite as real as he was when he was in the dark. In the dark, he was a fully formed man who, as Gram would say, cut a fine figure. He was strong and handsome. The mustache had even grown on me.

"Isabelle?" he asked.

"Can you see me?"

"Of course," he said, not realizing that the only source of light was him. "You can see me, can't you?"

"Yes. You look so real."

For the briefest instant we looked at each other and forgot about the treasure, the murder, Cliff, red-spotted shoes, the cook-off. For that spark of time, we both envisioned what might be. If only.

Jerome broke the spell. "I'm not real, Isabelle. I'm not. At least not real like you are real."

"Of course not." I flipped the lights on.

We both blinked with the glare. The moment was over.

"I remember!" Jerome said as he peered at the wall next to the large switch. "It's in the wall."

"What's in the wall?"

"Right next to you." Jerome walked toward me. "Right there." He pointed.

There was a hole in the wall. Inside the hole was a knob of some sort.

"There was a hand crank. Belinda kept it in the back. She didn't want people opening and closing the trapdoor. It was dangerous and it worried her."

A tire iron would do the trick, I thought. There were no cars parked close to the theater, though. The street had been closed.

But there was one vehicle — the van. I was certain we had a tire iron in the back of it. At least I hoped.

"Wait here," I said.

I ran through the auditorium and back out into the crowd. The judges were beginning to eat their food. It seemed as if everything was on schedule. The onlookers would be interested in the eating for a few minutes, but soon some of them would disperse and certainly go into the theater. I had to hurry. I dodged and darted and sidestepped.

Fortunately, the van was unlocked. I threw open the back doors and started rummaging. I threw a couple pans, some aprons, and a spatula out of the van and onto the ground. The tire iron was right where it should be: stored in a clip next to the tire. I yanked it out and, ignoring the mess I'd made, hurried back to the theater.

I didn't take the time to look up at the hanging platform as I ran with the tire iron. I focused on where I needed to go. But someone was looking down at me, wondering what I was doing with a tire iron, where I was going in such a hurry, and why I disappeared into the Jasper.

I was out of breath by the time I slipped the iron into the hole.

"It fits," I said, surprised.

"Turn it and let's see what happens," Jerome said.

I started slowly. Everything in the Jasper was old. The knob inside the hole might break at the slightest nudge.

But it didn't break. In fact, it felt strong and secure so I turned harder. The mechanisms screamed as I maneuvered. Age and time had almost frozen everything in place. But only almost.

Suddenly, the *J* started to move down, as

if a mouth was slowly opening.

"I can't believe it's working," I said.

"It's working just fine." Jerome stepped to the door and peered down. "Just a little more. Good. We need another light of some sort."

I cranked until the tire iron wouldn't move. I grabbed my cell phone from my pocket and went to my belly on the perimeter of the hole. I pushed a button and held the phone down into the dark space.

I was right about the spiderwebs and the jigsaw puzzle of wood planks. There was no sign of termite damage, but the wood was over a hundred years old. I wondered if it would crumble at the slightest touch. It wasn't basementlike moist, though. Instead, dusty, dry air hit my nose.

"Right there, in that corner — the corner that looks like it has an extra bump. That's where the treasure is, Isabelle. We did it! Good work."

"I'll be . . ." I said.

"You'll be what?" a voice from the auditorium said.

I looked up quickly, startled enough to drop my phone into the abyss below, and saw Miles moving toward us — though I presumed he saw only me — down the auditorium aisle. He pointed a gun directly at me.

"Run, Isabelle," Jerome said.

I glanced at the auditorium doors.

"They're locked. And I've locked the front doors, too," Miles said. "The only way to get out is around me."

Miles jumped up to the stage and peered into the hole. "I would have broken through the wall tonight, but thank you for saving me the work."

"Get behind me, Isabelle," Jerome said.

I looked at him. Ghosts couldn't stop bullets. He understood my hesitation.

"I'll try to make him see me," Jerome said. "If he does, he'll be distracted and you can run." Jerome moved himself in front of me more than I moved behind him.

"What happened?" I spoke around Jerome's shoulder — the shoulder that Miles still couldn't see. "Why, Miles?"

Miles laughed. "I moved here to find the treasure, Betts. I read about the legend years ago, and it became a part of me. It was destined to be mine. When the pool hall was put up for sale, I knew it was my way to be a part of the town. I had no idea that the treasure was buried right next to me this whole time. That is, until I caught Everett reading Belinda's obituary as he had a sandwich at my front counter one night. He started giggling like a schoolgirl and talking to himself. He had no idea I'd been searching for the treasure, too. I saw the obituary that night, but I also got it off his desk the day after I killed him. I came in through the roof. If the police saw it, they must not have thought it was important. I had no idea Everett had figured out the tie between Jerome Cowbender and Belinda. But it was my destiny to find the treasure, not Everett's."

"What about Jenna?"

"What about her?"

"She's a descendant of Jerome's."

"What?" Miles almost whinnied when he laughed. "You're making that up."

"No, I'm not."

"I had no idea. No idea at all. See, more destiny. It's why I was attracted to her — I was destined to find this treasure. Not Everett and certainly not you or your Gram."

"Did you put the coins in the tombstone? Did you put the paper in there, too?" I said.

Miles laughed again. "I put the coins there. And I had to point them out to you, not to the people I intended to see them! I put them there for Everett and Missouri to find. I thought it might throw them off, or just mess with their minds. I don't know anything about any paper."

"Well, it looks like you found the treasure fair and square. You won. It's all yours," I said.

"Right. I don't think so." Miles lifted the gun.

"Why did you shoot at me and Jake?" I asked, hoping to stall long enough for Jerome to become visible.

"I knew Everett's death would somehow lead to some archive somewhere that could give it all away. Your friend is a little too acquainted with Broken Rope's history. I figured it'd be easy to get rid of you both. Scratched the hell out of my arm, too. I slipped up there," he said, nodding upward. "If I hadn't fallen and started bleeding, I would have kept shooting until I got you both."

"How's it going, Jerome?" I muttered.

"Not so good," he said.

"What did you say about Jerome?" Miles asked.

"Nothing," I said.

"I'm too weak. If I can manage to make him see me, I'll probably disappear shortly thereafter," Jerome said. "Give Miz my love."

The entire scene was ludicrous. I wanted

to say good-bye but the setup was wrong. I wondered if maybe Jerome was just a figment of my, Gram's, and maybe Teddy's imagination. Was he really here, or was he something we collectively made up because we were citizens of Broken Rope, a place where almost nothing was like the rest of the world? Did my grandmother, brother, and I share some genetic mistake that made us have a collective hallucination?

"Good-bye, Jerome," I said.

"Good-bye, Jerome? Don't you mean 'Good-bye, Miles'?" And then he aimed the gun and pulled the trigger.

A sear of hot pain rode over the side of my neck and I went down.

"Isabelle!" Jerome went down with me.

"Damn," Miles said. "I need to try that again."

I was conscious and the pain was hot but not bad enough to keep me from moving or trying to figure out what to do next.

"You're okay, Isabelle. It didn't do much," Jerome said as he looked at my neck. I was looking over his shoulder at the man walking closer to me to get a better shot.

"It seems you're as bad at hitting your targets as Jerome was," I said.

"Oh, that's hysterical," Miles said.

Suddenly, I rolled once and then kicked

out my legs to knock Miles over. Unbelievably, it worked and he went down, too, the gun sliding to the other side of the stage. If I ran to get the gun, Miles could get up and beat me to it. So I pulled myself up and ran to the wall instead.

"Get ready, Jerome," I said as I pulled the big switch.

The theater was thrown back into darkness, and Jerome was glowing and three-dimensional again. He looked strong and powerful.

"He can't see me. He can't see you. I'm betting you can knock the crap out of him now. Well, maybe I'm not betting. I'm hoping. You look like you can," I said.

Miles used the same lighting technique I had a long few moments ago. He pushed a button on his cell phone and lit a path to the gun. The light was weak and not enough to extinguish Jerome's vitality.

Jerome didn't hesitate but took two long strides to Miles. As Miles was about to grasp the gun, Jerome put his hands on his shoulders and shoved. Miles flew through the air a brief moment and then landed on his back. Jerome seemed surprised by his new abilities, but he adjusted quickly.

I sat against the wall and held my hand to my bleeding neck and tried not to faint as

Jerome slugged Miles in the jaw and then in the gut. Miles made strange and unusual noises. He was hurt and confused, not understanding where the blows were coming from, and I had a front-row seat. I couldn't help but enjoy the show.

Finally, Jerome grabbed Miles's arm and pulled him toward the trapdoor hole. The fall probably wouldn't kill him unless he could bend in some impossible pose, but he wouldn't be able to get out unless there was a ladder close by or he managed to get through the wall. Jerome made it fast and clean as he dropped Miles in the hole. I heard a thump and a loud yell. At that moment, I didn't care how badly Miles was hurt.

"Isabelle, why didn't you run?" Jerome asked as he crouched beside me and pulled my hand from my neck.

"I would have had to turn the light on to see. The light would have ruined everything."

Jerome studied my neck. "You are going to be fine, I promise. Have a doctor throw a little whiskey on the cut, maybe a stitch or two, and you'll be good as new."

I nodded, smiled, and cried.

We both looked at my bloody hand in Jerome's. His hand felt like any other man's

I'd ever held, and the list wasn't long.

"How did you know? I mean, I didn't even know," Jerome said.

"You looked so real," I said. I felt a tear roll down my cheek. I wasn't a big crier, but considering the circumstances I thought a tear or two was appropriate.

"I had no idea," he said again as he put his other hand on my not bloodied cheek. He laughed. "Thank you. I didn't remember how wonderful a woman's skin felt. Thank you."

If he liked the feeling of skin, I was either about to push him into overload or make his day. I leaned forward and kissed him gently. He kissed me back and his mustache tickled me pleasantly. It was a sensation I'd remember forever.

"Isabelle," he said. "Isabelle."

"I know. You've got to go. I figured this would use up the last bit of your battery power. Go with my blessing, but come back someday. I know I'll need you."

"I'll do my best."

And then he was gone. The only light left in the auditorium was a small spit coming up from the trapdoor hole. I didn't know if it was from my cell phone or Miles's. I stood on my less than reliable legs and flipped the switch. The light hurt my eyes, but it didn't matter.

I made my way off the stage, through the auditorium, and into the lobby. Before I left the theater, I glanced at the picture of Belinda and said, "Lucky girl."

CHAPTER 23

Of course, everyone thought I was part of an Old West act; everyone except Jake, who saw me tumble down the street toward the hanging platform. He met me there, took my arm, and helped me into the saloon. A doctor, Jim, Gram, and Teddy were by my side in only a few minutes.

I explained everything to the best of my ability, but I suppose everyone will always wonder how I managed to beat up Miles without so much as a bruise or cut on my hands. I claimed that the bullet grazing my neck had pumped me with enough adrenaline to take down more than one homicidal pool hall owner if I'd needed to. I didn't even tell Jake and Gram the truth; it was something I needed to keep to myself for a while. Miles was so confused that he didn't know what to say.

Somehow we managed to continue the cook-off and keep the unlawful activities a secret from the tourists. The only hitch in their day was that one of the judges claimed to fall ill and had to leave the contest, leaving only four judges, which meant Gram would have to be the tie-breaking judge if needed.

Much to Gram's and my surprise, though, there was no need for a tie-breaker. Missy Landon won in a 4–0 victory. Her version of Gram's fried chicken had the judges swooning in their seats, and her chocolate cake with peanut butter frosting effectively sealed the deal.

Miles was hurt, but he would survive. He really didn't know that Jenna was Everett's daughter. He didn't know that both Everett and Jenna were descendants of Jerome's. Jenna didn't know it either. In fact, she hadn't even known she was adopted. She probably struggled the most with the information about her life that was suddenly heaped upon her. Fortunately, she had a good sense of humor and was interested in getting to know her birth mother, but none of us were sure how that would go. We all hoped for the best.

Everett had been leaving his home in Springfield early every morning and returning late, sometimes even after days had passed. He'd told his wife that he'd found a job in sales that kept him on the road. Though she'd been suspicious of his activities for a long time, it was when she found Gram's business card on his nightstand that she thought he might be having an affair. Her appearance and accusations the night of Everett's murder were merely the result of horrible timing.

When Everett and Gram hadn't noticed the coins in and on the tombstone, Miles was convinced that Everett's discovery of the treasure was imminent. Miles greeted Everett after Gram had gone back inside the school and told him he wanted to show him something in the supply room. Gram had spilled the food coloring and then got distracted by a student's question. Miles's timing had to be perfect so Gram wouldn't catch him. Miles claimed to kill Everett in a fit of obsessed rage. As Gram had concluded, he had walked through the food coloring and had to clean up the mess he'd made. He also cleaned off the soles of his shoes, but he wore them the night of the fire, when the singed chicken breast flew through the air. He changed them by the time the students were called back for questioning, though.

If only someone had noticed the red spots.

Miles shot at Jake and me for the reasons

he'd mentioned in the Jasper. He was convinced that whoever had access to the archives would somehow figure out that he was the one who'd killed Everett. He had no idea how confusing the archives had actually been. Jim claimed that Miles had become so caught up in himself that he thought everyone was seeing what he was seeing. When he wasn't able to kill us, he thought he could at least steal the archives. He said he thought he'd at least put Jake in a coma, but again my best friend had beaten the odds and survived Miles's second attempt to take him out of the picture.

Gram said that Everett had no idea that Jerome's treasure was hidden underneath the theater. She claimed that even finding Belinda's obituary hadn't given him the final clue. If he'd been "giggling like a schoolgirl and talking to himself" while reading the obituary at the pool hall it was just the result of finding something interesting or entertaining. The treasure hunt had turned into more of a fun diversion than a real hunt. Everett had taken Gram's business card so he could give it to his wife when he told her what he'd been up to. Everett thought Gram might be able to ease the blow of learning about Everett's "crazy idea."

Before Everett had come to Broken Rope, he had no idea that Jenna was his daughter. But not only did Jenna look like Belinda, she looked like Everett's mother, too. Before they were married, Everett and his wife had had a baby, a little girl they couldn't afford to raise and they thought would be better off with a family that could give her the best in life. The resemblance caused Everett to search further, and Gram claims that he somehow found out she was adopted and he hinted — though never admitted it to her — that he thought Jenna might be his daughter. Maybe he had contacts in Topeka, too, but none of us would ever know.

No one knew who placed the small pieces of paper, the copies of the word *Jasper,* in the tombstone and in Everett's desk. No one. Of course, I could never be sure, but something told me they came from the same place that Jerome was now, not from him exactly but from "that place," wherever it was. It was a disconcerting thought and not something I wanted to dwell on, but maybe someday I'd think about it more. Maybe someday I'd talk to Jerome about it. I hoped at least.

It turned out that the familial connections didn't mean much of anything when it came to Everett's murder. The only one who'd seemed to figure them out beforehand was Verna, and until the meeting I'd called with her and Gram, she never thought those connections meant anything important. She never admitted to the anonymous note, but come to think of it, I don't think anyone asked her outright.

I was fine. The doctor threw a little alcohol over my wound and put in a couple stitches for good measure. I hoped I'd have a scar.

Other than the bad things, it turned out to be a pretty good opening day.

Jerome's treasure was buried right where he'd said. It was gold — a lot of gold. Jim had it excavated without any damage to the Jasper and then he sealed off the area underneath the stage and theater. Never again would anyone be able to get into that space. Unless they were a ghost and could do those sorts of things. Later we'd learn that Amy had told Mabel that Everett had touched her inappropriately. It was a horrible accusation. And, it wasn't true according to the story Amy was now sticking to. Amy had said what she'd said because Everett wouldn't let her into a movie without paying. Mabel and Amy hadn't done anything to Everett, but Mabel admitted to thinking about it.

We'd all been called to a meeting in Jim's

office. Gram, Teddy, Verna, Jake, Cliff, and I were all there as Jim called the meeting to order.

"There are laws we must abide by. This is gold, folks, and someone else's gold at that. It's a historical find, and there are certain things we are required to do," Jim said.

None of us wanted the gold, had ever wanted it. In fact, Gram and I had been pushing Jim to give it all to Everett's widow if that was possible. It wasn't. There were laws and such.

"That makes sense," Verna said. Miles had tried to hire her as his attorney, but she'd refused. "Give us the scoop."

"This is what's been worked out with the authorities. I hope you're all in agreement. Even if you aren't, there's nothing we can do, though I feel they're being very generous," Jim said.

We looked at him and waited.

"Everett's widow will get some. Some will be given to Jake for archiving purposes only. I'd like Jake to put something together that shows our visitors who the real Jerome Cowbender was."

I swallowed hard and clenched my fist to keep my hand from reaching for the bandage at my neck or tearing up.

"I'd love to do that," Jake said.

"Verna, you're getting some to cover your attorney fees for Miz," Jim said.

"Hell's bells, Jim, I can pay," Gram said.

"I didn't do anything anyway. I wasn't going to charge her," Verna said.

"Yes you were," Gram said. "I wouldn't hear of you working for free."

"There, I fixed it. Verna, you're getting some," Jim said firmly. Gram and Verna both looked perturbed but didn't say anything more.

"Betts, you'll get a little for pain and suffering." Jim looked at me.

"I don't want any . . . wait, I take that back. I would like a small bit. One coin would be fine." I suddenly had the desire to carry one of Jerome's stolen coins with me.

"You'll get a few coins."

"You can give what you don't want to me," Teddy said with a big Teddy smile. "Kidding, sis, kidding."

"The rest will go to the state historical society. The town will receive some compensation, a finders' fee of sorts, but the amount is unclear. I thought we'd do repairs on the Jasper and the pool hall and whatever else might need a little something. Everyone good with the plan?"

We looked at each other and nodded.

"I think we're all for the plan, Jim. Good

work," Gram said.

The now-familiar metallic plunk sounded from the front of the jail. The handcuffs had fallen again.

"I do not understand what is going on with those handcuffs," Jim said.

I looked at Gram. She winked at me.

The meeting was adjourned and Cliff walked me out to my car. I still owned the Nova. I'd decided not to invest in the Mustang, no matter how wonderful it would have been.

"You okay, Betts?" Cliff asked as we stepped out into the bright sunshine and into a group of tourists who seemed to be headed toward the gunfight at the other end of the street.

"I'm fine. I might have a scar, but I'm just fine."

"I'm sorry about what you've been through. If there's anyone I want to protect, it's you."

I blinked.

"That was a bit much, huh?" Cliff said.

"No. Actually, it was great to hear. I'm just . . ." The words that were in my head were something about me being actually glad he was back but not knowing exactly why. Suddenly, I wasn't pining away for what we once had. Suddenly, I saw him as he was now, not as he was then. And suddenly, I was excited to get to know this him, one step at a time. "It was just great to hear."

"Good." He smiled.

"Hey, sis, Cliff." Teddy burst out the jail doors. "You two getting back together again anytime soon, or are we going to have to watch while y'all torture us all with your puppy-dog eyes and batting eyelashes?"

"Oh stop, Teddy," Gram said as she came out behind him. "Betts has never been an eyelash batter."

"Who says I was talking about Betts?"

We all laughed. It was good to laugh, and it was suddenly good to be a resident of a place that was full of surprises: Broken Rope, Missouri. Or as I liked to call it, home.

RECIPES

FRIED CHICKEN

My dad has often told me about how, when he was dating my mother, her mother would fry up some chicken and leave it warming in the oven just for him. He claims it was the best fried chicken he's ever eaten. Of course, I remember my grandmother's delicious chocolate chip cookies and her delicious Thanksgiving dinners. Sadly, those were the days when things like amazing fried chicken and chocolate chip cookie recipes didn't get written down. My grandmother cooked and baked by adding a little of this and a little of that. My mother had no interest in such things, so she never paid attention, and my grandmother died when I was nine, long before I had any cooking or baking interest myself.

I would love to have her fried chicken recipe, all of her recipes. I would love to share it with the world. But I don't. And it seems no one else does either.

So I went in search of the "best fried chicken recipe ever" to include in this book. What I found was something beyond ingredients and directions; I found tradition, family, and lots of love. A fried chicken recipe is one of those things that brings families together, puts future generations in touch with something that was theirs even before their time.

I think the following recipe is pretty darn good. I'm not done searching, though. Maybe I'll find something better, maybe I won't. If you have a fried chicken recipe in your family, I'll bet you think it's the best — and it is. And if you're lucky enough to have someone in your family who knows the recipe well, do me a favor: write it down and keep it close.

3 cups all-purpose flour
2 teaspoons salt
2 teaspoons freshly ground black pepper
1 teaspoon paprika
1 whole chicken cut into pieces, skin left on
Milk, I use whole
Vegetable oil

In a large shallow bowl or pie plate, mix together the flour, salt, pepper, and paprika.

Rinse the chicken pieces and pat them dry with a paper towel. Dip the chicken pieces in milk, and then dredge through your flour mixture. Let the chicken stand for 20 minutes, and then dredge again.

Fill a cast-iron skillet with about 1/2 inch vegetable oil, and heat it on medium high to 375 degrees F. Maintain this temperature throughout this first frying process. Make sure the skin browns, not burns.

Dip the chicken pieces, one or two pieces at a time, into the oil. Brown both sides. Remove to a platter until all the pieces have been browned.

Return all of the chicken pieces to the skillet. Reduce heat to low or medium low, and cover. Cook slowly and gently for about 20 minutes, or until the chicken is done all the way through and is fork tender.

Remove the cover. Turn up the heat to medium high, and recrisp the chicken, about 5 minutes, turning once, after the skillet is hot again.

Serve!

FAKE FRIED CHICKEN

I can't say the following recipe is healthy — flour is involved. It isn't fried but tastes almost like it is. This has turned into one of my son's favorite dishes. When I first made it, he couldn't get enough so I doubled it. This is the doubled version. It'll work if you have a large group or a teenage son or two. Not only does this make a satisfying dish for a meal, it's also a great appetizer to serve for a TV sporting event.

2 pounds skinless chicken strips
2 cups low-fat milk
1 tablespoon vegetable oil
2 cups all-purpose flour
2 teaspoons salt
2 teaspoons freshly ground black pepper
Vegetable spray

Wash and dry the chicken.

Place the chicken and milk in a gallon-size storage bag. Refrigerate for 30 minutes.

Preheat the oven to 400 degrees F.

Spread the vegetable oil on the bottom of a 13 × 9-inch baking dish until coated.

Place the flour, salt, and pepper in another gallon-size storage bag, seal, and shake until all ingredients are blended.

Remove the chicken from first storage

bag, drain, and then place it into the bag filled with the seasoned flour. I put in a few strips at a time. Shake to coat the chicken well.

Place the chicken in the prepared baking dish.

Coat the top of the chicken with a generous coat of vegetable spray — this is pretty important. Try to get a little spray on all exposed parts of the chicken. This gives it a great texture.

Bake in center of oven for 20–25 minutes, or until the chicken is browned on the outside and cooked through on the inside.

CHAMPAGNE COOKIES

To this day, I crave Barbara's Bake Shop champagne cake. I lived in Des Moines, Iowa, for a number of years when I was a kid. Barbara's was only a few blocks from our house, but once I discovered the shop's champagne cake, I was a convert. When I got to choose the cake, it was always champagne and it was always from Barbara's. Sadly, Barbara's closed a number of years ago.

I created this recipe with the champagne cake flavor in mind. I had some help with the frosting. Thank you, Heidi Baschnagel!

3 1/2 cups all-purpose flour
1/2 tablespoon baking powder
1/2 teaspoon baking soda
1/2 teaspoon salt
1/2 cup butter
1 cup sugar
4 ounces cream cheese
2 eggs
1/2 tablespoon vanilla extract
5 drops red food coloring
1/2 cup champagne (I use an affordable pink variety.)

Preheat the oven to 350 degrees F.

In large bowl mix the flour, baking powder, baking soda, and salt together.

In another large bowl cream together the butter, sugar, and cream cheese.

Add the eggs, vanilla, food coloring, and champagne. Blend to incorporate.

Add the flour mixture and mix until combined.

Chill in refrigerator for at least 2 hours.

On floured surface roll out the dough 1/4–1/2 inch thick. Cut into desired shapes, and place shapes about two inches apart on a cookie sheet.

Bake for about 12 minutes or until edges are slightly browned. Let the cookies cool on the cookie sheet for about 1 minute and then remove them to a cooling rack. While the cookies cool, make the frosting (recipe follows).

Makes about 24 two-inch-wide cookies.

Frosting

4 1/2 cups confectioners' sugar
3/4 pound (3 sticks) salted butter
2 tablespoons pink champagne
A few drops red food coloring
Up to 4 tablespoons water, for consistency
Edible silver glitter (optional)

In a large bowl, mix the sugar, butter, champagne, and food coloring. Add a little bit of water at a time to achieve the desired frosting consistency — I think thicker is better. Spread the frosting over the cooled cookies, and sprinkle with glitter (if desired).

MISSY'S PEANUT BUTTER FROSTING

Peanut butter frosting is a wicked creation. Because I love peanut butter, I've tried a number of different recipes over the years. Peanut butter frosting can be too thick, too crunchy, even too peanut buttery. I think I found a great balance of texture and taste with the following recipe. I recommend it on chocolate cake. While no Missouri Anna I know would ever do anything but make a cake from scratch, I'll admit to using this frosting on a box mix.

1/2 cup (1 stick) salted butter, softened
1 1/2 cups creamy peanut butter
2 cups confectioners' sugar
1/4 cup milk

In a large bowl, beat the butter and peanut butter until light and fluffy. Slowly beat in half of the sugar. Mix in the milk. Beat in the remaining sugar. If you find it necessary, add a little more milk to give it a spreading consistency.

Makes enough to frost one 2-layer 9-inch cake or one 9 x 13-inch cake.

Red Velvet Cake/Cupcakes

I think I've tried dozens of red velvet cake recipes. Most of the time, I've been terribly disappointed. They've been too dense, too dark, or just not flavorful enough. Then last year some friends of my son's made him a red velvet cake for his birthday. It was delicious. I was on the phone the next day, asking if I could include the recipe in this book. Thankfully, they agreed. So, thank you, Michael Kennedy-Yoon and Katherine Kennedy, for the best red velvet cake ever!

1/2 cup shortening
1 1/2 cups sugar
2 eggs
2 teaspoons vanilla extract
3 level tablespoons cocoa powder
1/2 ounce red food coloring
1 teaspoon salt
2 1/2 cups sifted cake flour
1 cup buttermilk
1 tablespoon white vinegar
1 teaspoon baking soda

Preheat the oven to 350 degrees F. Grease and lightly flour two 9-inch round cake pans or line a 24-cup pan with paper liners.

In a medium bowl cream together the shortening, sugar, eggs, and vanilla. In another medium bowl mix the cocoa and food coloring together with a spoon until pastelike consistency. Add it to the shortening mixture.

Add and mix the salt and flour alternately with the buttermilk into the shortening mixture.

In a small bowl mix the baking soda and vinegar, and add it to the batter. Mix until all ingredients are well blended and form a smooth batter.

Pour the batter into two greased and floured cake pans. Bake for 25–30 minutes.*
While the cake cools, make the frosting (recipe follows).

*Makes 1 cake or about 24 cupcakes. *Only bake for 17–21 minutes if making cupcakes.*

Frosting
6 ounces cream cheese, softened
3/4 cup (1 1/2 sticks) salted butter, softened
2 teaspoons vanilla extract
4 cups sifted confectioners' sugar
3 tablespoons cream
Red sugar sprinkles, for topping

In a large bowl, mix the cream cheese, butter, vanilla, cream, and sugar until smooth. Spread the frosting over the cooled cake or cupcakes, and top with sprinkles. Makes enough to generously frost one 2-layer 9-inch cake or 24 cupcakes.

Gram's secret ingredient is vinegar. When I was experimenting with recipes, none of them had vinegar, so I thought I'd found the magic. I have found vinegar in a number of recipes since then.

The employees of Thorndike Press hope you have enjoyed this Large Print book. All our Thorndike, Wheeler, and Kennebec Large Print titles are designed for easy reading, and all our books are made to last. Other Thorndike Press Large Print books are available at your library, through selected bookstores, or directly from us.

For information about titles, please call:
    (800) 223-1244

or visit our Web site at:
    http://gale.cengage.com/thorndike

To share your comments, please write:
    Publisher
    Thorndike Press
    10 Water St., Suite 310
    Waterville, ME 04901